TECH
ENGLISH

科技世代
一定會的英文

LINE

U0012407

CONTENTS

Part 1

Consumer Tech News
生活科技新聞

Part 2

Office Tech Conversations
職場科技對話

Part 3

Top Tech Brands
科技焦點品牌

在過去這 10 年中，蘋果於 2007 年推出了智慧型手機，然後 Facebook 也在 2008 年推出繁體中文版，FB 最近的「10 年挑戰」就幫大家回顧自己 10 年來的樣貌是否有所改變，常用的網路瀏覽器從 IE、Firefox 變成 Chrome，常用的聊天工具也從 Skype 變成了 LINE。

科技見證了時代，這個世代最精華的歲月彷彿是網路、社群媒體伴隨我們一同度過，於是我們決定做個科技特刊，一本讓恐懼科技者到科技達人都能受益的英文教學書，從「社群媒體演變史」開始，了解最早社群媒體的形式，學習 FB 和 Twitter 上的常用語言，生活科技新聞 (Consumer Tech News) 告訴你目前科技的最新進展，包括臺灣採用行動支付 (mobile payment) 速度緩慢、常用智慧型手機導致科技頸 (tech neck)，以及許多年輕人的夢想：成為知名 YouTuber，但你可能不知道，許多知名 YouTuber 竟然已有職業倦怠 (burnout)？

再來就是非常實用的「職場科技對話」Office Tech Conversations，8 個人人都可能在職場上遇到的辦公室情境，教你如何用英文說。包括整理投影片簡報（PowerPoint presentations）、用影印機掃描 (scan)、和同事抱怨用不慣蘋果電腦、電腦內的盜版軟體 (pirated software) 造成系統無法更新，還有行銷人一定會遇到老闆叫你增加臉書流量 (drive Facebook traffic)，或是請網紅拍攝 YouTube 開箱影片 (unboxing video)，來增加公司產品銷量。最後是一定要知道的傳輸大檔案的方式：用 gmail 或是放在雲端 (the cloud)，以及叫下午茶時一定要用的線上作業 Google 試算表 (Google sheets)，可以即時看到所有人的點餐狀態喔！

最後要來看看世界 10 大科技公司以及其創始人的崛起與發跡過程，他們的成長與個人歷練如何提供創業養分，開拓出科技江山。文章中會看到公司的概念、產品與服務，你會學到許多科技相關單字，Language Guide 上也提供清楚的說明，解釋這些科技概念，讓你不再一頭霧水，能夠快速晉身科技達人！文後並有閱讀測驗，考考你的理解力。不管是想學英文，還是想學好科技的朋友，這本書 has something for everyone。

P.S. 從本期開始，音檔將以 QR code 呈現，另也可翻至版權頁，下載全書音檔。

EZ TALK 主編 Amy

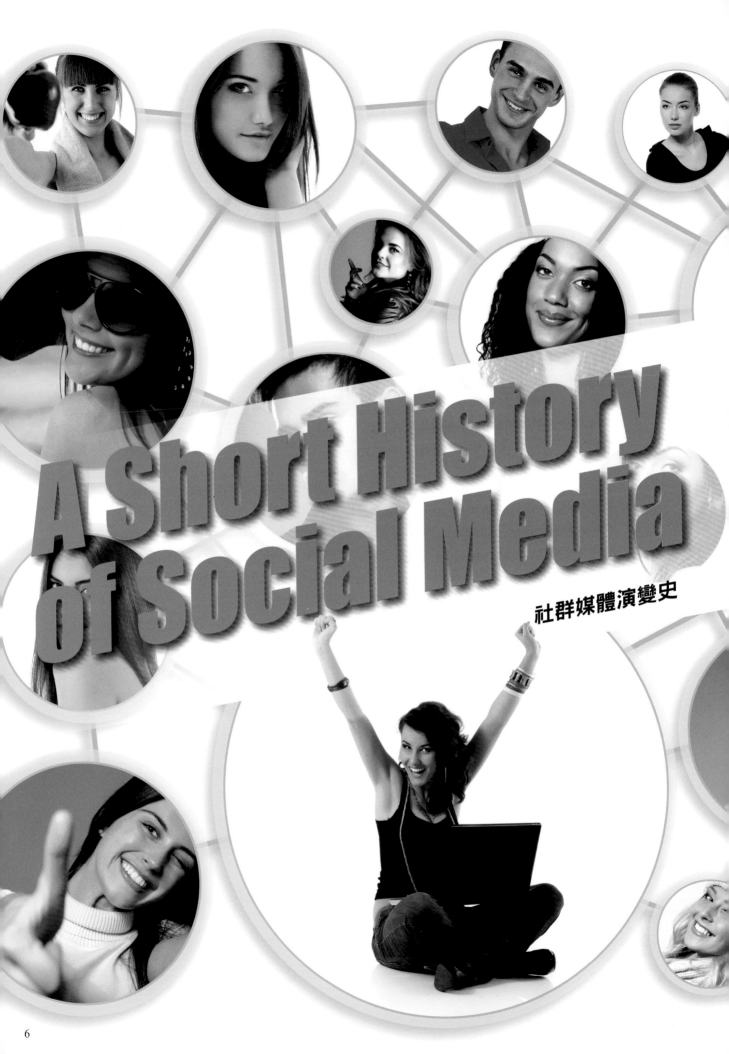

A Short History of Social Media

社群媒體演變史

文章 pp.6-10

A recent [1]invention
近期的發明

To young people today, it may seem like social media have been around forever. But social media, at least in the form that young people are familiar with, are actually a fairly recent invention. First, however, we need to go back to the beginning. Letters—written information that can be exchanged with other people over long distances—can be considered the earliest form of social media. During the [9]**heyday** of letter writing in the 18th century, most long distance [2]**communication** was [3]**carried out** by post. Some friendships were even maintained entirely by [4]**correspondence**, which of course required great patience—it could take weeks, or even months for letters to arrive.

對於現今的年輕人來說，社群媒體似乎存在已久。但社群媒體其實是近期發明的，至少以年輕人現在所熟悉的形式來說。不過首先我們要回到一開始，書信——人與人之間可以遠距離交換的書面訊息——可說是最早的社群媒體形式。18 世紀是寫信的全盛時期，大部分遠距離的通訊都是透過郵寄完成。有些友誼甚至完全藉由書信往來保持，這當然需要很大的耐心，因為當時的書信需要數週或甚至數月才能收到。

Communication speeds up
通訊速度加快

This all changed with the invention of the [5]**telegraph** in 1792. By the late 1800s, most of the world was connected by telegraph wires, and people could send messages over long distances in just minutes. Unfortunately, [6]**telegrams** had to be paid for by the word, so they weren't a great way to chat with friends in [7]**faraway** places. Next came the telephone in 1890, allowing people to talk to each other in [8]**real time**. But long distance calls were expensive, so telephones weren't an ideal form of social media either. It wasn't until the development of the computer in the 1940s and '50s that things really began to change.

這一切在 1792 年電報發明後改變了。到了十九世紀末，世界大部分地方都是靠拍電報聯繫，人們可以在幾分鐘內遠距離發送訊息。可惜電報是以字數計費，所以不是跟遠方朋友聊天的好方法。接下來是 1890 年發明的電話，可讓人們即時通話。但長途電話費依然昂貴，所以電話也不是社群媒體的理想形式。要等到 1940 和 1950 年代電腦發明後，一切才真正開始改變。

單字 pp.6-10

Vocabulary

1) **invention** [ɪnˋvɛnʃən] (n.) 創造，發明
2) **communication** [kə͵mjunəˋkeʃən] (n.) 溝通，傳播
3) **carry out** (phr.) 完成，執行，進行
4) **correspondence** [͵kɔrəˋspɑndəns] (n.) 通信，函授（課程）
5) **telegraph** [ˋtɛlə͵græf] (n.) 電報，電報機
6) **telegram** [ˋtɛlə͵græm] (n.)（一份）電報
7) **faraway** [͵fɑrəˋwe] (a.) 遙遠的，遠方的
8) **real time** (phr.) 即時，（電腦）即時處理

進階字彙

9) **heyday** [ˋhe͵de] (n.) 全盛期

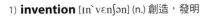

The Internet arrives
網路來臨

American scientists began looking for ways to link computers together, and by 1969, ARPANET—a military-funded [1]**network** that would [2]**eventually** become the Internet—began connecting the computer networks at American college campuses. A decade later, a network called Usenet allowed users, who had to connect with LG **dial-up modems**, to share articles and posts in LG "**newsgroups**." But because Usenet was limited to Unix systems, which were mostly found at universities, it was quickly replaced by LG **BBS**, or [3]**bulletin** board systems. Mostly [4]**hosted** on local networks, these systems allowed users to communicate on message boards, play online games and even share files. While BBS have mostly disappeared, they still survive in places like Taiwan, where LG **PTT** is still extremely popular with young people.

接下來美國科學家開始設法讓電腦互相連結，到了 1969 年，軍方資助的網絡 ARPANET 最終變成網際網路，開始連結美國各大學的電腦網路。十年後，Usenet 網路讓用戶透過撥接式數據機互相連結，在「新聞群組」上分享文章和貼文。但由於 Usenet 只限定 Unix 作業系統使用，而這種系統大多數在大學中使用，因此很快被電子佈告欄系統代替。這些系統的主機多數設在區域網路，讓用戶在留言板上通訊、玩線上遊戲，甚至分享檔案。雖然電子佈告欄系統大部分已經消失，但仍在臺灣等地保留下來，臺灣的批踢踢仍非常受年輕人歡迎。

Chatting in real time
即時聊天

The last development before the rise of social media as we know them today was the invention of instant messaging services like LG **IRC** and LG **ICQ**, which let people chat in real time on their computers, and were responsible for the spread of LG **emoticons** and [5]**abbreviations** like LOL and TTYL. Then, with the introduction of Internet service for the general public by companies like CompuServe and AOL, the first modern social media [6]**site**s began to appear. LG **Six Degrees**, which was created in 1997, was based on the "six degrees of separation" model—the idea that nobody in the world is separated by more than six steps. Six Degrees no longer exists, but like the sites popular today, it let users set up [7]**profiles**, add friends and create groups.

在現今的社群媒體興起前，最後一項發明是 IRC 和 ICQ 等即時通訊服務，能讓人們用電腦即時聊天，表情符號和 LOL、TTYL 等縮寫就是從這裡開始流傳開來（請見 p. 20「FB 和 Twitter 常見字」）。接著 CompuServe 和 AOL 等公司開始為一般大眾提供網路服務後，第一批現代社群媒體網站開始出現了。1997 年創辦的 Six Degrees 網站是基於「六度分隔理論」的模式－－世上任兩人透過最多六人就能聯繫上。Six Degrees 網站現已不存在，但它仍像現今流行的網站，能讓用戶設置個人資料、加好友和建立群組。

The "circle of friends" model
「朋友圈」模式

Six Degrees was soon followed by instant messaging services like MSN Messenger and Yahoo! Messenger, and early LG **blogging sites** like LiveJournal. Next came social media sites that used the "circle of friends" model, like

Friendster, which also served as a dating site, and MySpace, which allowed users to share music for free. This MySpace feature was a big [8]**hit** with music fans and musicians, and even helped start the careers of stars like Adele and Skrillex. MySpace went online a year before Facebook—which was created by Mark Zuckerberg in his Havard [9]**dorm** room in 2004—and was much more successful its early years. But then Facebook [10]**expanded** its [11]**membership** from college students to the general population, and by 2008 had become the most popular social media site in the world.

新聞群組 (newsgroup)

繼 Six Degrees 網站後，MSN 和雅虎奇摩即時通等即時通訊服務跟著出現，還有早期的部落格網站，比如 LiveJournal。接著運用「朋友圈」的社群媒體網站出現了，比如也是約會網站的 Friendster，以及讓用戶免費分享音樂的 MySpace。這項功能讓 MySpace 在音樂愛好者和音樂家的圈子風靡一時，甚至幫助愛黛兒和史奇雷克斯等明星展開職涯。MySpace 比 Facebook 早創辦一年，馬克祖克柏於 2004 年在哈佛大學的宿舍創辦 Facebook，初期時 MySpace 比 Facebook 更成功，但之後 Facebook 將會員資格從大學生擴大到一般民眾，到 2008 年已成為世上最受歡迎的社群媒體網站。

Vocabulary

1) **network** [ˈnɛt͵wɝk] (n.) 電腦網路，社群，電視網

2) **eventually** [ɪˈvɛntʃuəli] (adv.) 最後，終究

3) **bulletin** [ˈbʊlətɪn] (n.) 新聞快報，公報，**bulletin board** [ˈbʊlətɪn bɔrd] 即「佈告欄」

4) **host** [host] (v.) 為（網站）提供軟硬體支援

5) **abbreviation** [ə͵briviˈeʃən] (n.) 簡稱，縮寫

6) **site** [saɪt] (n.) 網站（=**website**）

7) **profile** [ˈprofaɪl] (n.)（人物）簡介

8) **hit** [hɪt] (n.) 成功、受歡迎的事物

9) **dorm** [dɔrm] (n.) 宿舍，為 **dormitory** [ˈdɔrmɪ͵tori] 的簡稱

10) **expand** [ɪkˈspænd] (v.) 擴大，擴展

11) **membership** [ˈmɛmbɚ͵ʃɪp] (n.) 會員資格、身分

New ways of sharing
與人分享的新方法

Now that just about everybody with an Internet connection had a Facebook account, it may have seemed like there was nowhere new for social media to go. But people like to connect and share in as many ways as possible, and new products kept appearing to meet these needs. With Skype, it became possible to make free video calls from your computer, and photo sharing services like Flickr have allowed photographers to share their work with other photographers all over the world. And if you enjoy videos, YouTube provides the perfect place to watch them and even create your own. Or if you like to blog, but don't have time to write long posts, Twitter is the place to go—each "tweet" is limited to 280 characters, just enough for a sentence or two.

這時幾乎所有能上網的人都有 Facebook 帳號，社群媒體似乎已經推不出更多新意。但人們希望盡量多用各種方式與他人聯繫和分享，因此不斷有新產品推出以符合這些需求。Skype 可讓你用電腦打免費視訊電話，Flickr 等相片分享服務能讓世界各地的攝影師分享彼此的作品。你若喜歡看影片，YouTube 是看影片的理想網站，甚至能創作你自己的影片。或者你若喜歡寫部落格，但沒有時間寫長篇文章，可以用推特，每條「推文」限制 280 字元，只能發一、兩句話。

The rise of the smartphone
智慧手機興起

Many of the most recent social media developments have been influenced by the rise of the smartphone, which people began buying in large numbers after the iPhone came out in 2008.

Some of these new services [1]**take advantage of** smartphone cameras, like 🄛🄖 **Instagram**, which lets you take photos and share them instantly with friends, and 🄛🄖 **Snapchat**, a [2]**multimedia** messaging app that lets you make video messages that disappear after they're sent. Others are location-based, like Tinder, a dating app that people can use to connect with nearby users. And new social media apps are being developed all the time. What's coming next? We'll just have to wait and see!

近期的社群媒體發展大部分受到智慧手機興起的影響，iPhone 在 2008 年推出以來就開始有大量人購買智慧手機。有些新的社群媒體服務會利用智慧手機相機，比如 Instagram，能讓你照相後立刻與朋友分享，Snapchat 則讓你製作影片訊息，並在發送後消失。另外還有定位式的服務，例如 Tinder，是能讓人用來跟附近用戶聯繫的約會 app。現在不斷有新的社群媒體 app 開發出來，接下來會有什麼？讓我們拭目以待吧！

Vocabulary

1) **take advantage of** (phr.) 利用…的機會
2) **multimedia** [ˌmʌltiˈmidiə] (a./n.) 多媒體（的）

social media 社群媒體

可以雙向溝通，相互交流、分享彼此的網路平台，能以各種形式來呈現，包括影像或音樂，不侷限以文字來表達，如 Facebook 和 Instagram 都是目前主流的社群媒體之一。

telegraph 電報

女子正在利用電報傳送摩斯密碼

利用「電流」來傳遞訊息，當時的技術無法做出能表達所有字母的設備，利用電流有無火花所產生的符號來替代，發展出我們所知的摩斯電碼 (Morse code)。現今的傳真技術，就是從這裡來。另一個字 telegram 也叫電報，這兩個字究竟有什麼不一樣呢？ telegraph 是指打電報的「機器」；telegram 則是利用電報所發送的電文。

dial-up modem 撥接數據機

dial-up 有「撥號上網」的意思，透過電話線來做數據傳輸，在撥接網路的過程會發出聲響，上網佔線的同時，電話便無法通話，費用昂貴且容易斷線，是 90 年代網路剛興起的連網方式。

newsgroup 新聞群組

這裡的「新聞」指的是各種主題的資訊交流，形式類似於現今的論壇，只要使用 Usenet 網路協定的電腦都能看見這些資料，這是早期的電腦網路系統之一。

BBS 電子布告欄系統

bulletin board system 的縮寫，發展至今都是使用 Talen 協定的純文字形式，被認為是網路論壇的前身，依照不同主題看板，提供給網友各種話題的資訊，是能雙向溝通的討論空間，可以發表及回覆自己的主張意見。**PTT**（批踢踢實驗坊）是目前台灣最大的 BBS 網站，「鄉民」們會在板上討論各種最夯最流行的時事話題。PTT 的使用者被泛稱為「鄉民」。

IRC / ICQ

IRC 和 ICQ 都是早期的通訊軟體。IRC 是 internet relay chat 的縮寫，透過特定的 IRC 伺服器，選擇頻道 (channel) 也就是聊天室，進行即時的團體討論，不過現在已經不盛行了。ICQ ——通訊軟體的老前輩，取名字

「I seek you」的諧音，意思就是「我找你」。前陣子趁著歡慶誕生 20 週年大改造，使用起來可不會輸給 LINE 喔！

emoticon 表情符號

是由 emotion 和 icon 組合的字，讀作 [ɪˋmotɪˏkɑn]，emotion 表「情感、情緒」，icon 則是「圖示、圖像」，顧名思義，emoticon 就是指用來表達情緒，大部分以圖片來呈現，例如 LINE 中的貼圖功能，是網路傳訊常會使用的功能。

Six Degrees 網站

六度分格理論 (six degrees of separation) 是指任何人之間的關係最多只間隔六個人。這是什麼意思呢，就是說只要透過六個人，就能連結世界任何人。Six Degrees 網站大約盛行於 1997 年至 2000 年間，是根據這個理論創立的社交網站。使用者可以和排名「前三度」的好友聊天、貼文分享心情，甚至再連結到其他使用者，就是可以連結到朋友的朋友，跟現今流行的社交網站非常相似。

blog 部落格

blog [blɑg] 是由「web」和「log」組合而來的，照字面翻就是「網路日誌」。在 Facebook 盛行之前，部落格有一段輝煌時期。早期的「無名小站」就是部落格的一種，有相簿功能，圖文並茂的紀錄方式，在當時非常流行。後來甚至出現專職在部落格發表文章的部落客 (blogger)，例如知名的網路圖文插畫家彎彎和馬克、兩性暢銷作家女王都是從這裡發跡。

年輕人愛用的社群媒體

不斷推陳出新，目前最受年輕人歡迎的社群媒體竟然不是 Facebook ！從照片到影片，只要短短十秒，輕鬆分享生活片段，這是 **Instagram** 和 **Snapchat** 帶來的新形態。更特別的是 Snapchat 的分享方式與主流平台不同，分享的貼文訊息不會永久保存，帶來不同的趣味性。

Social Media
Let's Get Social!

pp.12-13

你也有一天沒滑臉書就渾身不對勁的症頭嗎？網路帶起社群新型態，交朋友不一定要跨出門，不論是什麼樣的新鮮事，只消一個 **click**，即可全部掌握！這全都要多虧智慧型手機和社群網站的興起，現在就讓 **EZ TALK** 來跟你聊聊這些天天朝夕相處的便利科技吧！

社群網站 大家一起來哈啦吧！

社群媒體好用句

社群網站有很多，每種的功能不同，每個人偏愛的也不同，光是聊自己的喜好就有很多可以聊：

- Facebook is really convenient, but sometimes it can cause information overload.
  臉書很方便，但有時候訊息會爆量。

- I like Plurk better because the interface is easier to use.
  我比較喜歡用噗浪，因為介面比較好操作。

- I love photography, and Instagram makes it easy for me to edit and share photos.
  我很愛拍照，Instagram 讓我很容易就能編修照片並分享出去。

當然，也會有一些討厭用社群網站的原始人：

- I don't want to share every little detail of my life with everyone.
  我不想把生活大小事都分享給別人知道。

- Constantly updating your Facebook status is so meaningless.
  一直更新動態很沒意義耶。

- Nobody has any privacy anymore.
  已經沒人可以保有隱私了。

- I prefer interacting with people face to face.
  我比較喜歡與人面對面接觸。

用臉書上的訊息可是用來八卦、聯絡感情的熱門話題：

- Kate just updated her relationship status to "in a relationship"!
  凱特把感情狀態改為「穩定交往中」了！

- I saw on Facebook that my friends had a barbecue, but they didn't invite me!
  我在臉書上看到朋友相約去烤肉居然沒揪我！

- Mary's posts are all so negative! What's wrong with her?
  瑪麗發佈的動態都好負面喔！她怎麼了？

- I found out I have a lot of friends in common with Stella.
  我發現我跟史黛拉有好多共同朋友喔！

- I got unfriended by Kelly.
  我被凱莉刪好友了。

當然，除了分享心情之外，社群網站還有許多其他功能：

- I set up a Like page for my dog on Facebook.
  我幫我的狗狗在臉書上開了一個粉絲團。

- I'm addicted to playing games on Facebook.
  臉書上的小遊戲讓我沉迷。

- How do you start a Facebook group?
  我要怎麼在臉書架設社團？

- You can just send me a message if you don't want everyone to see what you write.
  如果你不想被大家看到訊息，可以傳私訊給我。

- How do I create an event?
  要怎麼開活動？

- Do you know how to place an ad on Facebook?
  我想在臉書上登廣告，該怎麼做？

社群網站上惱人的現象也很多，看到以下這些句子，想必你也心有戚戚焉：

- My boss wants to friend me. What should I do?
  我老闆要加我好友。怎麼辦？

- Those girls who always post selfies are so annoying.
  那些狂上傳自拍照的女生真的很煩耶。

- I wish they'd stop posting baby photos. They all look the same!
  我希望他們不要再一直 po 寶寶的照片了。看起來都一樣啊！

- Don't tag me in the photo—I'm supposed to be studying now.
  照片不要標示我喔，我現在應該在唸書才對。

- All these people I don't know keep friending me!
  一直有很多不認識的人加我好友！

- Why do people have to check in wherever they go?
  大家幹嘛去哪裡都要打卡啊？

- There are so many ads on Facebook. It's so intrusive!
  臉書上的廣告好多，好干擾！

- Rebecca keeps writing these whiny posts.
  蘿貝卡又在發表一些無病呻吟的動態了。

- I wish people wouldn't talk politics on Facebook.
  我希望大家可以不要在臉書上發政治文。

社群網站單字庫 Vocab Bank

社群分享網站

現在比較熱門的社群分享網站是這些，你都會唸嗎？

Facebook [ˈfesˌbʊk]

Twitter [ˈtwɪtɚ]

Tumblr [ˈtʌmblɚ]

LinkedIn [ˈlɪŋktˌɪn]

Plurk [plɝk]

Instagram [ˈɪnstəˌgræm]

Pinterest [ˈpɪntərɪst]

Flickr [ˈflɪkɚ]

Foursquare [ˈforˌskwɛr]

Myspace [ˈmaɪˌspes]

Yelp [jɛlp]

為什麼叫 Twitter？

Twitter 的中文名稱是「推特」，twitter 本來是小鳥的鳴叫聲，於是就用小鳥嘰嘰喳喳的意象來帶出大家在上面碎碎念的感覺，除了 logo 是一隻藍色小鳥，上頭發表的訊息也被稱作推文（tweet [twit]）。這種微網誌的好處是以文字抒發為主，不需長篇大論，也不會有過多紛雜的資訊。

什麼是社群網站？

social network（社群網絡）原為社會學用語，指人與人建立起來的社交圈。而我們現在常聽到的 social networking site（社群網站，亦可稱「社交網站」）即是一種讓人們得以聯繫、交流的網路互動平台，具有拓展社交圈和聯繫感情的作用。一般來說，像 Facebook、Twitter、Myspace 和 Plurk 等都稱為 social networking service（社群服務），不過由於它是藉由網站 (site) 來提供服務，所以大家也常會稱它們為 social networking site。

最常用的臉書功能：

status　動態
relationship status　感情狀態
news feed　動態消息
check in　打卡
share　分享
tag　貼標籤
like　按讚
unlike　收回讚
upload　上傳
friend　加入好友
unfriend　刪好友
block　封鎖
notification　通知
event　活動
group　群組
privacy settings　隱私設定
privacy checkup　隱私檢查
liked pages　粉絲頁面
mutual friends　共同好友
follow　追蹤

社群網站現象

探討社群網站現象，可能會用到這些單字，
快來學學免得跟不上時代。

鄉民 Internet user

A: Do netizens in your country have an
influence on politics?
貴國的鄉民對政治有影響力嗎？

B: What's a netizen? Is that like an
Internet user?
什麼是鄉民？你是指網路使用者嗎？

但 netizen 這個用法在歐美並不常見，我們也
稱網路使用者為「網友」，而網友的另一個
意思是網路上認識的朋友，英文則是 online
friend。

A: Do you ever meet with your **online
friends** face to face?
你有跟網友面對面聚會過嗎？

B: A few, but most of them are just
Facebook friends.
有那麼幾個，但大多都是只臉書上的朋友。

網軍 cyber warrior

A: Did you hear about the government program to train **cyber warriors**?
你有聽說政府招募訓練網軍的計畫嗎？

B: Yeah. We need them to protect our infrastructure from black hat hackers.
有。我們需要這種人保護國家基礎設施免受黑帽駭客攻擊。

我們這邊戲稱為「婉君」的所謂網軍，大多時候都只是數量龐大相互取暖的酸民及黑
特。嚴格來說，cyber warrior 是國家或政治團體發動的網路專業人士，專門向敵對陣
營的網站、網路留言板、臉書等發動攻擊，稱為「網路戰爭」cyber warfare。維護資
訊系統安全的網路高手是 white hat hacker（白帽駭客）；而利用網路技能犯罪者，
就是 black hat hacker（黑帽駭客）。

A: Do you believe that Russian hackers tried to influence the American
election?
你相信俄羅斯駭客試圖影響美國選舉嗎？

B: Yes. The Russians are experts at **cyber warfare**.
相信。俄羅斯可是網路戰爭專家。

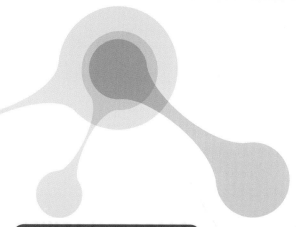

網紅 Internet celebrity

A: Did you know that Justin Bieber started out as an **Internet celebrity**?
你曉得小賈斯汀出道之初是一個網紅嗎？

B: Really? No, I had no idea.
真的嗎？我不知道耶。

Internet celebrity 或稱 online celebrity 是指因網路竄紅的名人，一般是受歡迎的部落客，或是靠上傳影片到 Youtube 引起廣大注意的人，這種人也被叫做 Youtuber。

網路爆紅 viral hit

A: Have you seen Carpool Karaoke with James Corden?
你有看詹姆士寇登的車上卡拉ＯＫ嗎？
（註：名人跟《詹姆斯科登深夜秀》(*The Late Late Show with James Corden*) 主持人一起開車上路，在車上唱歌的節目單元）

B: Of course. It's the biggest **viral hit** of the year.
當然有。這是今年網路上最爆紅的節目。

viral 是「病毒的」，hit 是「受歡迎的人事物」，viral hit 是從 viral marketing （病毒行銷），即透過網友彼此流傳或建立口碑，如同病毒般迅速蔓延的行銷手法。網路爆紅的動詞說法是 go viral。

A: Did your cute cat video **go viral**?
你的可愛貓咪影片在網路上爆紅了嗎？

B: Yeah. It already has millions of views.
有啊，已經有好幾百萬次點閱了。

酸民 troll

A: Are there a lot of **trolls** on that forum?
那個論壇上的酸民很多嗎？

B: Yeah. They're always starting flame wars.
多囉。那些人老是掀起論戰。

酸民是指憤世忌俗，故意留尖酸刻薄的言論討人厭，想要引發論戰（flame war），另一種「黑特」hater 則是討厭特定目標，比如仇恨某位明星，不管這個明星做什麼說什麼，他都要上影迷版亂罵一通。

A: Why do people say such negative things about such a successful singer?
怎麼有人會如此抹黑這麼成功的歌手？

B: Well, like Taylor Swift says, "**Haters** gonna hate."
哎，就像泰勒絲說的「黑特就是心懷仇恨。」

Conversation 1　社群網站該選哪個好？

Brenda: I'm thinking of joining a social media site. Any tips?

Allen: [1)]**Sign up for** Facebook! I mean, who doesn't have Facebook these days? I've used Facebook to get back in touch with lots of old friends.

Brenda: I actually have a Facebook [2)]**account**, but I don't use it very often. There's just too much [3)]**disorganized** information on there. I'm just looking for a place where I can express my feelings.

Allen: In that case, you should use Twitter or Plurk. They're a perfect way to 🄛 **get stuff off your chest**, and they won't give you information overload. There are even lots of [4)]**celebrities** on Twitter.

Brenda: Hmm, sounds like Twitter may be a good choice.

Allen: Oh yeah. Don't you like taking pictures? You can use Instagram. It lets you [5)]**apply** different [6)]**filters** to your photos and then share them [7)]**online**. Instagram is really popular now.

布蘭達：我在考慮來玩一下社群網站？有好推薦嗎？
艾　倫：用臉書啊！我說，現在誰還沒有臉書啊？而且我就是在臉書上找到很多失散已久的老朋友。
布蘭達：其實我有臉書帳號啦，只是很少上。上面訊息太雜亂了，我只想找個地方抒發心情而已。
艾　倫：那你可以用噗浪或推特啊！很適合讓你在上面吐嘈，也不會有過多資訊。連很多名人也都有在用推特。
布蘭達：嗯，聽起來推特可能是個好選擇喔。
艾　倫：對了，你不是很喜歡拍照？那你也可以用 Instagram 啊。它可以用不同濾鏡給照片做特效，然後即時分享。這應用程式現在超紅的。

Conversation 2　臉書狂潮

Alice: Here we are at the restaurant. Wait a sec while I check in.

Stacy: Remember to tag us all while you're at it.

Ron: Hey, how come Rob isn't here yet?

Stacy: He just [8)]**PMed** me saying he's gonna be late. He said to go ahead and order.

[food arrives at table]

Ron: Ooh, looks delicious! [12)]**Dig in**!

Alice: Hold on! Let me take a picture so I can [9)]**post** it on FB.

Ron: Why do you have to take pictures of everything you eat? My [13)]**wall** is covered with your food pictures!

愛麗絲：到餐廳了！等等，先來讓我打個卡。
史黛西：記得順便把我們都 tag 進去喔！
榮　恩：喂，羅柏怎麼還沒到。
史黛西：他剛才私訊我說會晚點到，要我們先點餐。
（餐點上桌）
榮　恩：耶！看起來好好吃噢，開動吧！
愛麗絲：等一下！先讓我拍照傳到臉書。
榮　恩：搞不懂你為什麼每次吃東西都要先照一堆相，我的首頁全都是你的食物照！

Language Guide

get...off one's chest 一吐為快

把東西從胸口倒出來」，就是「傾訴心聲，一吐為快」的意思。

Stan: Hey, Patty. ⓛⓖ **Why the long face?**

Patty: My boss found me on Facebook and sent me a friend request. I complain about work a lot on Facebook, so I want to ignore his request. But if I do that, he'll think I'm [14]**snubbing** him. Maybe I should just delete my account.

Stan: Whoa! ⓛⓖ **No need to go that far.** You can accept his invitation but limit the content he can see.

Patty: How do I do that?

Stan: You just divide your Friends List into "close friends" and "[10]**acquaintances**" and list your boss as an acquaintance. Then you set your privacy setting to Friends except Acquaintances, and only close friends can see your [8]**posts**.

Patty: It sounds a little [11]**complicated**, but it's better than closing my account and losing touch with my friends.

Stan: Exactly! Here, let me show you how to do it.

史　丹：嗨，派蒂。幹嘛臉這麼臭？

派　蒂：我老闆找到了我的臉書，還發了好友邀請。我很常在臉書上抱怨工作，我想忽略他的邀請。可是如果這麼做他又會覺得我冷落他。還是我乾脆刪帳號好了。

史　丹：哇，也不用做那麼絕啦。你可以接受他的邀請，但是限制他可以看到的內容。

派　蒂：要怎麼做？

史　丹：你只要把朋友名單分成「摯友」和「點頭之交」，把你老闆放在點頭之交就好了。然後你可以進行隱私設定，排除點頭之交，這樣就只有好友可以看到你上傳的內容。

派　蒂：聽起來有點複雜，但總比我關帳號，然後和一堆朋友失聯好。

史　丹：沒錯！來吧，我教你怎麼弄

Vocabulary

單字 pp.18-19

1) **sign up (for...)** [saɪn ʌp fɔr] (phr.) 註冊（帳號）

2) **account** [əˋkaʊnt] (n.) 帳戶，帳號

3) **disorganized** [dɪsˋɔrgənaɪzd] (a.) 雜亂無章的

4) **celebrity** [səˋlɛbrətɪ] (n.) 名人

5) **apply** [əˋplaɪ] (v.) 應用

6) **filter** [ˋfɪltə] (n.) 濾鏡

7) **online** [ˋɑnlaɪn] (adv./a.) 從網路上，在網路上，上網；線上的，網路上的

8) **PM** [ˏpiˋɛm] (n.) 私訊，全名為 **private message** [ˋpraɪvɪt ˋmɛsɪdʒ]

9) **post** [post] (v./n.) （在網站上）公佈，發布（資訊）；網站上公佈的資訊，帖子

10) **acquaintance** [əˋkwentəns] (n.) 相識人，舊識

11) **complicated** [ˋkɑmpləˏketɪd] (a.) 複雜的

進階字彙

12) **dig in** [dɪg ɪn] (phr.) 開動

13) **wall** [wɔl] (n.) Facebook 首頁

14) **snub** [snʌb] (v.) 冷落

Why the long face? 臉怎麼這麼臭？

A: What's wrong, man? Why the long face?
怎麼了？你臉怎麼那麼臭？

no need to go that far 不用做那麼過分

go far 除了字面上「走很遠」的意思外，也常引申指「過分」，例如有人開玩笑開過頭，你就可說 Your joke went too far（你玩笑開得太過分了。）

Understanding Facebook posts and Tweets

FB 和 Twitter 常用字

現在很氾濫的社群網路，像是 FB、Twitter 已經有 10 年的歷史，網路上已有自成的一套語言，不管是臉書功能還是網路縮寫，有些縮寫已經發展出原始定義以外的涵義了，快來了解這些網路語言的來源與用法！

網路縮寫這樣用

pp. 20-23

OMG 天哪！

Oh my God! 的縮寫，從網路發展出來，用在對話中表示驚訝或是厭惡。通常是少女會使用，由於覺得打出全名太麻煩而發明這樣的縮寫。

IDK 我不知道

為 I don't know. 的縮寫。

LOL 哈哈哈，也可寫作 lol

laughing out loud 的縮寫，在交談對話中用來表示極為好笑。

但現在這個字已經過度使用，常常在打出這個字時，根本不覺得好笑。現在這個字的使用情況可能包括：

1. 在對話中，不知道該講什麼的時候。
2. 我懶得讀你打的字，所以就打些沒什麼意義的話，讓你覺得我還有在看。
3. 你的話一點也不好笑，我打 LOL 只是假裝自己覺得好笑而已。
4. 有時只是沒什麼意思的語助詞，甚至在沒有意識的情況就打出來了。

TTYL 掰掰

為 talk to you later. 的縮寫，常用在多人線上遊戲或是聊天室。

ROFL 笑到在地上滾

為 roll on the floor laughing 的縮寫，強調比 LOL 更好笑。

JK 開玩笑的

為 Just kidding. 的縮寫。有時候對方真的是在開玩笑，但有時這句話前面會有一些不入耳的批評，然後最後說 JK，表示自己只是在開玩笑的，要你不要在意，但其實前面說的才是自己的內心話。

ILY 我愛你

大部分時間為 I love you. 的縮寫，但也可能是 I'm leaving you.（我要和你分手）的縮寫。

TMI 你說太多了

too much information 的縮寫，指對方講太多、太細了，你不想聽。

TBH 老實說…

to be honest 的縮寫。

FOMO 社交控，害怕錯過症

為 fear of missing out 的縮寫，指害怕錯過某些好玩活動的恐慌，通常是因社群網站上充斥親朋好友最近參與的最新、最酷的活動貼文所引發的。

FOMO 這個詞最早出現於 2004 年 8 月 12 日的加州《北岸週刊》（North Coast Journal）一篇報導中：艾卡西亞說：「那是場很棒的活動；我覺得我應該去，因為我可以免費參加。真正的原因是叫做 FOMO 的東西；它是一種疾病，害怕錯過症。」

TL;DR 太長了，沒看

也可用 TLDR 表示，為 "too long; didn't/don't read" 的縮寫，有兩種含意：

1. 別人給你的貼文、文章等，你覺得太長沒看時，可以用這個詞表示。
2. 自己寫了一篇長文，會先放這個詞後，再放上該文的簡短摘要。

SMH 傻眼，不 OK 吧

為 shaking my head 的縮寫，直譯的意思為「搖搖頭」，表示看到其他人的行為，覺得不以為然。

臉書功能與相關用語

#hashtag

hashtag [ˋhæʃˌtæg] (n.)

字符號

在 Facebook 和 Twitter 上，你一定看過 #，# 通常會出現在貼文和 tweet（推文）的最前面、要加強的重點內容，或是希望別人可搜尋到的內容。例如：#漫威，就可以搜尋到所有「漫威」相關的內容，# 後的字也會呈現粗體，要記住 # 後面的字中間不可以有空格或加標點符號喔。不過也有許多人認為，這個字已經被趕時髦的人濫用了。

這個字最早出現自 Twitter，但當時並非 Twitter 的功能。2009年，一台破損的飛機幸運地在哈德遜湖降落，有些 Twitter 用戶便發文，並在文章後加 #flight1549，這種用法很快就廣為流傳，蔚為風氣。

unfriend [ˌʌnˋfrend] (v.)

把朋友從 **Facebook** 帳號移除

有些人會定期清理臉書上的朋友名單，把沒有聯絡的朋友移除，但也可能是朋友的近況以及個人宣傳太惹人厭，你再也受不了看到這個人的一切。也有可能是他們的發言或留言惹到你，讓你不想再看到這個人。

unlike [ˌʌnˋlaɪk] (v.)

收回讚

這個詞發源自 Facebook，你公開表示 like「讚」，然後選擇收回「讚」，就是 unlike「收回讚」，這不表示你不喜歡某篇文章。

天哪！我被複製了！

HOLY CRAP

I'VE BEEN CLONED!

❤1436

💬 16

meme [mim] (n.)

通常指在網路上迅速傳播的有趣圖片，圖上有說明文字，又稱模因。

「模因」（meme）一詞的概念起源於 1976 年。當時，科普作家理察道金斯於其作品《自私的基因》中描述和定義模因，嘗試解釋文化資訊傳播的方式。模因的主題常和流行文化、政治相關，圖上的趣味說明也會在社群媒體散布時被人更動。

photobomb [ˋfotoˏbɑm]

（照片）亂入

在拍攝照片前，某人無預警地出現在鏡頭前，也因此入鏡，以至於畫面原本的重點被破壞。

女孩無預警地出現在爸媽的前面，使原本浪漫的婚紗照重點被破壞。

23

Tech Words

p. 24

科技衍生字

以下介紹一些由 **tech** 這個字衍生出來的相關字，想成為獨當一面的科技達人絕對要把這些字學好學滿！

tech nerd [tɛk nɝd]

科技呆子

相較於 nerd 指的是書呆子，tech nerd 指的是愛用科技、個性無趣的人，通常指愛用電腦的男性。

tech wreck [tɛk rɛk]

科技股崩盤

高科技產業的股價暴跌，相關詞為 tech bubble [tɛk `bʌbəl] 科技泡沫，指的是由於科技股投機活動增加導致的明顯和不持續的市場上漲。

technophobe [`tɛknəˌfob] (n.)

畏懼、不喜歡
且無法自信使用科技的人

tech support [tɛk səˋpɔrt]

技術支援

又作 technical support [ˋtɛknɪkəl səˋpɔrt]，由軟硬體公司提供服務，給予產品使用者協助和意見。

tech-savvy [ˋtɛkˋsævɪ] (a.)

形容對現代科技，
特別是電腦，懂很多的人

technophile [`tɛknəˌfaɪl] (n.)

科技狂人，科技達人

泛指熱愛科技，知道最新科技，並為科技著迷的人，為 technology（科技）和 -phile（喜愛⋯的人）結合的字，又可寫為 techie [ˋtɛki]，techie 也指在科技產業工作的人。

tech speak [tɛk spik]

科技行話

形容電腦專家、程式設計師、工程師說出來的話，通常聽起來很難懂，需要對電腦、硬體設計或是程式語言有更深的了解，才能理解。

Consumer Tech News

生活科技新聞

最生活化的科技產品、服務、
生活方式，以及伴隨而來的問
題與隱憂，人類是否有足夠的
智慧來掌控、整合與克服科技
所帶來的甜頭與挑戰？

文章 + 對話
pp. 26-29

Robots Replacing Waiters at Alibaba's Robot.He Restaurant

阿里巴巴的機器人餐廳以機器人取代服務生

24 小時的無人便利商店你去過了嗎？
還沒去體驗看看的朋友可就落伍囉！
這可能是 30 年前我們的從未想過的現在。
科技帶來的便利性，
無人經濟創造的無限未來，
人力被取代並不是不無可能，
不過這樣的經營模式究竟是如何落實，
讓我們一起來看看吧！

Alibaba [1)]**made its name** in online shopping, but is now turning its attention to [9)]**brick-and-mortar** stores. The Chinese [10)]**e-commerce** giant opened its first Hema (a [11)]**pun** on the Chinese word for hippo) supermarket in January 2016, and by the end of 2018 there will over 100 all across China. Products can be bought both online and [2)]**offline** from Hema, and even delivered in 30 minutes to customers who live within a 3 km [3)]**radius**. Inside the store, shoppers use the Hema **app** to [4)]**scan** items as they shop. Then, when they get to checkout, they can pay using **Alipay**, Alibaba's mobile [5]**payment** platform.

阿里巴巴因網路購物而成名，但現正將重心轉向實體店。這間中國電子商務巨頭於 2016 年 1 月推出第一家盒馬（中文河馬的諧音）超市後，到 2018 年底已經在中國各地開設逾一百家分店。顧客可上網或到盒馬實體超市購物，甚至住在超市方圓三公里內的顧客可在 30 分鐘內送貨到府。顧客在超市裡可使用盒馬 app 掃描要購買的商品，然後結帳時可用阿里巴巴的線上支付平臺支付寶結賬。

And now Alibaba is applying technology in another area to make shoppers' lives more convenient: restaurants. Inside one of their Shanghai Hema stores is Robot.He, a seafood restaurant where the waiters have been replaced by robots. At Robot.He, most of the work usually done by [6]**waitstaff** is handled by automated equipment and robot carts that travel on waist-high [7]**counters**; and seating, ordering and payment are [8]**taken care of** by smartphone apps.

阿里巴巴現正在另一個領域應用這項技術，使顧客的生活更便利：餐廳。他們在上海一家盒馬超市附設 Robot.He 機器人海鮮餐廳，服務生已由機器人取代。Robot.He 的大部分服務生工作由自動化設備和在與腰齊高的櫃檯來回行走的機器人推車完成；入座、點餐和付帳都透過智慧手機的 app 處理。

So how does this work for customers? When they arrive at the restaurant, they're still greeted by a host or hostess, who helps them use a personal QR code on the Hema app to find a seat. The diner then enters the supermarket to pick the fresh seafood they want the cooks to prepare. Their **QR code** is again scanned at checkout, and the items are placed on a [12]**conveyor** belt, and then placed in a refrigerator by a **robotic arm** to keep cool until the diner is seated and the cooks are ready to prepare the food.

那麼顧客要怎麼使用這家餐廳？顧客抵達餐廳時，仍有服務生接待，他們會協助顧客使用盒馬 app 上的個人 QR 碼找座位。然後顧客進入超市挑選讓廚師烹飪的新鮮海鮮，結帳時再用 QR 碼掃描食材，並將食材放在輸送帶上，然後由機器手臂放入冰箱保鮮，直到顧客入座，廚師準備烹調。

單字 pp. 26-29

Vocabulary

1) **make one's name** (phr.) 變得很出名
2) **offline** [ɑfˋlaɪn] (adv./a.) 離線；不連線的
3) **radius** [ˋredɪəs] (n.) 半徑，半徑範圍
4) **scan** [skæn] (v.) 掃描
5) **payment** [ˋpemənt] 支付，付款，
   mobile payment 即「行動支付」
6) **waitstaff** [ˋwetˏstæf] (n.) 服務生（統稱）
7) **counter** [ˋkaʊntɚ] (n.) 櫃檯

8) **take care of** (phr.) 處理，負責

進階字彙

9) **brick-and-mortar** [ˏbrɪkəndˋmɔrtɚ] (a.) 磚瓦加水泥
   （常用來比喻實體店面），實體的
10) **e-commerce** [ˋiˏkɑmɝs] (n.) 電子商務
11) **pun** [pʌn] (n.) 雙關語，俏皮話
12) **conveyor belt** [kənˋveɚ bɛlt] (n.) 傳送帶，傳輸帶

While waiting, the [1]**diner** can use the menu on the Hema app to order additional items, like rice. When the main course is ready, the kitchen staff places it, along with the additional items, on robot carts. Next, the carts [2]**glide** along the restaurant counters to the diner's table, using their QR code to find the correct location. The cover on the cart opens [3]**automatically**, and the diner can then remove the tray and enjoy his meal. It's usually considered [4]**impolite** to have your phone out during a restaurant meal, but this rule doesn't apply at Robot.He!

在等待上菜時，顧客可用盒馬 app 上的菜單點其他菜，例如米飯。主菜準備好時，廚房員工會將主菜和其他菜餚放在機器人推車上。接下來推車利用顧客的 QR 碼找到正確的座位，沿著餐廳櫃臺將餐點送到顧客桌上。推車

上的蓋子會自動打開，顧客可將拖盤取出，享用餐點。在餐廳用餐時拿出手機通常是不禮貌的，但這項禮儀在 Robot.He 不適用！

Vocabulary

1) **diner** [ˋdaɪnə] (n.) 用餐的人
2) **glide** [glaɪd] (v.) 滑動，滑行
3) **automatically** [͵ɔtəˋmætɪklɪ] (adv.) 自動地
4) **impolite** [͵ɪmpəˋlaɪt] (a.) 無理的，不禮貌的

Language Guide

app 應用程式

app 為 application 的縮寫，意思是應用程式。如同電腦一樣，在智慧型手機 (smartphone) 上安裝不同的應用程式，便可擴充裝置的功能。除照相、社群、搜尋功能的應用程式，近來還出現了像《Pokemon Go》與《太空戰士》等推陳出新的遊戲程式。app 這個字的正確唸法為 [æp]，而非台灣人常讀的 [e pi pi]，因此通訊軟體 WhatsApp 應該唸成 [wʌts æp]，正是取自 "What's up?" 這句問候語的諧音，表示這是一個用來聯絡感情的應用程式。

Alipay 支付寶

中國的第三方支付平台，最早是給淘寶網消費者的交易安全 (transaction security) 設定，為了降低用戶受騙的風險，防止買家收到不相符的商品。但要如何擔保買家的交易安全呢，買家下單後先將款項付款至由銀行代為管理的第三帳戶，淘寶收到付款資訊後，將商品寄至買家手上，由買家確認收到的商品無誤後，淘寶才會將款項轉帳 (transfer) 予賣家。如今，支付寶跨出阿里巴巴，合作廠商超過 30 萬家，含括生活日用、通訊服務、電玩遊戲等產業，搖身成為多元開放的付款平台，取代現金或信用卡，成為中國的主流付款方式之一，未來甚至不排除有發展虛擬貨幣 (virtual currency) 的可能性。

QR code 二維條碼

條碼在日常生活中的應用相當普遍，可以記錄許多資訊，資訊爆炸的現代，要想容納更多資訊，條碼勢必得越拉越長，於是便發明了第二代條碼技術，也就是二維條碼 (2D barcode，2D 表 two dimensional)，這種編碼方式可以連結到文字、聲音和圖形等資料，容量也較大，為黑白交錯的矩陣式（matrix）或條狀圖形。目前最常見的就是日本發明的 QR code（QR 表 quick response），只要下載掃描器，就可從中讀取網站、影音等資訊，相當方便。

robotic arm 機械手臂

仿真人手臂功能的機器裝置，以腕部以及手部的動作為主，能按照步驟規律運作，常使用在較具危險性的工業產業上，取代人力以降低作業風險或是應用在產線自動化方面。按照不同的型式及構造細分出不同類型的機械手臂，普遍是以三軸和多軸作為區分。產業的應用範圍也非常廣泛，從汽車工業、電子製造業開始，發展至今，更拓展至醫療、服務業等方面。

機械手臂正在裝箱

談論阿里巴巴旗下品牌

Rachel: Rachel: Hey, have you read about those new Alibaba supermarkets in China?

Fabio: No. I just know that they run Taobao. I hear it's the biggest online [1]**retailer** in the world now.

Rachel: Really? Bigger than Amazon? I mean, Jeff Bezos is the richest man in the world.

Fabio: Yeah, bigger than Amazon. They call Jack Ma "the Jeff Bezos of China." He helped make **LG Singles Day** the largest shopping day in the world.

Rachel: Singles Day? I've never even heard of it.

Fabio: It's like **LG China's Black Friday**. It started out as a day for people to [2]**celebrate** being single, but now it's all about shopping.

Rachel: Interesting. It says here that in Alibaba's Hema supermarkets all you need to shop is your smartphone—it's completely cashless. Is there anything like that in Taiwan?

Fabio: Well, there are a couple of [3]**unmanned** 7-Eleven stores where you can enter and pay using [4]**facial** [5]**recognition** or a [6]**cash card**.

Rachel: Wow! That sounds pretty [7]**futuristic**. But there are just a few?

Fabio: Yeah, and they're just **LG concept stores** at this point. Mobile payment isn't as popular in Taiwan as it is in China yet. Lots of people still prefer using cash.

瑞　秋：嘿，你看到中國的新阿里巴巴超市的新聞了嗎？

法比歐：沒有，我只知道他們經營淘寶網，聽說這是世上最大的網上零售店。

瑞　秋：真的？比亞馬遜還大嗎？我是說，傑佛瑞貝佐斯是世上最富有的人。

法比歐：對，比亞馬遜還大。他們稱馬雲是「中國的傑佛瑞貝佐斯」。他讓光棍節成了世上最大的購物日。

瑞　秋：光棍節？我從沒聽過。

法比歐：就像中國的黑色星期五。一開始是慶祝單身的日子，但現在成了購物日。

瑞　秋：有意思，新聞說阿里巴巴的盒馬超市可以用手機付帳，完全不用現金。臺灣有類似的東西嗎？

法比歐：有幾間 7-11 超商是無人商店，可以進去用人臉辨識或現金卡付帳。

瑞　秋：哇！聽起來很有未來感，但只有幾間而已嗎？

法比歐：對，而且目前只是概念商店。手機付帳在臺灣還不如中國流行。大多數人還是比較喜歡用現金。

Vocabulary

1) **retailer** [ˋritelɚ] (n.) 零售商，**retail** [ˋritel] (n./a./v.) 零售（的）

2) **cashless** [ˋkæʃləs] (a.) 不用現金的，刷卡的

3) **unmanned** [ʌnˋmænd] (a.) 無人的

4) **facial** [ˋfeʃəl] (a.) 臉部的

5) **recognition** [͵rɛkəgˋnɪʃən] (n.) 辨識，識別

6) **cash card** [kæʃ kɑrd] (n.) 現金卡

7) **futuristic** [͵fjutʃɚˋɪstɪk] (a.) 未來（主義）的，具未來感的

文章 + 對話
pp. 30-33

Make ¹⁾Fitness a ²⁾Priority This Year with a New Fitness Tracker

今年就用新的健身追蹤器，將健身列為頭等大事

健身追蹤器已經成為健身界的新寵兒，
還在找教練規劃督促實在太落伍啦！
現代人健康意識抬頭，運動觀念非常有，
光是這樣還不夠，還得利用智慧科技來
隨時掌握自己的健康資訊。
有趣的是，這股風潮還吹到寵物這來，
也有毛小孩版的健康追蹤器呢！

When it comes to health and fitness, your smartphone makes an excellent ³⁾**companion**. After all, there are apps available for just about everything, from diet and ⁴⁾**nutrition** to ¹⁶⁾<u>**cardio**</u> and ⁵⁾**yoga**. But a smartphone can be a burden when you're exercising—just ask anyone who's tried to run five miles with an iPhone ⁶⁾**strapped** to their arm. So if you've made a New Year's ⁷⁾**resolution** to lose weight or ⁸⁾**get fitter** in 2019, investing in some ⁹⁾**wearable** tech, like a fitness ¹⁰⁾**tracker** or a smartwatch, may be the perfect way to help you meet your goal.

說到健康和體能，手機是很棒的朋友。畢竟現在什麼都可用 app 處理，從飲食和營養到有氧運動和瑜伽。但運動時攜帶手機可能會是個累贅，只要問一下在五公里長跑時將蘋果手機綁在手臂上的人知道了。所以你在 2019 年的新年新希望如果是減重或健身，把錢花在穿戴型的科技產品，比如健身追蹤器或智慧手錶，這或許是幫你達到目標的最佳方式。

Fitbit has long been a leader in the fitness tracker market, and their latest model, the Fitbit Charge 3, is one of their best yet. The Charge 3 is lighter and thinner than previous [11]**versions**, and comes with a full **LG OLED LG touchscreen**. With the Charge 3, you can not only count steps, but automatically track different types of exercise, like running, biking and yoga. And because it's water-[17]**resistant** to 50 M, you can even track swimming. The Charge 3 also has a sleep tracking [12]**mode**, using its heart rate and **LG SpO2** [18]**sensors** to measure sleep quality.

健身手環 Fitbit 長久以來一直在健身追蹤器市場居於領先地位，他們的最新款 Fitbit Charge 3 也是最棒的一款。Charge 3 比之前的版本更輕薄，配備完整的 OLED 觸控螢幕。Charge 3 不但能幫你計算步數，還能自動追蹤不同類型的運動，比如跑步、騎自行車和瑜伽。由於它有 50 米防水範圍，你甚至可以追蹤游泳。Charge 3 還有睡眠追蹤模式，利用心率和血氧飽和度感應器測量睡眠品質。

Somewhere in between a fitness tracker and a smartwatch, the Garmin Vivoactive 3 Music is another excellent choice. The Vivoactive 3 can hold up to 500 songs [19]**locally**, making it easy to add music to your [13]**workout**. All you need is **LG Bluetooth** headphones and you're ready to go. With 15 sports apps—from golf to strength training—and many more available to download, you can choose how you like to get fit. And [20]**built-in** GPS lets you accurately record outdoor activities. Finally, you can [14]**monitor** your fitness level with the **LG VO2 max** and fitness age [15]**features**.

智慧手錶 Garmin Vivoactive 3 Music 是介於健身追蹤器和智慧手錶的絕佳選擇。Vivoactive 3 可儲存五百首歌，方便你在運動時聽音樂。你只需要藍牙耳機就行了。裡頭有 15 個運動 app，從高爾夫到重訓等，還有更多可以下載，你可以選擇自己喜歡的健身方式。還有內建全球定位系統，可以幫你精準紀錄戶外活動。最後，你可以用最大攝氧量和健身年齡功能監控健康狀況。

Fitbit Charge 3
Fitbit Charge 3 可偵測游泳的距離、速度、所花的時間和卡路里。

單字 pp.30-33

Vocabulary

1) **fitness** [ˈfɪtnɪs] (n.) 體適能，健康
2) **priority** [praɪˈɔrəti] (n.) 優先，重點
3) **companion** [kəmˈpænjən] (n.) 同伴，伴侶
4) **nutrition** [nuˈtrɪʃən] (n.) 營養，營養成分
5) **yoga** [ˈjogə] (n.) 瑜珈
6) **strap** [stræp] (v.) 用帶子繫（捆、綁）
7) **resolution** [ˌrɛzəˈluʃən] (n.) 決心，決定
8) **get fit** (phr.) 健身，塑形，使身體變健康
9) **wearable** [ˈwerəbəl] (a.) 穿戴式的
10) **tracker** [ˈtrækə] (n.) 追蹤器
11) **version** [ˈvɝʒən] (n.) 版本

12) **mode** [mod] (n.) 模式，方式
13) **workout** [ˈwɝˌkaut] (n.) （身體）鍛鍊、訓練
14) **monitor** [ˈmɑnɪtə] (v.) 監視，監控
15) **feature** [ˈfitʃə] (n./v.) 功能，特色；以…為特色，以…為號召

進階字彙

16) **cardio** [ˈkɑrdio] (n.) 有氧運動
17) **resistant** [rɪˈzɪstənt] (a.) 防…的，抵抗的
18) **sensor** [ˈsɛnsə] (n.) 感測器
19) **locally** [ˈlokəli] (adv.) 直接從內部地
20) **built-in** [ˌbɪltˈɪn] (a.) 內建的

Although the Apple Watch 4 is more smartwatch than fitness tracker, with a price to [1]**match**, it has more health and fitness features than any other smartwatch available. The Apple Watch 4 is basically an iPhone that's been turned into a [2]**stylish** watch—yes, you can use it to make calls, and call quality is good. The watch has all the automatic fitness tracking apps you'd expect, plus more for download, but it's the health features that really make it [3]**shine**. The new [6]**optical**/electric heart rate sensor monitors your heart with greater [4]**accuracy**, and can even take an [5]**ECG** you can save to [7]**PDF** and share with your doctor!

Apple Watch Series 4

雖然第四代蘋果手錶更偏向於智慧手錶而非健身追蹤器，價格也不便宜，但比其他智慧手錶的健康和健身功能還多。第四代蘋果手錶基本上是把蘋果手機變成時尚手錶，沒錯，這可以用來打電話，而且通話品質不錯。這手錶具備所有你想得到的自動健身追蹤 app，還有更多可以下載，不過以健康功能最出眾。新的光學／電子心率感應器可以幫你更準確監控心臟，甚至可以幫你做心電圖並存為 PDF 檔，與你的醫生分享！

Vocabulary

1) **match** [matʃ] (v.) 比得上的
2) **stylish** [ˈstaɪlɪʃ] (a.) 時髦的，流行的
3) **shine** [ʃaɪn] (v.) 表現突出，出眾
4) **accuracy** [ˈækjəəsi] (n.) 準確，精準
5) **ECG** [ˌisiˋdʒi] (n.) 心電圖，心電圖儀，為 **electrocardiogram** [ɪˌlɛktrəˋkɑdɪəˌgræm] 心電圖 或 **electrocardiograph** [ɪˌlɛktrəˋkɑdɪəˌgræf] 心電圖儀 的縮寫

進階字彙

6) **optical** [ˈɑptɪkəl] (a.) 視覺的，光學的
7) **PDF** [ˌpidiˋɛf] (a.) PDF 檔案，全名為 **portable document format** [ˈpɔrtəbəl ˋdɑkjəmənt ˋformæt] 可移植文檔格式

Language Guide

OLED 有機發光二極體

全名為 organic light-emitting diode，是目前的主流顯示器技術，提供為高解析度顯示器的使用，相較於液晶顯示器（liquid crystal display，簡稱 LCD）更省電、更輕薄、色彩更鮮豔，但價格也較 LCD 高了兩倍以上。

touch screen 觸控螢幕

沒事就滑一下，是現代人的習慣動作，可以「滑」手機，全托「觸控螢幕」的福。觸控螢幕為何物大家都曉得，但原理是什麼你們一定不知道吧！智慧型手機大多使用電容式 (capacitive sensing) 的觸控螢幕，利用人體會導電的特質，靠手指影響面板的電容量，推算出手指位置表達的功能，反應快速全在彈「指」之間。

SpO2 血氧飽和度

全名為 peripheral oxygen saturation，即血液中血氧的濃度，它是呼吸循環的重要生理參數。從事某些運動可能導致血氧飽和度降低，像是高空飛行、潛水等，使用者可藉由監控血氧飽和度，來調整運度強度，它也可用來測量睡眠品質和睡眠呼吸中止症 (sleep apnea)。許多疾病會造成氧供給的缺乏，這將直接影響細胞的正常新陳代謝，嚴重的還會威脅人的生命，所以動脈血氧濃度的實時監測在臨床救護中非常重要。

Bluetooth 藍牙

形成個人網域（personal area network，簡稱 PAN）來配對，以便進行近距離的資料交換或連線，是一種無線通訊的技術，不需要網路就能連接，目前是穿戴裝置或是智慧家庭常會使用的功能。

VO2 max 最大攝氧量

maximum oxygen volume 的簡寫，是指從事最激烈的運動時，所消耗的氧氣最大值。VO2 max 的數字愈高，表示能使用的氧氣就愈多，被認為是心肺耐力的指標。

談論健身追蹤器功能

Emma: Hey, I like your new watch.

Lucas: Thanks! It's actually not a watch. It's a Fitbit fitness tracker.

Emma: Cool. What does it do?

Lucas: Well, it's counting my steps right now. It can tell me how far I've walked and how many [1)]**calories** I've burned. And when we get to the gym, it'll track my exercise on the [2)]**stationary** bike too.

Emma: Do you have to switch [3)]**modes**?

Lucas: No. It has all kinds of exercise modes, but it uses **LG motion sensors** to detect what kind of exercise you're doing automatically.

Emma: Wow. Is that a touchscreen?

Lucas: Yeah. You can [4)]**navigate** the menu with [5)]**swipes** and taps.

Emma: That's convenient. What else can it do?

Lucas: All kinds of stuff, but my favorite is the sleep tracker. There's an SpO2 sensor to measure the [6)]**oxygen** in your blood, and the watch uses it to monitor your sleep quality.

Emma: Now *that's* something I could use!

艾　瑪：嘿，我喜歡你的新手錶。

盧卡斯：謝謝！這其實不是手錶，這是 Fitbit 健身追蹤器。

艾　瑪：酷，這有什麼功能？

盧卡斯：嗯，它正在計算我的步數，會紀錄我走了多遠，還有燃燒了多少卡路里。我們到健身房時，它還能追蹤我騎健身腳踏車的情況。

艾　瑪：你需要轉換模式嗎？

盧卡斯：不用，這有各種運動模式，但能利用移動感應器自動偵測你在做什麼運動。

艾　瑪：哇，這是觸控螢幕嗎？

盧卡斯：對，可以滑動和點擊來瀏覽選單。

艾　瑪：真方便，還有什麼功能？

盧卡斯：各式各樣，但我最喜歡的是睡眠追蹤。裡面有血氧飽和度感應器，可測量血液中的含氧量，用來監測睡眠品質。

艾　瑪：這正是我需要的功能！

Language Guide

motion sensors 移動感應器

移動感應器幾乎可以應用在任何會移動的物品上，從可穿戴的健身設備、智慧手錶、移動裝置到遊戲機都有，移動感應器主要由下列三種元素組成：感應器 (accelerometer)、磁場感應器 (magnetic sensor) 以及陀螺儀 (gyroscope)。

Vocabulary

1) **calorie** [ˈkælərɪ] (n.)（熱量單位）卡路里，卡

2) **stationary** [ˈsteʃəˌnɛrɪ] (a.) 靜止的，**stationary bike** 即「健身腳踏車」

3) **mode** [mod] (n.) 模式，方式

4) **navigate** [ˈnævəˌget] (v.) 瀏覽（網站）

5) **swipe** [swaɪp] (n./v.)（手指在螢幕上）滑動，刷（卡）

6) **oxygen** [ˈɑksɪdʒən] (n.) 氧，氧氣

文章＋對話
pp.34-37

Taiwan Slow to Adopt Mobile Payment

臺灣採用行動支付速度緩慢

不管是搭車還是買東西，
出門只要一支手機全部搞定。
使用行動支付讓消費變得更簡單，
也不用再為了找零錢而苦惱。
不僅如此，
它還能綁定多張信用卡，
幾乎是快完全取代錢包的功能。
雖然如此方便，
但台灣採用行動支付的速度卻十分緩慢，
究竟為何？讓我們來看看。

    With the highest rate of mobile payment [1]**usage** in the world, China is on its way to becoming the first cashless [2]**economy**. China accounts for 60% of mobile payments made worldwide, and 77% of the population regularly use mobile payment services. In addition, in a recent survey, 14% of Chinese [3]**consumers** said they refused to accept cash [4]**at all**. And other Asian countries are following China's lead. Mobile payment [5]**penetration** is 76% in India, 67% in Indonesia—currently the world's fastest growing mobile payment market—and 64% in Korea.

    行動支付使用率為全世界最高的中國正成為第一個無現金經濟體。中國的行動支付數量佔全球60％，77％的人口習慣使用行動支付服務。此外，近期一項調查顯示，14％的中國消費者表示完全拒絕接受現金，亞洲其他國家也開始效仿。行動支付在印度的普及率為76％，印尼為67％——目前是世上成長最快速的行動支付市場，韓國為64％。

In Taiwan, however, only 13% of the population uses mobile payment. Considering that Taiwan's economy began developing decades ahead of China and many other Asian countries, this figure may seem surprising. Taiwan has a smartphone ⁵⁾**penetration rate** of 93%, one of the highest in the world. And government data shows that over 80% of the population has ⁶⁾**access** to mobile Internet, with a similar ⁷⁾**percentage** willing to try or continue using **contactless payment**, a ⁸⁾**category** that includes **smart cards, contactless credit and** ⁹⁾**debit cards,** and payment made with mobile devices.

但在臺灣，只有 13% 人口使用行動支付。鑒於臺灣的經濟發展比中國和許多亞洲其他國家早起步數十年，這個數字可能令人驚訝。臺灣的智慧手機普及率為 93%，是全球最高普及率之一，而政府的數據顯示，有超過 80% 人口的手機可上網，類似的比例人口願意嘗試或繼續使用感應式支付，包括智慧卡、感應式信用卡和簽帳卡，以及用行動裝置支付。

 Taiwan's slow pace in adopting mobile payment can largely be explained by the fact that it has long had a well developed ¹⁰⁾**financial** system. The same is true for Japan, which also has a low mobile payment penetration rate of 27%. In Taiwan, consumers have many convenient non-cash payment choices, including **chip and PIN** ¹¹⁾**transactions** with credit and debit cards, as well as the popular EasyCard, which was originally designed for use on public ¹²⁾**transportation**.

Another reason for the slow mobile payment adoption rate is security concerns—many local consumers consider chip and PIN transactions to be more ¹³⁾**secure** than digital payment.

臺灣採用行動支付的速度緩慢，主要是因為長久以來已發展出完善的金融體制。日本也是同樣情況，他們的行動支付普及率也較低，為 27%。臺灣的消費者有許多方便的無現金支付選擇，包括信用卡和簽帳卡的晶片與個人辨識碼交易，以及受歡迎的悠遊卡，這原本是為了用於大眾運輸而設計。行動支付採用緩慢的另一個因素是安全疑慮，許多本地消費者認為晶片與個人辨識碼交易比數位交易更安全。

單字 pp.34-37

Vocabulary

1) **usage** [ˈjusɪdʒ] (n.) 使用，使用方法

2) **economy** [ɪˈkɑnəmi] (n.) 經濟（局勢）

3) **consumer** [kənˈsumɚ] (n.) 消費者

4) **at all** (phr.) （用於否定句和疑問句，表示強調）一點兒也

5) **penetration** [ˌpɛnəˈtreʃən] (n.) 穿透，滲入，
penetration rate 即「市佔率」

6) **access** [ˈæksɛs] (v./n.) 使用，進入，存取

7) **percentage** [pɚˈsɛntɪdʒ] (n.) 百分比，部分

8) **category** [ˈkɑtɪˌɡori] (n.) 種類，範疇

9) **debit** [ˈdɛbɪt] (n.) 提撥款項，**debit card** 即「轉帳卡」，是種具刷卡功能，但能直接從存款帳戶扣錢（扣完就無法再刷）的金融卡

10) **financial** [faɪˈnænʃəl] (a.) 金融的，財務的

11) **transaction** [trænˈzækʃən] (n.) 交易

12) **transportation** [ˌtrænspɚˈteʃən] (n.) 交通運輸（工具）

13) **secure** [sɪˈkjʊr] (a.) 安全的，無危險的

Since the government [1)]**relaxed** [2)]**regulations** on [3)]**third-party** payments in 2015, international mobile payment services like Apple Pay, Google Pay and Samsung Pay have entered the market. There are now [4)]**dozens of** **①** **mobile wallet** services operating in Taiwan, but the numbers of businesses that accept these forms of payment remain low. The government has recently introduced tax [5)]**incentives** to businesses that accept mobile payment, and has set a goal for 90% of smartphone users to adopt mobile payment by 2025. Whether this goal can be met remains to be seen.

自政府於 2015 年放寬對第三方支付的規定以來，Apple Pay、Google Pay 和 Samsung Pay 等國際行動支付服務已進入臺灣市場。現在臺灣有數十家行動錢包服務，但接受這些支付形式的商家數量仍很低。政府最近已

向接受行動支付的商家提供減稅優惠，並立下目標，要在 2025 年前讓 90%的智慧手機用戶採用行動支付。這目標是否能實現仍有待觀察。

Language Guide

contactless payment 感應式支付

要提到感應式支付，就不能不提到 RFID 和 NFC 這兩兄弟。NFC 全名為 near field communication，是一套可以「近距離無線通訊」的通訊協定技術，能讓兩個電子裝置（其中一個通常是行動裝置，例如智慧型手機）在幾公分內進行通訊。除了使用在手機裝置間的資料傳輸方式之外，更廣為流行綁定信用卡或是交通票證，開通手機中 NFC 的功能，手機就能快速感應付款。NFC 其實是從 RFID 射頻識別技術發展而來，RFID 是 radio frequency identification 的縮寫，就是智慧卡中的感應技術。

chip and PIN 智慧卡付款系統

讀作 [tʃɪp ənd ˋpɪn]，是指使用晶片信用卡或金融卡與個人密碼的支付方式，也就是「密碼刷卡」。PIN 意思為「識別碼」，是 personal identification number 的縮寫。相較之下，chip and signature 使用信用卡和簽名完成交易，不需要輸入 PIN 碼，方便使用卻沒這麼安全。

smart card 智慧卡

智慧卡其實就是晶片卡（intergrated circuit card，簡稱 IC 卡）的一種，具有資料存取、運算的功能，像是金融提款卡、健保卡和信用卡，都屬於智慧卡家族。

依照資料讀取方式分為接觸式 (contact card)、非接觸式 (contactless card) 和同時擁有這兩種介面的混合式 (hybrid card)。接觸式智慧卡讀取需藉由卡片上外露的微晶片；非接觸式的外觀則看不到微晶片，藉由紅外線或無線電波等射頻的方式讀取資料，像是我們搭捷運公車需要的悠遊卡 (EasyCard)；混合式則集前兩功能於一卡，我們皮包裡的信用卡和簽帳卡 (debit card) 大多是這類的卡片，當你準備付款時，店員將你的感應式信用卡 (contactless credit card) 放在感應器「嗶」一下就 OK 了，既快速又便利。

mobile wallet 電子錢包

在支付平台上建立一個虛擬的數位錢包，通常需要先儲值或是與實體帳戶、信用卡連結轉帳消費的功能。

聊使用行動支付

Aidan: Hey, Sandy. Can I use mobile payment at this [1)]convenience store?

Sandy: Yeah. They have [2)]stickers on the window there. Let's see, they accept Apple Pay….

Aidan: I have an 🔵 Android phone, see? So that's not gonna work.

Sandy: Oh, you have a Samsung phone. They accept Samsung Pay too.

Aidan: But I don't have that app [3)]installed on my phone. I only have Google Pay.

Sandy: Hmm, it doesn't look like they accept that. When I want to pay with my phone, I just use Line Pay.

Aidan: I thought Line was just a messaging app. How does it work?

Sandy: You just [4)]register your credit card with Line Pay, and then type in your password when you want to use it.

Aidan: Does it use an NFC reader like Google Pay?

Sandy: No. The app [5)]generates a barcode, and then the [6)]cashier scans it.

Aidan: Sounds [7)]complicated.

Sandy: Not at all. I'll show you how it works. This coffee[8)]'s on me!

艾　登：嘿，珊蒂，我能在這家超商用行動支付嗎？

珊　蒂：可以，他們的窗戶上有貼紙，來看看，他們接受 Apple Pay…

艾　登：我的是安卓手機，看到了嗎？所以不能用。

珊　蒂：噢，你用的是三星手機，他們也接受 Samsung Pay。

艾　登：但我的手機沒裝那種 app，我只有 Google Pay。

珊　蒂：呃，看來他們沒接受這個。我想用手機付帳時，就用 Line Pay。

艾　登：我以為 Line 只是通訊 app，怎麼用呢？

珊　蒂：只要在 Line Pay 註冊信用卡，然後使用時輸入密碼。

艾　登：它像 Google Pay 一樣用 NFC 讀卡器嗎？

珊　蒂：不是，這個 app 會產生一個條碼，然後讓收銀員掃描。

艾　登：聽起來很複雜。

珊　蒂：一點也不複雜，我來示範給你看，這杯咖啡我請客！

Language Guide

Android 安卓系統

Google 研發的手機操作系統，讀作 [ˈændrɔɪd]，原意為「人型機器人」，這個行動作業系統在 2017 年已成為全球最多人使用的手機系統。和蘋果的 iOS 比較，Android 系統較為開放，拿智慧型手機來說，Android 的市占率達八成，蘋果的 iOS 系統則不到兩成。

Vocabulary

1) **convenience** [kənˈvinjəns] (n.) 方便，便利設施，**convenience store** 即「便利商店」

2) **sticker** [ˈstɪkə] (n.) 貼紙

3) **install** [ɪnˈstɔl] (v.) 安裝，裝置

4) **register** [ˈrɛdʒɪstə] (v.) 登記，註冊

5) **generate** [ˈdʒɛnəˌret] (v.) 產生

6) **cashier** [kæˈʃɪr] (n.) 收銀員，出納員

7) **complicated** [ˈkɑmpləˌketɪd] (a.) 複雜的，難懂的

8) **be on sb.** (phr.) 某人請客

文章＋對話
pp. 38-41

New Companion Robots Show [1)]Promise

新陪伴型機器人前途無量

不斷創新的人工智慧技術，
為了高齡少子化的社會，
發展出更多的產物，
陪伴型機器人就是很典型的例子。
不僅如此，
打翻科技以往帶來的冷漠疏離感，
甚至推出「不實用」機器人，
什麼都不會做，能互動、單純陪伴，
就像真的有人陪一樣。

Science [2)]**fiction** has long been [10)]**obsessed** with walking, talking 🄛 **robots** that serve as [3)]**companions** for their human masters, and now science fiction is finally becoming science fact. No, we're not talking about 🄛 **sex robots**, although big advances have been made in that area as well. We're all familiar with robots like Sony's 🄛 **Aibo**, which is more like a cute toy, and a very expensive one at that. But the new [4)]**generation** of companion robots, from tabletop [5)]**devices** to [11)]**humanoid** bots—a number of which were on display at the 2019 🄛 **CES** in Las Vegas—promise to do much more.

科幻小說長久以來一直熱中於塑造會走路說話和陪伴人類主人的機器人，現在科幻小說終於要變成科學事實了。不，我們不是在說性愛機器人，雖然這方面也大有進展。我們都對索尼的 Aibo 機器狗很熟悉，這款比較像是可愛的玩具，而且價格非常昂貴。但新一代陪伴型機器人的功能更多，從桌面裝置到人形機器── 2019 年在拉斯維加斯舉行的消費電子展有許多人形機器人展出。

Perhaps the most impressive humanoid robot at CES is Walker, made by Chinese [12]**robotics** firm UBTECH. At five feet tall and 170 pounds, it's the size of a human being, and it acts like one too. With hands that can open doors and pick up objects, it can serve as a robotic [6]**household** helper. It's also voice-controlled, and displays human-like expressions on its touchscreen face when responding to commands. Walker will go on sale sometime in 2019, and the price tag, not announced yet, will be high. But for a robot that can help around the house, and provide everything from video [13]**surveillance** to friendship, the high price may be worth it.

消費電子展上最令人印象深刻的人形機器人，或許是由中國機器人公司優必選製造的 Walker 機器人，高五英尺，體重 170 磅，大小與人類一樣，行為也很像。機器人的手能開門、撿東西，可以當機器人家庭幫手。它也可以用語音控制，回應指令時，觸控式螢幕的臉會呈現出跟人一樣的表情。Walker 機器人會在 2019 年開始銷售，價格雖尚未公布，但一定很貴。但一個能在家中幫忙的機器人，包含從監視器到友誼等所有功能，價格昂貴或許是值得的。

For those who don't need, or want, their robots to look like people, Temi may be a better choice. [7]**Initially** designed to help the elderly, Temi is more like a [8]**tablet** on wheels than an android. The production model is a **telepresence** robot you can use to play music and videos, and even make video calls. Temi also has Alexa built in, so it can respond to voice commands and be used to control other smart devices. But most impressive is the way it moves. With 16 sensors in its base, it can avoid [9]**obstacles**, and its ability to recognize people and faces means it can follow you around the house. The Temi is now in stores and priced at $1,500.

若不需要或不想看到人形機器人，Temi 可能是更好的選擇。Temi 最初是為了幫助老人而設計，更像是有輪子的平板電腦，而不是機器人。生產模型是遙現機器人，可用來播放音樂和影片，甚至打視訊電話。Temi 也內建智慧語音助理 Alexa ，所以可以回應語音指令，也可用來控制其他智慧裝置。但最厲害的是它移動的方式。Temi 的底座有 16 個感應器，可避開障礙物，能辨識人和臉，所以能跟著人在家裡四處走動。Temi 現已上市，售價為 1500 美元。

Temi

單字 pp.38-41

Vocabulary

1) **promise** [ˋprɑmɪs] (n.) 前途，指望

2) **fiction** [ˋfɪkʃən] (n.) 小說，**science fiction** 即「科幻小說」

3) **companion** [kəmˋpænjən] (n.) 同伴，伴侶

4) **generation** [͵dʒɛnəˋreʃən] (n.) 代，世代

5) **device** [dɪˋvaɪs] (n.) 設備，裝置

6) **household** [ˋhaʊs͵hold] (a.) 家庭的，家用的

7) **initially** [ɪˋnɪʃəli] (adv.) 最初，初步

8) **tablet (computer)** [ˋtæblɪt] (n.) 平板電腦

9) **obstacle** [ˋɑbstəkəl] (n.) 障礙（物）

進階字彙

10) **obsessed** [əbˋsɛst] (a.) 著迷的，入迷的

11) **humanoid** [ˋhjumənɔɪd] (a./n.) 像人的，人形的；類人動物

12) **robotics** [rəˋbatiks] (n.) 機器人學

13) **surveillance** [səˋveləns] (n.) 監視，盯哨

桌面機器人 Elli-Q

[1]**Last but not least** is a tabletop bot called the Elli-Q. Made by [2]**Intuition** Robotics, the Elli-Q is designed to keep the elderly mentally [3]**alert** with features like video chat, games and [4]**reminders**. Throughout the day, the bot will [5]**prompt** users to do things like drink a glass of water, take their [8]**meds** or call a family member. It can even sense when the user is [6]**annoyed** and stop [7]**engaging** as much. Elli-Q looks more like a desk lamp with a [9]**detachable** tablet than a robot, but with an 🄛🄖 **LED** face and a head that moves when it talks, it's cuter than it sounds. The bot will go on sale in summer 2019.

還有一款桌面機器人也值得一提，名為 Elli-Q，是由直覺機器人公司製造，是為了讓老年人保持頭腦靈敏而設計，功能包括視訊聊天、電玩和提醒功能。在一天當中，機器人會提醒使用者做一些事情，比如喝水、服藥，或打電話給家人，甚至可以感應到使用者感到厭煩而停止互動。Elli-Q 的外型比較像是帶有可拆式平板電腦的桌燈，而不是機器人，不過有 LED 螢幕的臉，還有說話時會動的頭，比印象中更可愛。這款機器人會在 2019 年夏季上市。

Vocabulary

1) **last but not least** (phr.) 最後但同樣重要的
2) **intuition** [ˌɪntuˈɪʃən] (n.) 直覺
3) **alert** [əˈlɜt] (a.) 機警的，敏捷的
4) **reminder** [rɪˈmaɪndə] (n.) 提醒，提示
5) **prompt** [prɑmpt] (v.) 提示
6) **annoyed** [əˈnɔɪd] (a.) 生氣的，煩惱的
7) **engage** [ɪnˈgedʒ] (v.)（使）參與，互動

進階字彙

8) **meds** [mɛdz] (n.)（口）藥物
9) **detachable** [dɪˈtætʃəbəl] (a.) 可拆式的，可分開的

Language Guide

robot 機器人

可以用 bot 來稱呼，為 robot 的非正式說法。在英文中 robot 是模擬人類行為或思想，並能夠自動執行任務的裝置機器，並沒有「人」的涵義在裡面，那麼為什麼中文習慣翻成「機器人」呢？或許是因為大多數的 robot 都設計成類人形的外型。機器人可以作一些重複性高或是比較危險、人類不想做的工作，也可以做一些因為環境限制，人類無法作的工作。文中提到的性愛機器人 (sex robot)，從性愛娃娃在全球的銷售量不斷增長的現象可見，它們擁有一定的市場，且能有助於解決非自願獨身人口所面對的問題。

Aibo 愛寶

日本索尼 (Sony) 公司在 1999 首次推出的陪伴型機器寵物，具有聲控功能，風靡一時。隨著人工智慧蓬勃發展，原先在 2006 年停產的 AIBO 在 2018 年重出江湖，名字由大寫改為小寫 aibo，導入學習的互動能力，讓新一代愛寶可以透過與人的互動發展出不同的「性格」，也能藉由它來管理家中設備，成為生活小幫手。

CES 國際消費類電子產品博覽會

全名為 Consumer Electronics Show，是知名國際性最新電子產品和科技的商展，每年吸引來自世界各地的主要公司和業界人士參加。消費型電子展每年 1 月於美國內華達州的拉斯維加斯會議中心舉行，不開放一般民眾入場，展覽期間通常會舉行多場產品預覽會和新產品發表會。

telepresence 遠程出席

讀作 [ˈtɛləˌprɛzəns]，也可譯作「網真」，利用高畫質影像系統，讓在遙遠的彼方，有如同親臨現場的感受。2017 年 12 月 21 日，行政院政務委員唐鳳因受中共打壓，無法出席聯合國網路治理論壇，靠著遠程出席機器人 (telepresence robot) 直播發言，成功突破政治阻力。

LED 發光二極體

讀作 [ˌɛliˈdi]，全名為 light-emitting diode，是一項將電能轉為光能的半導體技術，相較於需先將電能轉換為熱能，再變為光能的傳統燈泡，LED 省去轉換過程耗損的電能，更能發揮光能的價值，燈泡使用壽命也更久。

CFL
省電燈泡

LED
LED 燈

聊聊陪伴型機器人的功能

Carter: Hey, Jenny. Meet Temi, my new [1)]**butler**.

Jenny: Whoa, you got a robot! Can he actually open the door for people?

Carter: He doesn't have arms, so no. But he can [2)]**interact** with all my smart devices, so when I come home, he greets me by turning on the lights and [3)]**adjusting** the [4)]**thermostat**.

Jenny: That's pretty [5)]**neat**. What else can he do?

Carter: Here, let me give you a [6)]**demo**. Temi, play some Cardi B. *[music starts]*

Jenny: Wow, the sound is great! Listen to that [7)]**bass**.

Carter: Yeah, I [8)]**upgraded** to the Harman Kardon speakers—and the ⒧Ⓖ **4K** screen so I can watch videos too.

Jenny: But can't your home theater do all that?

Carter: Yeah, but my home theater can't follow me around the house like Temi does.

Jenny: True. You said Temi is a butler, so can he serve drinks?

Carter: Of course. There's a tray behind his screen, and I [9)]**input** a map of the house so he can go to any room I tell him to. Oh, and the tray even [10)]**doubles as a** [11)]**wireless** charger.

Jenny: Cool! The [12)]**charge** on my iPhone is a little low.

卡　特：嘿，珍妮，來見見我的新管家 Temi。

珍　妮：哇，你有機器人！他真的能幫人開門嗎？

卡　特：他沒有手臂，所以不行。但他可以跟我所有智慧裝置互動，所以我回家時，他會開燈和調節恆溫器。

珍　妮：那很棒，他還能做什麼？

卡　特：來，我示範給你看。Temi，播放卡迪 B 的歌。（音樂開始）

珍　妮：哇，聲音太棒了！聽那個低音。

卡　特：對，我升級到哈曼卡頓音箱，還有 4K 螢幕，這樣也可以看影片了。

珍　妮：但你的家庭劇院不是已經都有這些功能了嗎？

卡　特：對，但家庭劇院不能像 Temi 那樣跟著我在家裡走來走去。

珍　妮：這倒是真的。你說 Temi 是管家，那他會端飲料來嗎？

卡　特：當然，他的螢幕後面有托盤，我已經輸入這房子的平面圖，這樣他就能照我的指令到任何房間。噢，這托盤還有無線充電器的功能。

珍　妮：酷！我的 iPhone 電量剛好有點低了。

Language Guide

4K 4K 解析度

4K 解析度的簡稱，英文全名為 4K resolution，畫面像素 (pixel) 是 FHD 的四倍。FHD 代表 full high definition，就是我們常講的「高畫質」，代表畫面的水平像素 * 垂直像素為 1920*1080，也能以「1080p」來表示，4K 解析度則是 3840*2060。

1080p (1920×1080)	1080p (1920x1080)
1080p (1920×1080)	1080p (1920×1080)

Vocabulary

1) **butler** [ˋbʌtlə] (n.) 男管家

2) **interact (with)** [ˌɪntəˋækt] (v.) 互動，互相影響

3) **adjust** [əˋdʒʌst] (v.) 調整

4) **thermostat** [ˋθɝməˌstæt] (n.) 溫度自動調節器，恆溫器

5) **neat** [nit] (a.)（口）美妙的，很棒的

6) **demo** [ˋdemo] (n.) 示範，證明（**demonstration** [ˌdɛmənˋstreʃən] 的非正式用法）

7) **bass** [bes] (n.) 貝斯吉他，低音提琴

8) **upgrade** [ˋʌpˌgred] (v.) 升級，改善

9) **input** [ˋɪnˌpʌt] (v./n.) 輸入（資料）

10) **double (as)** [ˋdʌbəl] (v.) 充當，兼任

11) **wireless** [ˋwaɪrlɪs] (a.) 無線的

12) **charge** [tʃɑrdʒ] (n./v.) 儲電量；充電

The Latest in VR Tech

文章 + 對話
pp. 42-45

最新的虛擬實境科技

玩家正在使用 Oculus Quest

說到虛擬實境，十有八九會先想到電競遊戲，令大家意想不到的是，隨著這項技術不斷地進步，它的應用領域也相當廣泛，重現犯罪現場幫助判決、以身歷其境的方式來閱讀新聞或是預覽新品發表，甚至跨足至醫療應用…等等，逐漸成為主流科技。

Although 🔴 [1]**virtual reality** has been around for decades, VR tech has had trouble finding a [2]**mainstream** audience. Whether because of high prices for [3]**headsets** or a limited [4]**library** of games, mainstream gamers just haven't been [5]**enthusiastic** about VR. 🔴 **Augmented reality** games for smartphones,

of course, are another story. Pokemon Go has become an international [6]**phenomenon** since it was released in 2016, and popular AR mobile games are coming out all the time. But as VR technology continues to improve, big brands like Oculus (now owned by Facebook) and HTC are slowly [7]**winning** gamers **over** to VR, and new players like Pico Interactive are creating attractive choices for the [8]**enterprise** market.

雖然虛擬實境科技已經存在幾十年，但仍難以找到主流顧客群。不論是因為頭戴顯示器價格昂貴或電玩作品量有限，主流玩家就是不熱中虛擬實境。當然智慧手機的擴增實境遊戲又是另一回事了。《精靈寶可夢 GO》自 2016 年發行以來已風靡國際，也不斷有新的熱門 AR 手遊推出。但隨著虛擬實境科技不斷改進，Oculus（現為臉書所有）和宏達電等大品牌正逐漸說玩家玩 VR 遊戲，Pico Interactive 等新電玩公司也正為企業市場打造有吸引力的選擇。

So what's new for VR headsets in 2019? One of the most promising new headsets is the 🔠 **Oculus Quest**. While the Oculus Rift is a great VR headset for PC gaming [5]**enthusiasts**, the [13]**standalone** Quest doesn't require a gaming PC to work. The Oculus Go isn't [14]**tethered** to a PC either, but the new Quest has a more powerful [15]**processor** and two controllers, which provides a more [16]**immersive** VR experience. And unlike the Oculus Go, the Quest supports 🔠 **six degrees of freedom** (DOF), meaning it can track your movements in all directions.

那麼 2019 年有什麼新的虛擬實境頭戴顯示器推出？其中前景最看好的是 Oculus Quest。對熱愛電競遊戲的人來說，Oculus Rift 是很棒的 VR 頭戴顯示器，而單獨的 Quest 不需電競電腦就能使用。Oculus Go 也不需要連接到電腦，而新款 Quest 的處理器更強大又配兩個控制器，可提供更加身歷其境的 VR 體驗。與 Oculus Go 不同的是，Quest 支援六自由度，這表示能追蹤所有方位的移動。

With its popular Vive and Vive Pro headsets, HTC has become one of the most well-known names in virtual reality gaming. And with the 2019 🔠 **Vive Pro Eye**, HTC is adding a new [9]**dimension** to the VR experience. The Eye is basically the [17]**flagship** Vive Pro with the addition of 🔠 **Tobii** eye tracking. What are the benefits? You can use your eyes to [10]**navigate** menus, and hand-eye [11]**coordination** makes the gaming experience more [12]**realistic**. In addition, just like your brain, the processor uses more power to [18]**render** the areas you look at, leaving other areas [19]**blurry**, which makes what you see more vivid.

宏達電憑藉受歡迎的 Vive 和 Vive Pro 頭戴顯示器成為最知名 VR 遊戲品牌之一，加上 2019 年的 Vive Pro Eye，宏達電為 VR 體驗增添了新特點。Vive Pro Eye 基本上是旗艦產品 Vive Pro，但是多加了 Tobii 眼動控制器。這有什麼好處？你可以用雙眼瀏覽選單，而且手眼協調的方式使遊戲體驗更逼真。此外，處理器就像大腦一樣，用更多處理能力來呈現你所看到的區域，讓其他區域變得模糊，讓你所看到的畫面更生動。

單字 pp.42-45

Vocabulary

1) **virtual** [ˋvɝtʃuəl] (a.) 虛擬的，**virtual reality** 即「虛擬實境」

2) **mainstream** [ˋmen͵strim] (a./n.) 主流（的）

3) **headset** [ˋhɛd͵sɛt] (n.) 頭戴裝置，頭戴式顯示器，耳機

4) **library** [ˋlaɪ͵brɛri] (n.) 產品庫，收藏

5) **enthusiastic** [ɪn͵θuzɪˋæstɪk] (a.) 熱中的，熱情的，名詞 **enthusiast** [ɪnˋθuzɪ͵æst] 即「熱中者」

6) **phenomenon** [fəˋnɑmə͵nɑn] (n.) 意想不到、非凡的人事物，現象

7) **win over** (phr.) 爭取，說服

8) **enterprise** [ˋɛntə͵praɪz] (n.) 企業，公司

9) **dimension** [dɪˋmɛnʃən] (n.)（長、寬、厚、高等）量度，尺寸

10) **navigate** [ˋnævə͵get] (v.) 瀏覽

11) **coordination** [ko͵ɔrdəˋneʃən] (n.) 協調，**hand-eye coordination** 即「手眼協調能力」

12) **realistic** [͵riəˋlɪstɪk] (a.) 逼真的，栩栩如生的

進階字彙

13) **standalone** [ˋstændə͵lon] (a.) 單機，獨立的電腦

14) **tether** [ˋtɛðə] (v.) 連接，連結

15) **processor** [ˋprɑ͵sɛsə] (n.)（電腦的）處理器

16) **immersive** [ɪˋmɝsɪv] (a.) 身臨其境的

17) **flagship** [ˋflæg͵ʃɪp] (a.) 旗艦的

18) **render** [ˋrɛndə] (v.) 畫圖，描繪，呈現

19) **blurry** [ˋblɝi] (a.) 模糊不清的

While the above two headsets are aimed at the gaming market, there are also new [1]**options** for business customers. The best of these may be the Pico G2 4K. Like the Oculus Quest, the G2 4K is a standalone headset, but with the added benefit of [2]**crisp** 4K resolution. It also has several features designed specifically for the enterprise market, including [5]**Kiosk** Mode, which allows the headset to be locked for use in a single application. And the face pads are [3]**replaceable**, making it well suited to [4]**multiple** users.

玩家正在使用 Pico G2 4K

以上兩款頭戴顯示器都是以遊戲市場為目標，也有適合商業顧客的新選擇，其中最好的可能是 Pico G2 4K。就跟 Oculus Quest 一樣，G2 4K 是單獨使用的頭戴顯示器，但多了清晰 4K 解析度的優點，還專為企業市場設計幾種功能，包括攤位模式，讓頭戴顯示器鎖定使用單一應用程式。面罩墊也可替換，適合不同的使用者。

Vocabulary

1) **option** [ˋɑpʃən] (n.) 選項，可選擇的東西
2) **crisp** [krɪsp] (a.)（畫面或聲音）清晰明瞭的
3) **replaceable** [rɪˋplesəbəl] (a.) 可替換的，可更換的
4) **multiple** [ˋmʌltəpəl] (a.) 多重的，不只一個的

進階字彙
5) **kiosk** [ˋkɪˌɑsk] (n.) 攤位，小亭

Language Guide

VR & AR

VR（虛擬實境）是 virtual reality 的縮寫，透過高真實感的 3D 模擬空間，讓人有身處其境的錯覺；augmented reality 簡稱為 AR，中文稱作「擴增實境」，可說是 VR 的衍生技術。如果說 VR 是接近現實的虛擬環境，那麼 AR 則是利用投影將虛擬物件與「真實」環境結合。

Oculus Quest

Oculus 是 Facebook 旗下的一間虛擬實境科技公司，2019 最新推出的 Oculus Quest 是一款無線的 VR 裝置，不需連結手機或電腦，只要戴顯示器和控制器，隨時都能使用，地點完全不受限，並且擁有一個稱作「Insight」的感測技術，比起傳統的追蹤系統更敏銳。

six degrees of freedom
六自由度

自由度，又簡稱做 DOF，是指物體在運動進行中的自由程度，依據在空間中的移動模式而不同，可分做平面的三自由度和三軸的六自由度。六自由度是指在三維空間中，可以上下、前後、左右平移之外，也能旋轉，依據旋轉方向稱做俯仰 (pitch)、偏擺 (yaw) 及翻滾 (roll)。在 VR 裝置中的六自由度，特別是指頭部戴顯示器後的 6 種移動模式追蹤。

Vive Pro Eye

作為 Vive Pro 的新一代，是宏達電 (HTC) 的虛擬實境產品，Vive Pro Eye 新增「眼動追蹤」(eye tracking) 的功能，在無控制器模式中以眼球視覺操控，提供更直覺的互動方式。美國職業大聯盟 (MLB) 更將此功能整合進最新一款電玩遊戲裡，不用任何控制器，玩家也能輕鬆操作選單。同時藉由眼球視覺位置，能減少浪費非視線集中處的畫面效能。眼球追蹤這項技術是源自與一家瑞典的高科技公司——Tobii Technology 合作，專門開發與眼動控制相關的產品，甚至推出一款不須戴上特定裝置，只要有 USB 連接線，玩家眼睛只要對準遊戲中的目標物就能瞄準，更能享受射擊遊戲的快感。

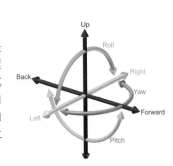

Up
Roll
Right
Back
Yaw
Left
Forward
Pitch

聊虛擬實境電玩顯示器

Robert: Hey, you[1]'re into gaming, right? You got any [2]recommendations for a VR headset?

John: Um, let's see—are you talking PC or [3]console?

Robert: I usually play games on my Xbox, but I have a PC too.

John: I don't think they even make VR headsets for the Xbox. I have a PlayStation VR, and I really like it.

Robert: Yeah? What's it like?

John: The **LG** [4]**refresh rate** is pretty good and the **LG** **head tracking** is smooth. It hasn't been updated since 2016 though, so the resolution is a lot lower than the newer models.

Robert: Hmm, that's a long time. And I don't have a PlayStation anyway, so I guess I should get a PC headset.

John: Do you have a [5]**decent** gaming PC?

Robert: No, just a regular desktop.

John: In that case, you should probably just go wireless and get a standalone headset.

Robert: What's a good model?

John: I tried a friend's Oculus Go, and it's almost as good as my Rift, but it's much cheaper. Lots of cool games available too.

羅伯特：嘿，你是電玩迷，對吧？你會推薦哪種 VR 頭戴顯示器？

約翰：　嗯，我想想，你是在說電腦還是遊戲機？

羅伯特：我通常用 Xbox 玩遊戲，但也用電腦。

約翰：　他們好像沒有發行 Xbox 用的 VR 頭戴顯示器。我有 PlayStation 的 VR 頭戴顯示器，我真的很喜歡。

羅伯特：是嗎？用起來怎麼樣？

約翰：　畫面更新率很好，頭部追蹤也順暢，但從 2016 年就沒再更新了，所以解析度比新型號低很多。

羅伯特：嗯，那已經過了很久了。反正我也沒有 PlayStation，所以我想我該買電腦用的頭戴顯示器。

約翰：　你有好用的電競電腦嗎？

羅伯特：沒有，就是一般桌機。

約翰：　這樣的話，你或許該用無線的，買個單獨用的頭戴顯示器。

羅伯特：哪種型號比較好？

約翰：　我試過朋友的 Oculus Go，幾乎跟我的 Rift 一樣好，而且更便宜，也有很多很酷的遊戲。

Language Guide

refresh rate 畫面更新率

就是每秒鐘畫面更新的次數，單位為赫茲（hertz，簡稱為 Hz），螢幕的垂直更新率越高，畫面就越穩定，反之，螢幕閃爍的情形就越嚴重。長時間注視顯示器，如螢幕有閃爍的現象，會導致眼睛疲勞甚至於頭痛的現象。一般來說，顯示器的畫面更新率至少要在 60Hz 以上，玩家眼睛才不至於不舒服。

head tracking 頭部追蹤

追蹤使用者頭部的運動，然後根據頭部的姿勢移動所顯示的內容。簡而言之，如果戴上一台 Oculus Rift，看看上下左右，那麼虛擬世界的一部分就呈現在相應的位置上。

Vocabulary

1) **be into** (phr.) 熱中於…

2) **recommendation** [ˌrɛkəmɛnˋdeʃən] (n.) 推薦，建議

3) **console** [ˋkɑnˌsol] (n.) 遊戲機

4) **refresh** [rɪˋfrɛʃ] (v.) 更新、刷新（畫面，網頁等）

5) **decent** [ˋdisənt] (a.) 像樣的，還不錯的

文章 + 對話
pp. 46-49

Is Your Smartphone a Pain in the Neck?

你的智慧手機會造成肩頸痠痛嗎？

你有沒有手機滑一滑，突然肩膀僵硬的經驗？幾乎所有人，滑手機的姿勢都不良。長時間使用科技產品早已融入你我的生活當中，魔鬼就藏在細節裡，記得中間一定要站起身來，伸伸懶腰，活動活動筋骨，不要年紀輕輕就染上文明病啦，現在還不趕快檢查自己的姿勢？！

According to a recent study, the world's 3.5 billion smartphone users—nearly half the global population—may be at risk of [1)]**chronic** neck and back pain. Frequent use of smartphones, and tablets and [2)]**laptops** as well, puts stress on the [3)]**spine** and [4)]**alters** the natural [5)]**curve** of the neck, which increases the chances of soft tissue [6)]**discomfort**, commonly [7)]**referred** to as " **IG** **tech neck**." While using a device such as a smartphone, the neck is typically bent at a 60-degree angle, which puts stress on the neck equal to the weight of two bowling balls, or around 27 kilos.

根據近期一項研究，全世界 35 億使用智慧手機的人，幾乎是全球一半人口，可能都面臨慢性頸部和背部疼痛的風險。頻繁使用智慧手機、平板和筆記型電腦會對脊椎造成壓力，改變頸部的自然曲線，因此會增加軟組織不適的機會，這種症狀通常稱為「科技頸」。使用智慧手機一類的裝置時，脖子通常會彎曲 60 度角，造成脖子承受約兩個保齡球重量的壓力，或約 27 公斤。

The recently published study, which was carried out by [8]**researchers** from Khon Kaen University in Thailand and the University of Southern Australia, [9]**highlights** the [19] ⓛⓒ **ergonomic** risks to smartphone and tablet users. These risks are especially high for young people, who are experiencing neck pain earlier than previous generations. In the study, video recordings of 30 smartphone users in Thailand, aged 18-25, who spend up to eight hours a day on their phones, were [10]**analyzed** using the RULA (Rapid Upper Limb [11]**Assessment**) method.

這項近期公布的研究是由泰國孔敬大學和南澳大學的研究員所做，強調智慧手機和平板使用者的人體工學風險。這些風險對年輕人來說特別高，他們出現肩頸痠痛的年齡比上一代更早。這項研究是以影片記錄泰國 30 名智慧手機使用者，年齡為 18 到 25 歲，每天使用手機多達八小時，利用快速上肢評估法分析他們的狀況。

RULA has been used to measure the ergonomic impact of desktop computer and laptop use for over a decade, but this is the first time the tool has been used to [11]**assess** the ergonomic risks of [12] ⓛⓒ **excessive smartphone use**. The researchers found that the average score of [13]**participants** was 6, much higher than an acceptable score of 1-2. The results revealed

[14]**awkward** neck, [15]**trunk** and leg [16]**postures**, which can lead to [20]**musculoskeletal** [17]**disorders**. [18]**Symptoms** were worse in participants who used their devices five hours or more a day, and especially those who smoked or got little exercise.

快速上肢評估法十年多來一直用於評估桌上型和筆記型電腦使用者的人體工學影響，但這是該方法首次用於評估過度使用智慧手機的人體工學風險。研究員發現，參與者的平均分數是六分，遠遠高於可接受的一至二分。研究結果顯示不良的頸部、軀幹和腿部姿勢，而這樣的姿勢會導致肌肉骨骼疾病。一天使用手機超過五小時的參與者，症狀更為嚴重，尤其是那些抽菸或較少運動者。

單字 pp.46-49

Vocabulary

1) **chronic** [ˈkrɑnɪk] (a.)（疾病等不好的事物）慢性的，長期的

2) **laptop (computer)** [ˈlæpˌtɑp] (n.) 筆記型電腦

3) **spine** [spaɪn] (n.) 脊椎，脊柱

4) **alter** [ˈɔltɚ] (v.)（輕微地）改變，使變化

5) **curve** [kɝv] (n.) 曲線，彎曲處

6) **discomfort** [dɪˈskʌmfɚt] (n.) 不適，不舒服

7) **refer (to)** [rɪˈfɝ] (phr.) 指的是

8) **researcher** [rɪˈsɝtʃɚ] (n.) 研究者，調查者

9) **highlight** [ˈhaɪˌlaɪt] (v.) 強調，凸顯

10) **analyze** [ˈænəˌlaɪz] (v.) 分析

11) **assessment** [əˈsɛsmənt] (n.) 評估，評價，動詞為 **assess** [əˈsɛs]

12) **excessive** [ɛkˈsɛsɪv] (a.) 過度的，過多的

13) **participant** [parˈtɪsəpənt] (n.) 參與者

14) **awkward** [ˈɔkwɚd] (a.) 笨拙的，不靈活的

15) **trunk** [trʌŋk] (n.) 軀幹

16) **posture** [ˈpɑstʃɚ] (n.) 姿勢，姿態

17) **disorder** [dɪsˈɔrdɚ] (n.) 失調症，病症

18) **symptom** [ˈsɪmptəm] (n.) 症狀

進階字彙

19) **ergonomic** [ˌɝgəˈnɑmɪk] (a.) 人體工學的，名詞為 **ergonomics** [ˌɝgəˈnɑmɪks] 人體工學

20) **musculoskeletal** [ˌmʌskjələˈskɛlətəl] (a.) 肌肉與骨骼的

What can be done to [1)]**relieve** neck pain and avoid the musculoskeletal disorders that come with long hours of smartphone or tablet use? Asking people to reduce device usage probably isn't realistic, but developing good posture habits can definitely help. To keep your neck from [2)]**leaning** forward, keep the screen of your device at [3)]**eye** level. And if this is too tiring, try looking down with just your eyes instead of bending your head forward or [4)]**slouching**. Tech breaks are important too—just a few 2-3 minute breaks every hour can make a big difference.

要怎麼做才能舒緩和避免因長時間使用智慧手機或平板而造成的頸部痠痛和肌肉骨骼病症？要求大家減少使用智慧裝置可能不切實際，但養成良好姿勢習慣肯定有幫助。為避免頸部往前傾，將裝置螢幕的高度保持在視線水平的位置。如果這樣太累，就用眼睛往下看，而不是低頭或垂肩。暫時抽離科技產品也很重要，每小時休息兩、三分鐘就能改善不少。

觀看手機的正確與錯誤方式

Language Guide

tech neck 科技頸

形容花長時間看手機、平板或其他無線裝置而導致頸部痠痛，這個名稱原本叫做 text neck（簡訊頸），但後來發現不只是打簡訊的問題，而是使用各種科技產品過度所產生的症狀，所以也更名為 tech neck。

ergonomics 人體工學

字根 ergon- 表「工作、勞動」；nomos 意思則是「規律」。人體工學是指依人體模型，配合身心理學的研究，做出最高舒適度的產品設計，讓人能更便利地使用，以提高效率。形容詞是 ergonomic，意思為「符合人體工學的」。

excessive smartphone use 過度使用智慧手機

你有沒有仔細想過自己一天就花多少時間在手機上？被手機綁架的我們，不知不覺成為無手機恐懼症 (nomophobia) 的一員了。世界上持有手機者，只有不到一成的人每天用不到 1 小時，花 3 個小時約三成，超過 5 小時的居然有超過四成，比例真的很高。台灣人也愛黏手機，一天平均花近 3.5 個小時，幾乎每 10 分鐘都要看瞄手機一眼，不過，巴西和印度也不遑多讓，每天大約都花 5 個小時以上。

從 2008-2018，科技產品的使用增長

科技十年間，產品不斷推陳出新，新科技帶來新生活，有一項很有趣的研究調查，它比較 2008 年和 2018 年占用產品的時間比例，結果發現使用桌上型電腦的比例居然減少了，從原本的 69% 降到只剩 28%，因為大家都把時間拿去滑手機了，原本只有 17% 居然攀升至 78%，這個幅度真的很驚人！然後看電影也不愛用 DVD 播放器了，反而是智慧電視從 5% 上升到 42%，更不用說其他新出的產品了。這樣想想，十年的變化真的很大，會不會再過十年，手機就消失了呢？因為被更新更好的產品取代。

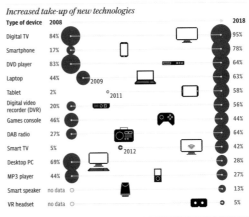

Increased take-up of new technologies

Type of device	2008	2018
Digital TV	84%	95%
Smartphone	17%	78%
DVD player	83%	64%
Laptop	44%	63%
Tablet	2%	58%
Digital video recorder (DVR)	20%	56%
Games console	46%	44%
DAB radio	27%	64%
Smart TV	5%	42%
Desktop PC	69%	28%
MP3 player	44%	27%
Smart speaker	no data	13%
VR headset	no data	5%

SOURCE: TELECOMS AND NETWORKS/OFCOM TECHNOLOGY TRACKER

聊長時間滑手機對身體的壞處

Daniel: Ouch, my neck is [1)]**killing** me!

Audrey: Sounds like a case of tech neck.

Daniel: Tech neck? What do you mean?

Audrey: It's what happens when you have your face buried in your phone all day. Why do you think your neck is so sore?

Daniel: Hmm, you do [2)]**have a point**. But what can I do about it? Smartphones are [3)]**indispensable** these days.

Audrey: Tech neck is caused by bending your neck forward for long periods of time, so try holding your phone higher, or look down with your eyes instead of your head.

Daniel: Does that actually work?

Audrey: Yeah. I put my desktop [4)]**monitor** at eye level, and now I hardly ever get a sore neck.

Daniel: It must be harder to change your smartphone habits though.

Audrey: True, but it's still possible. When I'm on the MRT, I listen to 🆖 podcasts instead of watching YouTube videos now. That way I can lean back and relax instead of [5)]**hunching** over my phone.

Daniel: That's a great idea. I'll have to try that. Now if I can just cure my Facebook [6)]**addiction**....

丹尼爾：哎喲，我的脖子痛死了。

奧黛麗：聽起來像是科技頸。

丹尼爾：科技頸？什麼意思？

奧黛麗：整天低頭看手機就會有這種情況，不然你覺得你的脖子為什麼會這麼痠痛？

丹尼爾：嗯，妳說得有道理。但我能怎麼辦？現在手機已經是必需品了。

奧黛麗：科技頸是因為長時間頸部往前彎造成的，所以試著把手機拿高一點，或眼睛往下看，不要低頭。

丹尼爾：這樣真的有用嗎？

奧黛麗：有，我把桌上電腦的螢幕調到視線高度，我脖子現在幾乎不會痠痛了。

丹尼爾：但改變看手機的習慣一定更難。

奧黛麗：沒錯，但還是有可能做到的。我現在搭捷運時就聽播客，不看 YouTube 影片。這樣我就可以放鬆往後靠，而不是駝背看手機。

丹尼爾：這真是個好主意，我會試試看。只要我能戒掉看臉書的癮……

Language Guide

podcast 播客

iPod 和 broadcast（廣播）的混合字，以數位格式儲存的電台節目，聽眾可經由電子裝置訂閱音訊，以下載方式收聽。下載後的媒體檔則儲存在用戶的電腦或其他裝置內，以便在離線時聆聽或觀看。用 podcast 訂閱喜愛的英文頻道，也是練聽力的好方法喔，大家不妨試試看。

Vocabulary

1) **kill** [kɪl] (v.) 使非常疼痛、痛苦

2) **have a point** (phr.) 有道理

3) **indispensable** [ɪndɪ`spensəbəl] (a.) 不可少的，必須的

4) **monitor** [`mɑnɪtə] (n.) 顯示器，監視器

5) **hunch** [hʌntʃ] (v.) 弓背，彎腰

6) **addiction** [ə`dɪkʃən] (n.) 成癮，入迷

文章 pp. 50-53

Burnout Common Among Top °YouTubers

職業倦怠是 YouTube 熱門網紅的常見現象

「我想當 YouTuber」，
逐漸成為許多人的夢想職業，
不過想加入這個行列，
光有「哏」還不夠！
搞創意已是踏進網紅業界的基本配備，
抓住維持人氣的秘訣才是長久之道，
難怪這些網紅絞盡腦汁也要每天生出一段影片，
不然一下子就被擠出排行外了。

Since the first video—shot at the San Diego Zoo by YouTube [1]**co-founder** Jawed Karim—was uploaded in 2005, the [2]**content** of YouTube videos has changed and [3]**evolved**. Although [4]**random** pet [5]**clips** are still popular, they're being increasingly buried under billions of hours of [6]**tutorials**, ⓵**unboxing** videos and ⓵**mukbangs** from active YouTubers, or "⓵**creators**," as the company calls them. And having a creative [7]**outlet** isn't the only [8]**motivation**. Creators who attract large numbers of [9]**viewers** can [17]<u>**monetize**</u> their videos, and those with over 100,000 [10]**subscribers** can even make a living as a YouTuber.

自從 YouTube 共同創辦人賈德卡林姆在 2005 年上傳第一支在聖地牙哥動物園拍攝的影片以來，YouTube 影片的內容就一直在演變。雖然隨著上傳的寵物短片仍相當受歡迎，但也被越來越多活躍 YouTube 網紅（或 YouTube 公司所稱的「創作者」）的數十億小時影片所淹沒，例如教學、開箱影片和吃播。有創作的宣洩管道不是唯一的動力，能吸引大量觀眾的創作者還能靠影片賺錢，若擁有十萬以上訂閱人數，甚至能以 YouTube 網紅的身分謀生。

And at the top of the YouTube ¹¹⁾**food chain** are the " **⓵ influencers**," those who have millions of subscribers—enough to bring them fortune and ¹²⁾**fame**. It may appear that these influencers have it all: a job doing what they love, creative control, more money than they can spend and ¹³⁾**loyal** fans. But there's a dark side to being a famous YouTuber. It's not easy staying at the top of a highly ¹⁴⁾**competitive** game, and the long hours and pressure involved in creating the content needed to maintain and grow one's fan base can lead to ¹⁸⁾**burnout**.

在 YouTube 這個食物鏈的頂端是「意見領袖」，他們擁有數百萬訂閱者，足以因此致富和出名。表面上看來，這些意見領袖擁有一切：做著自己熱愛的工作、擁有創作控制權、花不完的錢和忠實的粉絲群。但身為知名 YouTube 網紅也有黑暗的一面。要在競爭激烈的遊戲中保持領先並不容易，而且為了維持和發展粉絲群，需長時間創作內容並承受壓力，這可能導致職業倦怠。

Over the past few years, more and more creators have burned out and taken breaks from their channels, some never to return. And in the past year, a number of famous influencers have taken breaks and ¹⁵⁾**opened up** about burnout. In her video, "Burnt Out At 19," Canadian influencer **⓵ Elle Mills** (1.6 M subscribers) described how the pressure of creating content and interacting with fans was affecting her mental health, and announced she'd be taking a break. And even YouTube's biggest star, **⓵ PewDiePie** (86 M subscribers) has admitted that the stress of his YouTube career nearly caused him to ¹⁶⁾**call it quits**.

過去幾年越來越多創作者因職業倦怠而暫時退出自己的頻道，有些人再也沒回來。過去一年來，一些知名意見領袖也暫停創作，並公開自己的倦怠感。加拿大意見領袖艾兒米爾斯（160 萬訂閱人數）在她的影片「19 歲倦怠」中表示，創作內容以及與粉絲的互動都為她帶來壓力，影響到她的心理健康，並宣布她要休息。就連 YouTube 最大的明星 PewDiePie（8600 萬訂閱人數）也承認，他曾因為 YouTube 的職涯壓力而差點退出。

韓國美女在網路上直播吃飯秀，每天面對鏡頭吃 3 個小時，就能賺到 9000 美元（約 27 萬台幣）。

單字 pp.50-53

Vocabulary

1) **co-founder** [ˋko͵faʊndɚ] (n.) 共同創辦人

2) **content** [ˋkɑntɛnt] (n.) 內容

3) **evolve** [ɪˋvɑlv] (v.) 演變，演化

4) **random** [ˋrændəm] (a.) 隨機的

5) **clip** [klɪp] (n.) 一段影片，剪輯片段

6) **tutorial** [tuˋtɔrɪəl] (n.) 教學單元，個別指導

7) **outlet** [ˋaʊt͵lɛt] (n.) 發洩精力、感情的途徑，發揮創意的管道

8) **motivation** [͵motɪˋveʃən] (n.) 動機，原因

9) **viewer** [ˋvjuɚ] (n.) 觀看者，電視觀眾

10) **subscriber** [səbˋskraɪbɚ] (n.) 訂閱者，訂戶

11) **food chain** [fud tʃen] (n.) 食物鏈

12) **fame** [fem] (n.) 聲望，名聲

13) **loyal** [ˋlɔɪəl] (a.) 忠誠的，忠心的

14) **competitive** [kəmˋpɛtətɪv] (a.) 競爭性的，有競爭力的

15) **open up** (phr.) 傾吐心聲，打開心扉

16) **call it quits** [kɑl ɪt kwɪts] (phr.) 停止做，退出，辭職

進階字彙

17) **monetize** [ˋmʌnə͵taɪz] (v.) 從中賺錢

18) **burnout** [ˋbɝn͵aʊt] (n.) 倦怠，片語為 **burn out**

Part of the blame for this burnout lies in YouTube's [6]**algorithm**, which [1]**recommends** new videos from creators who post new content frequently, especially those who post every day. Faced with growing [2]**criticism**, YouTube has responded by encouraging creators to take breaks and enjoy weekends and vacations, just like they would with any job. Also, as part of its 🅛🅖 Creator [3] 🅛🅖 Academy, YouTube has introduced a series of videos designed to teach YouTubers how to avoid [4]**fatigue**. But [5]**apparently**, not many creators are aware of them—the video on burnout has less than 40,000 views.

職業倦怠的部分原因要歸咎於 YouTube 的演算法，這種演算法會推薦經常發佈新內容的創作者所做的新影片，尤其是每天發佈影片者。面對日益增加的批評，

YouTube 的回應是鼓勵創作者休息，享受週末和假期，就像其他一般上班族。此外，YouTube 的創作者學院也推出一系列影片，是為了教導網紅避免疲倦而設計的。但顯然沒有多少創作者知道有這些影片，因為職業倦怠影片的觀看次數不到四萬次。

Vocabulary

1) **recommend** [ˌrɛkəˈmɛnd] (v.) 推薦，建議
2) **criticism** [ˈkrɪtəˌsɪzəm] (n.) 批評，評論，挑剔
3) **academy** [əˈkædəmi] (n.) 學院，大學
4) **fatigue** [fəˈtig] (n.) 疲憊，勞累
5) **apparently** [əˈpærəntli] (adv.) 似乎，據說，顯然

進階字彙

6) **algorithm** [ˈælgəˌrɪðm] (n.)（尤指電腦使用的）演算法，計算程式

Language Guide

YouTuber YouTube 網路紅人，YouTube 影片創作者

為 YouTube 與英語詞尾 "er"（表某職業之意）的組合字，通常指知名網紅，若只是在 YouTube 上分享與個人相關瑣事的人，則較適合用「創作者」(creator) 稱呼，網路上的意見領袖，稱為 influencer，泛指對潛在消費族群有影響力的人。

Unboxing 開箱文，開箱影片

把最近購買的新產品，尤其是消費電子產品，自包裝盒內逐步地解開封裝，並且以相機或是攝影機詳細說明與記錄，寫成開箱文或是拍攝成開箱影片，再上傳到網際網路。早期的開箱影片多為電子產品或是時尚用品，然而，自從上傳開箱文的風氣開始盛行以後，任何產品都有人做開箱影片。

mukbang 直播吃飯，吃播

讀作 [ˈmʌkbæŋ]，為韓語 mukneun「吃飯」和 bangsong「播放」的結合字，是直播主在網路平台上直播吃飯給觀眾看的一種娛樂，直播主通常會吃下大量食物。直播吃飯於 2010 年在南韓開始流行

Elle Mills 艾兒米爾斯

艾兒米爾斯是位菲裔加拿大人的影音部落客 (vlogger，video blogger 的合成字)，常在 YouTube 上分享許多關於「自己」的事，自然不做作的親切風格以及動人的說書功力，吸引許多粉絲瀏覽訂閱。2017 年，她拍攝一支關於自己如何「出櫃」(come out) 影片，點閱率衝高，躍升為百萬訂閱者的 YouTube 紅人。2018 年拍完「19 歲倦怠」後的米爾斯，暫停影片製作，一個月後才開始重新上傳影片。

YouTube 明星 PewDiePie

PewDiePie 本名 Felix Kjellberg，是名瑞典的遊戲實況主 (streamer)，「pew」字取自於電玩射擊遊戲中的聲響。他大約從 2010 年開始經營自己的頻道，以分享各種遊戲經驗為主，起初是玩恐怖遊戲而受到矚目。他在 2016 年的訂閱數衝破 5,000 萬人數，是 YouTube 史上達成此成就的第一人。

Creator Academy

提供 YouTube 創作者免費線上課程，幫助他們瞭解如何製作精彩影片、推動頻道成長、賺取收益。

談論如何經營 YouTube 頻道

Ethan: Hey, Casey, how's your career as a YouTuber [1]coming along?

Casey: Not bad, although I'd hardly call it a career.

Ethan: Well, you're making money from your channel, aren't you?

Casey: Yeah, but not enough to **LG** **make ends meet**. I haven't quit my day job yet, ha-ha.

Ethan: I'm sure your [2]**fan base** will keep growing. I love your cats in sweaters videos! I was thinking of starting my own channel. Can you tell me how to do it?

Casey: Sure. Just sign into your Google account, go to YouTube and you can set up a channel. It's important to choose a good name.

Ethan: I'm thinking "Dogs in Sweaters."

Casey: Ha-ha, not bad. Then you want to choose a good channel icon and [3]**banner** art.

Ethan: OK. And then I can start shooting, right? Can I use my iPhone?

Casey: Sure. I use a **LG** **DSLR** now, but I started with my smartphone. Now, after you make videos, you should create [4]**thumbnails** that make people want to click on them.

Ethan: Is that hard to do?

Casey: No. There are plenty of tutorials online that show you how.

Ethan: Great. I guess I'd better start knitting some sweaters for my dogs!

伊　森：嘿，凱西，妳的 YouTube 網紅事業做得怎樣？

凱　西：還不錯，雖然我覺得還不算是事業。

伊　森：妳經營頻道有賺錢，不是嗎？

凱　西：有，但還不夠維持生計，我還沒辭掉正職，哈哈。

伊　森：我相信妳的粉絲群會繼續增加的，我喜歡妳的「穿毛衣的貓」影片！我也在考慮開個個人頻道，妳能教我怎麼做嗎？

凱　西：可以啊，只要登入 Google 帳號，到 YouTube 網站，就可以設置頻道，選個好的名稱很重要。

伊　森：我考慮用「穿毛衣的狗」。

凱　西：哈哈，不錯。然後你要選個好的頻道圖示和橫幅圖案。

伊　森：好，那我就可以開始拍攝影片了吧？我能用 iPhone 拍攝嗎？

凱　西：可以，我現在用數位單眼相機拍，但一開始是用智慧手機。你製作完影片後，應該製作縮圖，吸引大家去點擊。

伊　森：那會很難做嗎？

凱　西：不會，網路上有很多教學影片教你怎麼做。

伊　森：太好了，我想我最好開始替我的狗狗織些毛衣了！

Language Guide

make ends meet 維持生計

此片語照字面上解釋是「使兩端相接」，可以想成記帳時「收入」與「支出」兩欄的數字至少要「入能敷出」，所以 make ends meet 可解釋為「收支平衡、勉強餬口」。

A: How's the pay at your company?
你在這間公司的薪資待遇如何？

B: Pretty bad. I'm barely making enough to make ends meet.
很差。我賺的錢少到幾乎無法維持生計。

DSLR 單眼數位相機

全名為 digital single lens reflex camera，單眼相機跟一般數位相機就使用上來說，最大的差異就是單眼相機可以「交換鏡頭」跟「更快速的對焦」。可藉由更換超廣角鏡頭把高聳的建築物完整的收進畫面裡，也可讓畫面主題更鮮明。

Vocabulary

1) **come along** (phr.) 進展，進行

2) **fan base** [fæn bes] (n.) 粉絲群

3) **banner** [ˈbænɚ] (n.) 橫幅圖案、廣告

4) **thumbnail** [ˈθʌmˌnel] (n.)（電腦螢幕上的）縮圖

文章 + 對話
pp. 54-57

Facebook's Latest Privacy Scandal

臉書最近的隱私權醜聞

你有在用臉書嗎？
台灣有許多人是臉書的重度使用者，
超過 1900 萬人都愛滑臉書，
資訊安全議題跟你我都切身相關。
這也就是為什麼 2018 年正式上路的歐盟
一般資料保護法規 GDPR 如此受到關注，
這個號稱史上最嚴格的個資法的出現，
不難看出大家對於資安問題的重視。

Since it was revealed last March that [1)]**consulting** firm Ⓛ**Ⓖ Cambridge Analytica** improperly used Facebook data to build tools that Ⓛ**Ⓖ aided President Trump's 2016 election** [2)]**campaign**, the social media giant has been hit by a series of [3)]**privacy** [4)]**scandals**. And now, according to a *New York Times* report, the company has been involved in even more serious privacy [5)]**breaches**. [6)]**Documents** [7)]**obtained** by the paper show that Facebook gave over 150 companies access to the data of its users without their permission. Facebook claims, however, that this access has been shut down over the past few months.

自從去年三月爆發顧問公司劍橋分析不當使用臉書數據建立工具，以協助川普總統的 2016 年競選活動以來，這個社群媒體巨擘便一直受到一連串隱私權醜聞的抨擊。現在根據《紐約時報》報導，該公司涉及更嚴重的隱私權侵害。該報取得的文件顯示，臉書允許超過 150 家公司在未經許可下存取用戶的資料。但臉書聲稱已在過去數月關閉存取功能。

These latest [8]**revelations** show that Facebook gave these companies—mostly tech businesses, but also media organizations and even automakers—more [9]**extensive** access to users' personal data than it previously admitted, letting them read private messages and see the names of friends without [10]**consent**. The newspaper detailed arrangements between Facebook and companies such as Spotify, Netflix and Microsoft that enabled them to harvest user data through apps on the platform even when users [11]**disabled** sharing. Apps from many of these "[12]**integration** partners" weren't even shown in user application [13]**settings**, as Facebook considered them an [14]**extension** of its own network.

這些最新揭露的消息顯示，臉書允許這些公司存取的用戶個人資料，比起過去所承認的範圍更廣，讓他們能在未經同意下讀取私人訊息、看到好友名單，這些公司大部分是科技企業，但也有媒體組織，甚至汽車製造商。該報詳細報導臉書與這些公司的協議，例如 Spotify、網飛和微軟，就算用戶停用分享功能，他們也能透過平臺上的 app 收集用戶資料。其中有許多「合作夥伴」的 app 甚至未出現在用戶的應用程式設定中，而臉書認定這些 app 是自己網路的延伸。

The deals with these companies go back as far as 2010, and were all active in 2017, with some still [15]**in effect** in 2019. 🎧 Spotify and Netflix, for example, were able to read and even delete Facebook users' private messages, and see everyone on a message [16]**thread**. While Netflix turned off features that enabled message access, Spotify could look at the messages of more than 70 million users a month. According to the *Times* report, Facebook also let Microsoft's Bing search engine see the names of Facebook users' friends without consent. And Yahoo had the ability to show Facebook users' news feeds, including posts by their friends, on its home page. Yahoo [17]**eliminated** this feature in 2012, but still had access last year to the data of nearly 100,000 users a month.

臉書與這些公司的協議可追溯至 2010 年，全部在 2017 年生效，有些至 2019 年仍有效。例如 Spotify 和網飛可以讀取甚至刪除臉書用戶的私人訊息，也可看到一條訊息串的所有人。雖然網飛已關閉可存取訊息的功能，但 Spotify 每月仍可以看到七千萬名用戶的訊息。根據《紐約時報》報導，臉書也讓微軟的搜尋引擎 Bing 在未經同意下看到臉書用戶的好友名單。雅虎可以在首頁上顯示臉書用戶的動態消息，包括朋友貼文。雅虎已於 2012 年刪除此功能，但去年每月仍可存取近十萬名用戶的資料。

單字 pp.54-57

Vocabulary

1) **consulting** [kənˋsʌltɪŋ] (a.) 咨詢、顧問業，顧問工作

2) **campaign** [kæmˋpen] (n.) 活動，運動

3) **privacy** [ˋpraɪvəsi] (n.) 隱私

4) **scandal** [ˋskændəl] (n.) 醜聞

5) **breach** [britʃ] (n.) 違反，破壞

6) **document** [ˋdɑkjəmənt] (n.) 文件，公文

7) **obtain** [əbˋten] (v.) 取得，獲得

8) **revelation** [ˏrɛvəˋleʃən] (n.) 顯示，揭露

9) **extensive** [ɪkˋstɛnsɪv] (a.) 廣泛的，廣大的

10) **consent** [kənˋsent] (n./v.) 同意，答應

11) **disable** [dɪsˋebəl] (v.) 關閉、禁用（功能）

12) **integration** [ˏɪntəˋgreʃən] (n.) 整合

13) **setting** [ˋsɛtɪŋ] (n.) 設定

14) **extension** [ɪkˋstɛnʃən] (n.) 延伸，延長

15) **in effect** (phr.) 有效

16) **thread** [θred] (n.) （網路論壇等的）討論串

17) **eliminate** [ɪˋlɪməˏnet] (v.) 刪除，消滅

Facebook responded to the *Times* report in a blog post, stating that while the [1]**partnerships** did allow "messaging integration," nearly all have been shut down in recent months. The social media giant further claimed that none of the deals with outside companies [2]**violated** users' privacy. The company also said a separate feature called "instant [3]**personalization**," which gave Bing access to user data, was shut down in 2014.

針對《紐約時報》的報導,臉書在部落格一篇貼文中回應並指出,雖然合作協議確實允許「訊息整合」,但幾乎所有公司近幾個月都已關閉此功能。這個社群媒體巨擘進一步聲稱,與外部公司的協議都未違反用戶隱私權。該公司還表示,允許 Bing 存取用戶資料的另一項「即時個人化」功能,已在 2014 年關閉。

Vocabulary

1) **partnership** [ˈpɑrtnɚˌʃɪp] (n.) 合夥、合作（關係）
2) **violate** [ˈvaɪəˌlet] (v.) 違反,侵犯
3) **personalization** [ˌpɝsənələˈzeʃʌn] (n.) 個人化

Language Guide

Cambridge Analytica 劍橋分析公司

是一家成立於 2013 年的政治顧問公司,因不當使用臉書用戶資料,2018 年 5 月在美國及英國申請破產,停止所有營運,甚至因媒體負面輿論及龐大的律師訴訟費,連帶影響英國母公司策略溝通實驗室集團(Strategic Communication Laboratories,簡稱 SCL Group)關門大吉。SCL 過去曾和美國政府合作,提供海外反恐及反假消息相關的研究分析,是資料數據分析的大公司。

Facebook data aided President Trump's 2016 election
臉書數據協助川普的 2016 年競選活動

從 2013 年底,劍橋分析獲得川普支持者、保守派金主默瑟 (Robert Mercer) 投資,Facebook 被劍橋分析假借學術研究名義,利用美籍俄裔心理學家科甘所設計的心理測驗等 FB 應用程式,在 FB 上收集用戶數據。在 2014 到 2015 年間蒐集 5000 萬用戶個人資料,存取使用後給第三方分析,針對用戶的政治立場投放特定廣告,企圖影響美國總統大選選情。

Spotify

2006 年成立於瑞典的音樂串流服務公司,是目前全球最大的音樂串流品牌,提供方案分為免費及付費(premium)兩種,差別在於廣告的播放、切換歌曲的次數、離線收聽功能以及音質的差異。付費方案的費用視各國為主,台灣的定價為每月新台幣 $149。Spotify 專有的播放軟體,使用數位版權管理(DRM,digital rights management),透過這項存取控制技術,防止音樂被未經授權的使用。

談論臉書侵權問題

Steve: Hey, we should friend each other on Facebook.

Jamie: I would, but I quit Facebook recently.

Steve: You mean you're taking a break from social media?

Jamie: No. I **LG deleted my Facebook account**. Lots of people are doing it—even celebrities like Cher! It's become a **LG** [1]**movement**.

Steve: But why? Everybody in Taiwan is on Facebook.

Jamie: To protect your personal data, of course. Haven't you seen all the Facebook privacy [2]**violations** in the news?

Steve: Yeah, but if I haven't done anything wrong, why should I worry about them having my data? I just use Facebook to keep in touch with my friends and [3]**relatives**.

Jamie: But they sell your data to other companies. You know what they say: If you're not paying, you're the product. And they [4]**censor** views they don't like.

Steve: Well, the company has to make money somehow.

Jamie: You know about Cambridge Analytica, right? They used data Facebook gave them access to to help the Trump campaign. Would you want your data used to help elect a [5]**candidate** you don't like?

Steve: Hmm, I see your point now. Maybe I should use Line to [6]**stay in touch** with my friends, or write more e-mails.

Jamie: Yeah, but don't use Gmail—they've admitted to giving other companies access to your [7]**inbox**!

史提夫：嘿，我們應該互加臉書好友。

潔　米：我是願意，但我最近退出臉書了。

史提夫：你是說你暫時不用社群媒體？

潔　米：不是，我刪除了我的臉書帳號。很多人都已經這麼做了，甚至像雪兒這樣的名人！這已經變成一種運動了。

史提夫：但這是為什麼？臺灣每個人幾乎都在用臉書。

潔　米：當然是為了保護個人資料。你沒看到那些臉書侵犯隱私權的新聞嗎？

史提夫：看到了，但我若沒做錯什麼事，我何必擔心他們取走我的資料？我只是用臉書跟我的朋友和家人聯繫。

潔　米：但他們會把你的資料賣給其他公司。你知道他們說什麼：你若沒付錢，你就是產品。他們會封鎖他們不喜歡的觀點。

史提夫：這個嘛，可能臉書也要想辦法賺錢吧。

潔　米：你知道劍橋分析公司吧？他們利用臉書允許他們存取的資料幫川普競選。你想讓你的資料被用來幫你不喜歡的候選人當選嗎？

史提夫：嗯，我懂你的意思了，也許我該用 Line 跟朋友聯繫，或多寫電郵。

潔　米：對，但不要用 Gmail，他們已經承認允許其他公司存取你的收件夾！

Language Guide

delete Facebook movement
刪除臉書帳號運動

臉書醜聞爆發後，許多企業及名人皆開始發響刪除臉書的活動，「#deleteFacebook」這個主題標籤 (hashtag) 不斷增加。特斯拉始人馬斯克也是這個活動的主要參與人物之一，他表示不會利用臉書為自己的產品做宣傳。同樣對臉書失望透頂的《花花公子》(PlayBoy) 雜誌也公開發表停止臉書平台活動官方聲明，原因是因為不想讓愛護他們的粉絲朋友暴露在隱私危險之中。

Vocabulary

1) **movement** [ˋmuvmənt] (n.)（思想、社會等）運動

2) **violation** [ˏvaɪəˋleʃən] (n.) 違反，侵犯

3) **relative** [ˋrɛlətɪv] (n.) 親戚，親屬

4) **censor** [ˋsɛnsɚ] (v.) 審查，（審查員）刪改、封鎖

5) **candidate** [ˋkændɪˏdet] (n.) 候選人，攻讀學位者

6) **stay in touch** (phr.) 保持聯絡

7) **inbox** [ˋɪnˏbɑks] (n.)（電子郵件的）收件箱

文章 + 對話
pp.58-61

CRISPR [1] Gene-edited Baby Project [2] Declared Illegal

當局宣布 CRISPR 基因編輯嬰兒計畫屬違法

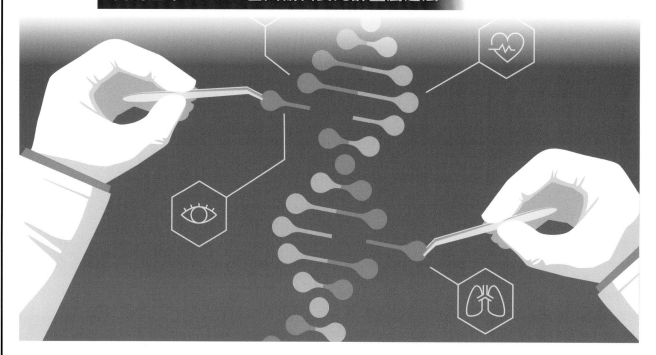

基因編輯寶寶的誕生，
意味著中國在基因編輯技術用於疾病預防
領域有歷史性的突破，
但為何會引發全球強烈反彈及撻伐呢？
這項宛如「人體活實驗」以科學的角度來
說，
它能有效幫助人類對於遺傳疾病的改革，
但卻有可能引發「人種進化」的倫理問題。
這也就是為什麼進行科學研究之前，
需要進行「倫理審查」，
就是為了要杜絕類似這種的情況發生。

Chinese [3]**authorities** have declared the work of He Jiankui, who shocked the scientific world in November 2018 with his claim of successfully creating the world's first ⑯ **gene-edited** babies, an illegal act carried out [4]**in pursuit of** personal fame and fortune. According to a report by China's official Xinhua News [5]**Agency**, [6]**investigators** have finished the first stage of a [17]**probe** that began in November following He's claims, and say the researcher faces serious punishment for his violations of the law.

賀建奎在 2018 年 11 月聲稱已成功創造出世界第一對基因編輯的嬰兒，震驚了科學界，而中國當局已宣布這項成果是為了追求個人名利而進行的非法行為。根據中國官方新華通訊社報導，賀建奎去年 11 月發表聲明後，調查員便展開調查，現已完成初步階段，並表示這位研究員將因違法而面臨嚴重懲處。

After completing a Ph.D. in [18]**biophysics** in the U.S., He taught at Shenzhen's Southern University of Science and Technology. The scientist previously led a team at the school to research use of the 🔊 **CRISPR** gene-editing tool—which enables the [7]**removal** of specific genes by acting as a [8]**precise** pair of [1]**genetic** scissors—in the treatment of cancer and other diseases. In addition, he also received 🔊 **angel funding** from the Chinese government, which he used to found two [19]**biotech** 🔊 **startups**, one to develop 🔊 **single-molecule sequencing** tools, and the other to offer 🔊 **genome sequencing** to cancer patients.

賀建奎在美國完成生物物理博士學位後，在深圳的南方科技大學教書。這位科學家之前在該校帶領一個研究小組，研究運用 CRISPR 基因編輯技術——就像一把精準的基因剪刀，可移除特定基因——來治療癌症等其他疾病。此外，他也獲得中國政府提供的天使資金，他用這筆資金創辦兩間生物科技新興公司，其中一間是研發單分子定序技術，另一間是為癌症病患提供基因體定序。

The trouble began when He [20]**fabricated** [9]**ethics** [10]**approvals**, which he used to [11]**recruit** eight couples to participate in [12]**clinical** [13]**procedures** between March 2017 and November 2018. The goal was to use CRISPR to delete the CCR5 gene—which 🔊 **HIV**, the virus that causes 🔊 **AIDS**, requires to enter blood cells—from human [21]**embryos**, resulting in babies [14]**immune** to HIV [15]**infection**. The project led to two [16]**pregnancies**, including one that resulted in the birth of twin girls, Lulu and Nana. Five couples failed to achieve [22]**fertilization**, and one pair left the experiment.

這起風波始於賀建奎偽造倫理審查的批准文件，他在 2017 年 3 月至 2018 年 11 月期間，用這份文件招募八對夫妻參與臨床程序，旨在運用 CRISPR 編輯技術移除人類胚胎中的 CCR5 基因——這是導致愛滋病的 HIV 病毒侵入血球所需的管道——讓嬰兒對 HIV 感染免疫。這項實驗計畫最終使兩人懷孕，其中一人生下雙胞胎女兒，名為露露和娜娜。另外五對夫妻未成功受精，另有一對夫妻退出實驗。

中國生物物理學者，賀建奎

單字 pp.58-61

Vocabulary

1) **gene** [dʒin] (n.) 基因，形容詞為 **genetic** [dʒə`nɛtɪk] 基因的

2) **declare** [dɪ`klɛr] (v.) 宣告，宣布

3) **authority** [ə`θɔrəti] (n.)（多為複數）當局，警方，管理機關，專家

4) **in pursuit of** (phr.) 追尋，追求

5) **agency** [`edʒənsi] (n.) 行政機構，局，署，處

6) **investigator** [ɪn`vɛstə,ɡetə] (n.) 調查者，研究者

7) **removal** [rɪ`muvəl] (n.) 移除，消除

8) **precise** [prɪ`saɪs] (a.) 精確的，準確的

9) **ethics** [`eθɪks] (n.) 道德規範，倫理學，道德學

10) **approval** [ə`pruvəl] (n.) 批准，認可

11) **recruit** [rɪ`krut] (v.) 招募，招收

12) **clinical** [`klɪnɪkəl] (a.) 臨床的

13) **procedure** [prə`sidʒə] (n.) 醫療程序，手術

14) **immune** [ɪ`mjun] (a.) 免疫的，不受影響的

15) **infection** [ɪn`fɛkʃən] (n.) 傳染，感染

16) **pregnancy** [`prɛɡnənsi] (n.) 懷孕，妊娠

進階字彙

17) **probe** [prob] (n.) 調查，探查

18) **biophysics** [,baɪo`fɪzɪks] (n.) 生物物理學

19) **biotech** [`baɪo,tɛk] (n.) 生物科技

20) **fabricate** [`fæbrɪ,ket] (v.) 偽造，捏造

21) **embryo** [`embri,o] (n.) 胚胎

22) **fertilization** [,fɜtələ`zeʃən] (n.) 受精

He's project has caused a wave of criticism among scientists across the [1]**globe**. Many believe that using CRISPR on human embryos is still dangerously [5]**unethical** at this stage, as it may cause [2]**severe** genetic damage. Some scientists have even proposed a [6]**moratorium** on CRISPR until clear [3]**guidelines** can be developed, while others [4]**urge** the development of safer and more [5]**ethical** methods to move the technology forward. At the present time, gene-editing of human embryos for [7]**reproductive** purposes is [8]**prohibited** in many countries, including the U.S. and China.

　　賀建奎的計畫引來全球科學家的批評聲浪。許多人認為現階段在人類胚胎上運用 CRISPR 仍相當危險且不道德，因為可能對基因造成嚴重損害。一些科學家甚至提議，在制訂明確的方針前，暫停運用 CRISPR，另有些人則敦促開發更安全、更符合道德的方式推動這項技術。目前世上有許多國家都禁止以生殖為目的的編輯人類胚胎的基因，包括美國和中國。

Vocabulary

1) **globe** [glob] (n.) 地球，地球儀，球體
2) **severe** [səˋvɪr] (a.) 嚴重的，劇烈的
3) **guideline** [ˋgaɪd͵laɪn] (n.) 指導方針，指導原則
4) **urge** [ɜdʒ] (v.) 督促

進階字彙

5) **unethical** [ʌnˋɛθɪkəl] (a.) 不道德的，反義字為 **ethical** [ˋɛθɪkəl] (a.) 道德的，倫理的
6) **moratorium** [͵mɔrəˋtɔrɪəm] (n.) 暫停，中止
7) **reproductive** [͵riprəˋdʌktɪv] (a.) 生殖的，生育的
8) **prohibit** [prəˋhɪbɪt] (v.) 禁止

Language Guide

gene-editing 基因編輯技術

基因編輯技術就是運用 Cas9 酵素剪下某段基因，來進行修改或刪除，控制操作生命體的 DNA。這項基因編輯技術是利用 CRISPR 能記憶的細菌免疫防衛機制而發展出來的，CRISPR 簡稱為 clustered regularly interspaced short palindromic repeats，讀作 [ˋkrɪspə]，藉由擷取曾受攻擊的病毒基因片段，待被同病原再度感染時，辨識這些基因片段，對目標染原體進行 DNA 雙鍊斷裂（double-strand break，簡稱為 DSB）作用，進而摧毀，達到抵禦外來致病原的效果。

angel funding 天使投資

angel 這個說法是來自於百老匯劇院 (Broadway theater)，用來形容提供戲劇演出資金的出資人，否則演出將無法進行。天使投資人（angel investor，另稱為商業天使 business angel）是指在公司草創初期就挺身揖注的投資者，通常會投入一筆資金來換取一部份股權，大多的天使投資人都不會干預公司的營運，但對於新創事業的投資，風險相對較高。

startup 新創公司

讀作 [ˋstɑrt͵ʌp]，指快速發展的創新公司。這些公司為創立初期的階段，公司的資金及人力都相當有限，正處於商業發展以及市場調查的階段，目的是要在短時間內達到擴張及快速成長，其中許多為網際網路公司。在創投界投資人會把成立不到 10 年但估值超過 10 億美元的新創公司稱為獨角獸 (unicorn)，把規模達到 1,000 億美元的新創公司稱為超級獨角獸，如：Airbnb、Uber、Dropbox 等。

single-molecule sequencing 單分子定序技術

molecule [ˋmɑləkjul] 是化學物質中的基本單元，譯作「分子」；sequence 原意為「安排…的順序」，若在專業的生物領域議題，則解釋作「測定 DNA 的序列」。單分子定序技術是屬於第三代定序技術 (3rd generation sequencing technology)，技術比前兩代更趨進步，不需要利用擴增子就能解讀更長片段的 DNA 分子，以 SMRT (single molecule real time) 和奈米孔定序 (nanopore sequencing) 為主要技術。擴增子（amplicon，[ˋæmplɪ͵kɑn]）是指擴增現象後所得的 DNA 片段，主要用於物種的鑑定。

genome sequencing 基因體定序

genome [ˋdʒi͵nom] 意思為「基因組，染色體組」。genome sequencing（基因體定序）被認為是人體基因解碼，開啟研究人體基因的大門，對於遺傳學 (genetics) 和基因變異有更深入的研究，目前常見的兩種技術為全基因體定序 (whole genome sequencing) 和全外顯子體定序 (whole exome sequencing)。

HIV /AIDS

HIV 全名為 human immunodeficiency virus，中文稱作「人類免疫缺乏病毒」，是一種專門攻擊人類免疫細胞的病毒，感染 HIV 病毒後，導致免疫系統被破壞，也是造成愛滋病的主因，正式病名為「後天免疫缺乏症候群」，英文為 acquired immune deficiency syndrome，縮寫 AIDS。

聊基因編輯嬰兒的道德疑慮

Jane: Have you seen the news about those gene-edited babies in China?

Zack: Yeah. Wasn't there some project where a couple gave birth to gene-edited twins?

Jane: Right. The latest news is that the Chinese government's declared the project illegal.

Zack: Why would they do that? Weren't their genes [1)]**modified** to give them [2)]**resistance** to HIV?

Jane: Yes. But apparently, the researcher faked his **LG** ethics [3)]**application approval**. And also, a lot of scientists think using the CRISPR tool on human embryos is unethical.

Zack: Why? It seems like there's lots of [4)]**potential** benefits.

Jane: Of course, but when you edit genes with CRISPR, there's a risk of causing genetic damage.

Zack: So a baby could be born with birth [5)]**defects**?

Jane: Possibly. But even if no damage is caused, there are still ethical concerns.

Zack: For instance?

Jane: Well, if you look at the history of **LG** eugenics, it was used by the **LG** Nazis to try and improve the "**LG** master race."

Zack: Hmm. Making improvements to babies sounds good, but when you put it like that, it seems pretty [6)]**creepy**.

Jane: Yeah. And if rich people are able to make their babies smarter and healthier, we may end up with even more [7)]**inequality** in the world.

珍： 你有看到中國基因編輯嬰兒的新聞嗎？

扎克： 有，是不是有一項實驗計畫讓一對夫妻生了一對基因編輯的嬰兒？

珍： 對，最新消息是中國政府宣布這項計畫違法。

扎克： 他們為什麼要這麼做？他們修改基因不是為了要抵抗 HIV 病毒嗎？

珍： 對，但那位研究員據說假造倫理審查申請書的批准。而且許多科學家認為將 CRISPR 技術用在人類胚胎上是不道德的。

扎克： 為什麼？這似乎有很多潛在的好處。

珍： 當然，但用 CRISPR 編輯基因時，基因有受損的風險。

扎克： 所以嬰兒出生時可能會有天生缺陷嗎？

珍： 有這可能，但就算基因沒有受損，還是有道德疑慮。

扎克： 比如說呢？

珍： 這個嘛，若回顧一下優生學史，納粹就曾利用優生學試圖改良「優越人種」。

扎克： 嗯，對嬰兒進行改良聽起來很不錯，但你換成那種說法時，讓人感覺不寒而慄。

珍： 對，而且若有錢人能讓自己的寶寶更聰明健康，我們的世界最後可能變得更不平等。

Language Guide

ethics review 倫理審查

只要是有人類為研究對象的生物醫學研究與行為研究，皆須通過人體試驗審查委員會 (institutional review board, IRB) 的審查，才能進行。人體試驗審查委員會會檢視研究者提出的研究方法是否符合倫理，然後將會同意或否決、監控與審查各個研究。該委員會的目的為確保研究對象的權益和福利獲得充分保障。

eugenics 優生學

又名「人種改良學」，讀作 [juˋdʒɛnɪks]，利用非自然的手段來改良人類的遺傳素質，19 世紀時，法蘭西斯高爾頓 (Francis Galton) 開始使用「優生學」一詞，主張人類的健康心理與強健身體是能透過遺傳延續的。這個說法引發了英國的優生學運動，支持者呼籲政府擬定法規藉由選擇性生育來改善人種素質，希望能夠打造比較健康強壯的人民。1933 年，德國納粹黨（Nazis [ˋnɑtsiz]）以留下「優等名族」(master race) 為由，宣稱心理和身體有缺陷者「不配活下」，要求他們絕育，最後更變成安樂死。1941 年，種族優生行動已屠殺了二十五萬人。由於納粹黨的濫用，世界各地的優生學計畫大部分都被捨棄。

Vocabulary

1) **modify** [ˋmɑdə͵faɪ] (n.) 修改，更改

2) **resistance** [rɪˋzɪstəns] (n.) 抵抗力

3) **application** [͵æpləˋkeʃən] (n.) 申請（書）

4) **potential** [pəˋtɛnʃəl] (a./n.) 潛在的，可能的；潛力，可能性

5) **defect** [ˋdifɛkt] (n.) 瑕疵，缺陷，缺點

6) **creepy** [ˋkripi] (a.) 令人毛骨悚然的，恐怖的

7) **inequality** [͵ɪnɪˋkwɑləti] (n.) 不平等，不均等

文章 + 對話
pp.62-65

Taiwan ¹⁾Warming Up to ^{LG}Blockchain

臺灣逐漸接受區塊鏈

世界一直在改變，
數位化讓我們的生活不斷更新，
貨幣的使用也出現不同的樣貌，
自我機制的虛擬貨幣、行動支付的普及，
數位貨幣的未來，
是你我都想像不到的。

🔲 **Bitcoin**, the world's most popular 🔲 **cryptocurrency**, had a bad year in 2018. In just 12 months, the digital ²⁾**currency** lost over 70% of its value, falling from US$19,870 per bitcoin to under US$3,500. Why have Bitcoin and other cryptocurrencies experienced such a sharp ³⁾**decline**? Reasons include the use of 🔲 **crypto** in 🔲 **money laundering** and other criminal activities, the fact that its value isn't backed by real ⁴⁾**assets**, and increasing regulation by governments that want more control of the currencies used within their borders.

世上最受歡迎的加密貨幣比特幣在 2018 年表現欠佳。這個虛擬貨幣在一年內損失超過 70％ 價值，從每一比特幣兌換 1 萬 9870 美元跌到 3500 美元以下。為何比特幣和其他加密貨幣會經歷如此慘跌？原因包括虛擬貨幣被用於洗錢等犯罪活動，沒有實際資產支撐，加上政府為了進一步控制在境內流通的貨幣而加強規範。

While countries like China and India have begun to [5]**crack down** on cryptocurrencies, others like Estonia and Japan—the world's largest crypto market—have continued to [6]**embrace** them. Taiwan, like South Korea, has decided to take the middle road, allowing limited trading of cryptocurrencies on local [7]**exchanges**, and at the same time creating a ⑯ **fintech** [15]**regulatory** environment that encourages the development of new uses for blockchain, the ⑯ **distributed ledger technology** that makes crypto possible. Blockchain is basically "blocks" of digital information stored in a public ⑯ **ledger** (the "chain"). The blocks contain data about transactions, along with [8]**identifying** codes called "⑯ **hashes**," and are [16]**encrypted** to ensure security.

雖然中國和印度等國家已開始制裁加密貨幣，愛沙尼亞和日本等其他國仍繼續接受，而日本是世上最大加密貨幣市場。臺灣則和南韓一樣，決定走中間路線，允許本地交易所進行有限的加密貨幣交易，同時建立金融科技監管環境，鼓勵開發新的區塊鏈用途，區塊鏈即是促成加密貨幣的分散式帳本技術。區塊鏈基本上是儲存在公共分賬（「鏈」）中的數位資訊「區塊」。區塊包含交易數據，以及稱為「散列」的識別碼，並加密以確保安全。

[9]**In light of** blockchain's potential applications in a wide range of industries, from finance and [17]**logistics** to medicine and [10]**hospitality**, Taiwan's government has set the goal of turning the island into a regional blockchain center. At the Asian Blockchain [11]**Summit** in Taipei last July, [12]**Minister** Chen Mei-ling of the National Development [13]**Council** said that blockchain would play an important role in the development of Taiwan's [14] ⑯ **digital economy**, and that the government would provide support for local blockchain firms. Last October, the government [15]**launched** the Asia Blockchain ⑯ **Accelerator**, with the goal of creating NT$1 billion in blockchain business value over the next two years.

鑑於區塊鏈在各種行業的潛在應用，從金融業和物流業到醫藥業和旅館業，臺灣政府已立訂目標，讓臺灣成為區域區塊鏈中心。去年七月在台北舉行的亞洲區塊鏈高峰會上，國家發展委員會主任委員陳美伶表示，區塊鏈在臺灣的數位經濟中將扮演要角，政府也將為本地區塊鏈企業提供支援。去年十月，政府推動亞洲區塊鏈加速器，目標是在未來兩年創造台幣十億元的區塊鏈商業價值。

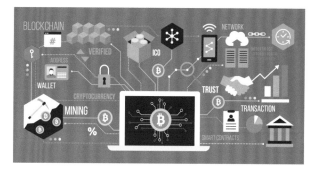

單字 pp.62-65

Vocabulary

1) **warm up (to)** (phr.) 逐漸接受，開始喜歡

2) **currency** [ˋkɝənsi] (n.) 貨幣，錢

3) **decline** [dɪˋklaɪn] (v./n.) 下跌，衰退

4) **asset** [ˋæsɛt] (n.) 資產，財產

5) **crack down** (phr.) 鎮壓，取締，打擊

6) **embrace** [ɪmˋbres] (n./v.) 擁抱，接納

7) **exchange** [iksˋtʃendʒ] (n.) 交易所，市場

8) **identify** [aɪˋdɛntəˏfaɪ] (v.) 識別，辨識

9) **In light of** (phr.) 鑑於，根據

10) **hospitality** [ˏhɑspɪˋtæləti] (n.) 好客，酒店業

11) **summit** [ˋsʌmɪt] (n.) 高峰會，最高級會議

12) **minister** [ˋmɪnɪstə] (n.) 部長，大臣

13) **council** [ˋkaʊnsəl] (n.) 委員會，理事會

14) **digital** [ˋdɪdʒɪtəl] (a.) 數位的

15) **launch** [lɔntʃ] (v./n.) 推出，發行

63

But Taiwan's blockchain industry seems to be doing well even without government [1]**assistance**. Founded in 2010, 🅛🅖 **AppWorks** is a Taipei-based accelerator that has assisted in the creation of over 800 startups, mostly tech-related. Worth noting is that out of AppWorks' most recent [2]**batch** of startups 17 out of 33 are blockchain related. And what's more, over half these blockchain startups are international, with founders coming from the U.S., Sweden, Austria, Poland, South Africa, Vietnam, Malaysia and Hong Kong.

但臺灣的區塊鏈產業就算沒有政府協助,似乎也表現良好。2010 年創辦的 AppWorks 是總部設在台北的加速器,已協助逾八百間新興公司創業,大部分是科技相關公司。值得一提的是,AppWorks 最近一批 33 間新興公司中,有 17 間與區塊鏈有關。此外,這些區塊鏈公司中有超過一半是國際公司,創辦人來自美國、瑞典、奧地利、波蘭、南非、越南、馬來西亞和香港。

AppWorks Accelerator 是位於台北的創業加速器

Vocabulary

1) **assistance** [ə`sɪstəns] (n.) 幫助,協助
2) **batch** [bætʃ] (n.) 一批,一群

Language Guide

bitcoin 比特幣

要聊到比特幣,一定要先提到加密貨幣,英文是 **cryptocurrency** [ˋkrɪptoˋkɝənsi],縮寫為 **crypto** [ˋkrɪpto],是一種運用密碼學原理來保障交易 (transaction) 安全的數位貨幣 (digital currency),非政府發行、完全無須仰賴金融體系控管。這樣的性質源自於區塊鏈技術。比特幣不需任何中介者,只要透過網路就能傳送。同時能使用任何幣別來購買,買下的比特幣會存在你手機或電腦裡的電子錢包。

money laundering 洗錢

「洗錢」可不是要把鈔票拿去用水洗啊,不過跟 laundering 倒是很有關係。這個字的來由源自於 20 世紀的芝加哥黑幫老大艾爾卡彭 (Al Capone),他利用經營自助洗衣店,謊稱是投幣式洗衣機的現金收入,使其不法款項重返「正規」金融體系。它的定義是指透過銀行或其他金融機構加以轉移,將其款項包裝成為合法所得,意圖隱匿其不法之來源去向的犯罪行為,不只如此,收受和使用此不法之款項,也都算是洗錢的行為喔。

blockchain 區塊鏈

區塊鏈的去中心化就是不需中心運作便能發行比特幣的核心技術,分散式帳本技術 (**distributed ledger technology**) 以會計分類帳 (**ledger** [ˋledʒɚ]) 的概念,將處理完成的帳目寫至另一帳本中,讓使用者都能持有最新且完整的帳務資料。基於密碼學原理設計,運用散列 (hash) 將資料保密且難以被推測,帳本內容無法被改寫,沒有假帳的可能。看到這裡,千萬不要認為區塊鏈就是虛擬貨幣,不只跟金融界相關,它的演化能改變我們的生活模式,像是股權的智慧合約、紀錄醫療或戶政資訊還有慈善捐募款項的流向等,不會被竄改且公信力足夠,區塊鏈的應用有無限的可能性。

fintech 金融科技

唸作 [ˋfɪnˏtek],全名為 financial technology,利用高科技技術賦予金融業顛覆傳統的創新金融工具,使得金融服務更有效率。最具體的例子就是行動支付,手機就能完成所有金融大小事。

digital economy 數位經濟

又稱為「網路經濟」(Internet economy),泛指以數位電腦科技為基礎的經濟,一般人普遍認為這是以網路市場經商的模式。這個概念最早是 90 年代,一位日籍教授在經濟衰退時所提出的。

accelerator 加速器

提供各種資源,輔助新創公司在短期內能達一定的經營規模或商業目標,加速創業的過程。又被稱為 startup accelerator「新創公司加速器」 或 business accelerator「企業加速器」。

AppWorks

2010 年,創始合夥人林之晨發現台灣數位產業的發展遠遠落後歐美,在全球經濟舞台上逐漸被邊緣化,於是從紐約回台成立 AppWorks,希望透過輔導網路創業團隊,來提升台灣的轉型動能。經過多年的努力,AppWorks 已經成為大東南亞地區領先的創投加速器。

Chloe: Hey, Mark. How are your [1]**investments** doing?

Mark: Not great. Taiwan's [2]**stock** market is up since the [3]**crash** last October, by all my stocks are still [4]**in the red**.

Chloe: That's too bad. Have you ever considered investing in crypto?

Mark: You mean cryptocurrencies?

Chloe: Yeah, like Bitcoin or 🄛🄖 **Ethereum**. I have a friend who's [5]**made serious bank** in crypto.

Mark: I seem to remember an article saying that Bitcoin lost most of its value last year.

Chloe: He actually sold close to the peak, and then started buying again after the [6]**sell-off**.

Mark: Trying to [7]**time** the market is too risky for me. And then there's the issue of [8] 🄛🄖 **liquidity**. I keep hearing about people having trouble [9]**cashing out** of cryptocurrencies.

Chloe: Well, cryptocurrencies are currencies after all, so you can always just spend them.

Mark: Yeah, but cryptocurrency payments aren't really common in Taiwan.

Chloe: But I stayed at a [10]**hostel** that accepts Bitcoin a couple months ago.

Mark: They're probably 🄛🄖 the [11]**exception that proves the rule**.

Chloe: Hmm, I guess you'd know better than I would.

Mark: The government does want to turn Taiwan into a blockchain [12]**hub**, so maybe crypto will be big in the future.

克蘿伊：嘿，馬克，你的投資情況如何？
馬　克：不太好，臺灣的股市從去年十月崩盤後已經上來一些，但我所有股票還是在虧損。
克蘿伊：太慘了，你考慮過投資加密嗎？
馬　克：妳是說加密貨幣嗎？
克蘿伊：對，例如比特幣或以太幣，我朋友投資加密貨幣賺了大錢。
馬　克：我好像記得有文章提到比特幣去年幣值慘跌。
克蘿伊：他其實是在接近高點時賣掉，然後在拋售後又開始買。
馬　克：選擇時機進出市場對我來說風險太大了，還有流動性的問題。我一直聽說兌現虛擬貨幣很麻煩。
克蘿伊：呃，加密貨幣畢竟是貨幣，還是可以花掉的。
馬　克：對，但用虛擬貨幣支付在臺灣不常見。
克蘿伊：但我幾個月前住過收比特幣的旅館。
馬　克：他們可能是特例。
克蘿伊：嗯，我想你應該比我瞭解。
馬　克：政府確實想把臺灣變成區塊鏈中心，所以未來虛擬貨幣可能會大受歡迎。

Language Guide

Ethereum 以太幣

以太幣是一個有智慧型合約功能的公共區段鏈平台。透過其專用加密貨幣以太幣 (ether) 提供去中心化的虛擬機器來處理對等合約。創辦人為程式設計師維塔利克布特林 (Vitalik Buterin)，受比特幣啟發後提出，目前為市值第二高的加密貨幣。

liquidity 流動性

又作 market liquidity（市場流動性），指資產能夠以合理的價格順利變現的能力，在投資的世界中，流動性本身，就是一種價值，投資標的的流動性越高，價值也越高。

the exception that proves the rule
反證規矩的例外，足以證明普遍性的例外

指某件事的涵義被解讀或曲解為不同的方式，指某種特例的存在反而表露出一般的規則。

A: Have you seen our hot new CEO? I thought CEOs were all old and bald.
你看過新上任的執行長嗎？他真是塊小鮮肉。我以為執行長都是又老又禿。

B: Yeah, he's gorgeous. I guess he's the exception that proves the rule, ha-ha.
沒錯，他真的很帥。小鮮肉執行長其實凸顯出大多數執行長還是又老又禿。哈哈。

Vocabulary

1) **investment** [ɪnˋvɛstmənt] (n.) 投資（額、標的），動詞為 **invest** [ɪnˋvɛst]

2) **stock** [stɑk] (n.) 股票，**stock market** 為股票交易市場

3) **crash** [kræʃ] (n./v.)（股市、公司等）崩盤，垮枱，破，崩潰

4) **in the red** (phr.) 虧損，赤字

5) **make bank** (phr.)（口）賺大錢

6) **sell-off** [selˋɑf] (n.)（股票等的）拋售，低價出售

7) **time** [taɪm] (v.) 確定好…的時機

8) **liquidity** [lɪˋkwɪdətɪ] (n.) 流動性

9) **cash out** (phr.) 兌現

10) **hostel** [ˋhɑstəl] (n.) 旅社，客棧

11) **exception** [ɪkˋsɛpʃən] (n.) 例外的人事物

12) **hub** [hʌb] (n.)（活動的）中心

All About Cell Phones

Cell Phone Functions
手機功能

- send text message 傳簡訊
- check voicemail
  聽取語音信箱
- use voice commands
  使用聲控
- use GPS
  使用衛星定位系統
  GPS 全名為 global positioning system
- access Internet 上網
- add / save / delete contact
  新增 / 儲存 / 刪除聯絡人
- change ringtone 換鈴聲
- adjust volume 調整音量
- set alarm 設鬧鐘

Cell Phone Parts
手機各部位

- earpiece 聽筒
- screen 螢幕
- microphone 麥克風
- camera 照相機
- battery 電池
- memory card 記憶卡
- SIM card SIM 卡
  SIM 為 subscriber identity module（用戶識別模組）

Cell Phone Accessories
手機配件

- (Bluetooth) headset
  （藍芽）耳機
- (car) charger
  （車用）充電器
- case 手機套
- faceplate 手機面版
- strap 手機掛繩
- charm 手機吊飾
- ring holder 手機釦環
- speaker 喇叭
- USB cable USB 傳輸線
  USB 為 universal serial bus
  （通用串列匯流排）

近年來不論是在路上還是公車捷運上，人人都成了低頭族 (smartphone addict)，許多資訊的流通和傳輸都在「彈指間」即可獲得，智慧型手機不僅是便捷的掌上型電腦，同時還結合了行動電話 (cell phone) 的通訊功能。這項高科技的出現，也掀起一波風潮，讓許多人甚至得了手機上癮症，一秒都離不開。

Cell phone Phrases 手機常用句

用手機時，你常會說⋯⋯

- My [1]**battery** is running low / about to die.
  我的電池快沒電了。

- I need to [2]**recharge** my battery.
  我必須幫電池充電。

- I'll add you to my contacts.
  我會把你加入我的聯絡人。

- I want to change my ringtone.
  我想要更換我的手機鈴聲。

- The [3]**reception** is really bad—I can barely hear you.
  收訊很差，我幾乎聽不到你的聲音。

- Hold on a second, I have another call.
  稍等一下，我有插撥。

手機的規格和功能更新速度非常快，因此很多人買不到幾年就想換一台，以下這些話可能就是他們的口頭禪：

- I'm thinking of getting a cell phone.
  最近想買手機。

- I've been thinking of switching cell phones.
  最近想換手機。

- My smartphone is getting really slow.
  我的智慧手機變得很慢。

- My phone doesn't have enough memory.
  我手機的容量太小了。

- I want a phone with a bigger screen.
  我想要螢幕大一點的手機。

運氣太背，沒做好功課，結果買到爛手機，難免會想要跟朋友吐苦水：

- It's a piece of crap. 爛手機。

- It's a lemon. 這台超難用。

- The batteries don't last long. 電池很容易沒電。

- Don't buy a / an _____ phone; they're hard to use.
  不要買 ____ 牌的手機，很難用。

Vocabulary

單字 p. 67

1) **battery** [ˋbætəri] (n.) 電池
2) **recharge** [riˋtʃɑrdʒ] (v.) 充電
3) **reception** [rɪˋsɛpʃən] (n.) 收訊，接收效果

All About Cell Phones

Internet [1] on the run
在外面上網

句子 pp. 68-69

網路又掛了

如果想在熱門時段上網，很容易連不上線：

- The [2]**Wi-Fi** here is [3]**spotty**. I keep losing the [4]**signal**.
  這裡的無線網路時好時壞，老是會斷線。

- The Wi-Fi connection keeps [5]**dropping**.
  我的連線一直斷掉。

- The connection is terrible. I can't even get online.
  連線狀況好差。我沒辦法連上網。

這裡有無線網路嗎？

不是每個人都有吃到飽方案，這時無線網路就很重要了：

- Does your café have free Wi-Fi?
  你們咖啡廳有免費的無線網路嗎？

- Can you tell me the Wi-Fi password?
  你可以告訴我無線網路密碼嗎？

- Are there any public Wi-Fi [6]**hotspots** around here?
  這附近有公共的上網熱點嗎？

- I don't have [7]**unlimited** data, so I need to find a hotspot.
  我沒有加入吃到飽方案，所以我要找熱點。

最近的插座究竟在哪裡

手機快沒電啦，隨身電源也忘了帶，只好趕快找插座：

- Is there an [8]**outlet** where I can charge my phone?
  有插座可以讓我幫手機充電嗎？

- Is it OK if I plug my phone in here?
  請問這裡可以讓手機充電嗎？

Cell Phone Plans
手機方案

綁約門號

綁約門號者，你常會說……

- Can you recommend a good cell phone company / [9]**carrier**?
  你可以推薦一家好的電信公司嗎？

- Is there a trial period?
  這有試用期嗎？

- I'd like to change my plan.
  我想要更換方案。

- Did I go over my minutes?
  我有超過分鐘數嗎？

- Is there a [10]**termination** fee?
  終止合約需要收費嗎？

- I have a question about my bill.
  我對我的帳單有點疑問。

易付卡門號

易付卡門號者，你常會說……

- How can I [11]**activate** my prepaid minutes?
  我如何啟用我的預付分鐘數？

- I need to buy more minutes.
  我需要多買一點分鐘數。

- I'd like to get a text messaging plan.
  我想買簡訊方案。

- Can I sign up for automatic [12]**renewal**?
  我可以辦理自動續約嗎？

- Let's keep this short—I'm [13]**running** low on minutes.
  我們長話短說吧！我的分鐘數快用完了。

Vocabulary

單字 p. 69

1) **on the run** (phr.) 移動中，忙碌中

2) **Wi-Fi** [ˋwaɪ.faɪ] 無線寬頻連線

3) **spotty** [ˋspɑtɪ] (a.) 時好時壞的

4) **signal** [ˋsɪɡnəl] (n.)（用於傳輸聲音、圖像或其他資訊的）電波信號

5) **drop** [drɑp] (v.)（電話、網路）斷掉、斷線

6) **hotspot** [ˋhɑt.spɑt]（可接上無線寬頻上網的）熱點

7) **unlimited** [ʌnˋlɪmɪtɪd] (a.) 無限制的，無限量的

8) **outlet** [ˋaut.lɛt] (n.) 電源插座

9) **carrier** [ˋkærɪɚ] (n.) 電信公司

10) **termination** [.tɝməˋneʃən] (n.) 終止，動詞為 **terminate** [ˋtɝmə.net] 結束，終止

11) **activate** [ˋæktə.vet] (v.) 啟用

12) **renewal** [rɪˋnuəl] (n.) 續訂，更新，動詞為 **renew** [rɪˋnu]

13) **run low (on)** (phr.) 即將用盡

對話 pp.70-71

Contract Plans
綁約門號

Conversation 1

顧客 Hi. I'm thinking of buying a new cell phone. Can you tell me about your contracts?
嗨，我正在考慮買一隻新手機，你可以說明一下你們的合約嗎？

店員 Certainly. We have one- and two-year plans available.
沒問題。我們有一年和兩年的方案可供選擇。

顧客 Two years sounds like a long time. What's the difference between the plans?
兩年聽起來好久喔，這兩種方案有何不同呢？

店員 If you sign up for a two-year contract, you'll get a better price on a phone. Some are even free.
如果你申辦兩年的合約，你可以用比較優惠的價錢買手機，有些手機甚至免費。

Conversation 2

M/男 I was just [1]**going over** my phone bill. I spend a lot of time chatting with my girlfriend, and it's getting expensive!
我剛看了一下我的電話帳單，我花了非常多時間跟我的女朋友聊天，電話費變得好貴！

F/女 If your girlfriend switches to Verizon too, you can talk as much as you want for free.
如果你的女朋友也轉到威訊，你們想聊多久都免費了。

M/男 Really? Can we talk anytime, or only during certain times of the day?
真的嗎？我們可以隨時講，還是只限定在一天的某些時段？

F/女 It's always free to talk with someone [2]**on our network**.
與我們網內任何人通話，全時段都免費。

Vocabulary

單字 pp.70-71

1) **go over** (phr.) （重新）檢查、審視
2) **on one's network** (phr.) 網內

Are You Ready for 5G?
準備迎接 5G 了嗎？

文／ Brian Foden

M/男 I'm going shopping for a new smartphone. You want to ¹⁾**tag along**?

我要買新的智慧手機，妳想跟我一起去嗎？

F/女 Wait, what? Didn't you just get a new phone last year?

等等，什麼？你去年不是剛買新手機嗎？

M/男 Yes, but my old phone is already starting to ²⁾**lag**. And I want one with more ³⁾**storage** ⁴⁾**capacity**.

對，但我的舊手機已經開始速度變慢了，而且我想換一個儲存空間更大的。

F/女 Oh yeah, I forgot. You're always playing ⁷⁾**multiplayer** games and ⁸⁾**streaming** videos.

喔，對，我忘了。你老是在玩多人遊戲和看串流影片。

M/男 Yep. I'm already on the best unlimited data plan, but my data speeds are just too slow.

對，我已經在用最好的無限流量方案，但流量速度還是太慢。

F/女 You might want to wait then. I hear they're ⁵⁾**rolling** out 🅛🅖 5G next year.

你可以先等一等，我聽說明年會推出 5G。

M/男 So if I wait and buy a 5G phone I can get faster speeds?

所以我若是等到明年買 5G 手機，速度會更快？

F/女 Much faster. The download speeds for 5G are gonna be at least 20 times as fast as 🅛🅖 4G.

會快更多，5G 的下載速度會比 4G 至少快 20 倍。

M/男 Whoa, that means no more ⁹⁾**latency** issues. Sounds like it's worth waiting for.

哇，這表示不會有延遲問題，看來很值得等。

F/女 For sure. But I'm not sure how long the rollout will take, so ⁶⁾**coverage** may be limited at first.

這是肯定的。但我不確定要等多久才發布，一開始覆蓋範圍可能會有限制。

Vocabulary

1) **tag along** (phr.) 跟著某人

2) **lag** [læg] (v.) 延遲，落後

3) **storage** [ˋstɔrɪdʒ] (n.) 儲存（空間）

4) **capacity** [kəˋpæsətɪ] (n.) 容量，容積

5) **roll (sth) out** (phr.) 推出（新產品、服務等），名詞為 **rollout**，首次提供（產品或服務）

6) **coverage** [ˋkʌvərɪdʒ] (n.) 涵蓋範圍

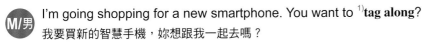
進階字彙

7) **multiplayer** [ˋmʌltɪˏpleɚ] (a.)（遊戲）多人的

8) **stream** [strim] (v.) 線上收聽、收看，串流，名詞為 **streaming** [strimɪŋ] 是一項影音多媒體檔案的傳輸技術，藉由分段傳送，穩定且快速像流水般送達至用戶端

9) **latency** [ˋletənsi] (n.) 延遲

真實辦公室情境對話，包括：
科技產品簡易使用教學、如何
提升粉絲團流量與線上檔案共
享，看了以後馬上烙兩句！

Office
Tech Conversations
職場科技對話

Putting Together PowerPoint Presentations

整理投影片簡報

文／ Leah Zimmermann

F/女 Can you believe it? I have to ¹⁾**put in** ¹¹⁾**overtime** again tonight!

你能相信嗎？我今晚又要加班了！

M/男 Oh no, not again. What is it this time?

糟糕，怎麼又來了，這次又是什麼事？

F/女 The boss is giving a PowerPoint ²⁾**presentation** tomorrow on the latest market ³⁾**analysis**.

老闆明天要做最新市場分析的投影片報告。

M/男 And you're ⁴⁾**in charge of** putting together the ⁵⁾**slides** for his presentation? That's what you get for being a PowerPoint ¹²⁾**whiz,** ha-ha.

所以妳要負責幫他整理投影片嗎？這是身為投影片簡報高手的妳才能勝任的工作啊，哈哈。

F/女 I wish I could laugh. I have tons of work to do. First I have to ¹³⁾**tweak** the slide ⁶⁾**layouts**, and then make sure all the ⁷⁾**transitions** are smooth.

我希望我笑得出來。我有一堆工作要做。首先我要調整投影片的版面，然後確保所有轉場都很順暢。

M/男 Is that it?

就這樣嗎？

F/女 I wish. I also have to make sure the ⁸⁾**graph** ⁹⁾**templates** are set up right and add some ¹⁴⁾**clipart** so that the graphs really ¹⁰⁾**pop**.

最好是，我還要確保圖表模板設置正確，然後加一些插圖，好讓圖表更顯眼一點。

M/男 Well, **LG** **look at the bright side**. At least you know the boss values your skills, ha-ha.

嗯，往好處想，至少妳知道老闆很看重妳這項專長，哈哈。

F/女 Yeah, I guess. Well, enough ¹⁵⁾**chit-chat**. I better get back to work if I want to get out of here before midnight.

對，我想是吧。嗯，閒聊夠了，我要是想在半夜前下班，最好繼續趕工了。

Language Guide

look at/on the bright side
往好處想

一體總有兩面，背光的一片漆黑，就表示向光面就在另一方。常用這個句子來激勵人「眼前的逆境其實也有好處」，鼓勵人要樂觀一點。

A: I can't believe my fiancé was cheating on me!
真不敢相信我的未婚夫背著我劈腿！

B: Look at the bright side. At least you found out before you got married!
往好處想吧，至少妳結婚前就發現了！

Vocabulary

1) **put in** (phr.) 投入（時間、努力等）

2) **presentation** [ˌprɛzənˈteʃən] (n.) 簡報，報告，演講

3) **analysis** [əˈnæləsɪs] (n.) 分析

4) **in charge (of)** (phr.) 負責，掌管

5) **slide** [slaɪd] (n.) 投影片，幻燈片

6) **layout** [ˈleˌaʊt] (n.) 版型，排列

7) **transition** [trænˈzɪʃən] (n.)（投影片）轉場，切換

8) **graph** [græf] (n.) 圖，圖表

9) **template** [ˈtɛmplɪt] (n.) 範本，模板，樣板

10) **pop** [pɑp] (v.) 顯眼，突顯

進階字彙

11) **overtime** [ˈovəˌtaɪm] (n./adv./a.) 加班，超時

12) **whiz** [wɪz] (n.) 奇才，高手

13) **tweak** [twik] (v.) 微調，調整

14) **clipart** [ˈklɪpˌɑrt] (n.) 美工圖案，素材集

15) **chit-chat** [ˈtʃɪtˌtʃæt] (n.) 閒話，閒聊

A Multifunction Printer [1] to the Rescue!

多功能事務機來解救

文／Brian Foden

 Quick, what's the phone number of the [6]**courier** service we use? I need to deliver this [2]**sketch** to the designer ⓛ**ⓖ on the double**.
快點，我們用的快遞服務電話號碼是多少？我要盡快將這份草稿拿給設計師。

 Let me see that, Sally. I've got a much better idea. Follow me.
讓我看看，莎莉，我有更好的辦法，跟我來。

 Why are you putting it in the printer? I don't need a copy of it.
為什麼要放進影印機裡？我不用影印。

 Oh, this is much more than just a printer. It's a [7]**multifunction** machine.
噢，這不只是影印機，這是多功能機種。

 So it's got a [3]**scanner** and a fax machine [4]**built** into it then?
所以這也是掃描機和傳真機？

 Yup. But there's no need to fax your sketch. You can just scan it to your PC or laptop and then e-mail it to the designer. Adjusting the [5]**format** is easy as well. I'll make it into a PDF file for you.
對，但不用傳真妳的草稿，妳可以把草稿掃描進妳的電腦或筆電，然後用電郵傳給設計師。調整檔案格式也很容易，我可以幫妳轉成 PDF 檔。

 Or I could save it to a [8]**USB drive** and then [6]**courier** it to the designer!
或者我可以存進隨身碟裡，然後請快遞交給設計師！

 Um…I think you're ⓛⓖ **missing the point**, Sally.
呃…我想妳搞錯我的重點了，莎莉。

Language Guide

on the double 立即，馬上

on the double 意指「立刻，迅速地」，可以想像為用「加倍」的速度來做事，意思就是要你快一點。

A: **I need that report on the double!**
我馬上就需要那份報告！

B: **Yes sir, I'm almost finished.**
好的，我快要好了。

miss the point 未能理解，未能領會

沒有正確理解或是抓到重點，反義的片語為 get the point。

A: **I told Ellen she should get to know Ken better before marrying him, and now she thinks I'm against her getting married.**
我告訴艾倫她應該要對肯更了解以後再嫁給他，結果她以為我反對他們結婚。

B: **It sounds like she missed the point completely.**
聽起來像是她完全搞錯重點了。

Vocabulary

1) **to the rescue** (phr.) 某人或某物扭轉情況，化險為安
2) **sketch** [skɛtʃ] (n.) 草圖，素描
3) **scanner** [ˋskænɚ] (n.) 掃描機
4) **build (in/into)** [bɪld] (phr.) 使包括，使成為組成部分
5) **format** [ˋfɔrmæt] (n.) 形式，樣式

進階字彙

6) **courier** [ˋkʊrɪɚ] (n./v.) 快遞，遞送員；透過快遞遞送
7) **multifunction** [ˌmʌltɪˋfʌŋkʃən] (n.) 多功能
8) **USB drive** [ˌjuesˋbi draɪv] (n.) 隨身碟

[1)]Making the Case for Macs

說說蘋果電腦的優點

文／Brian Foden

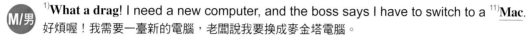

M/男 [1)]**What a drag!** I need a new computer, and the boss says I have to switch to a [11)]**Mac**.
好煩喔！我需要一臺新的電腦，老闆說我要換成麥金塔電腦。

F/女 What's the problem? Macs are great. They're much more [2)]**user-friendly**. I really love my MacBook Pro. The [12)]**SSD** makes it really fast.
這有什麼問題嗎？麥金塔電腦很棒，更好用。我好喜歡我的 MacBook Pro 筆電，固態硬碟讓它跑得超快。

M/男 Well, that's because you're a designer. I do data collection and analysis.
嗯，那是因為妳是設計師，我的工作是收集數據和分析。

F/女 It's true that most designers favor Macs. I mean, the colors are truer and the [3)]**graphics** software is superior.
確實大部分設計師偏愛麥金塔電腦。我是說，顏色更真實，繪圖軟體更高級。

M/男 See, that's what I mean. That's your [4)]**bias**.
看吧，我就是這個意思。那是妳的偏見。

F/女 Wait; you didn't let me finish. It's a [5)]**myth** that only designers like Macs. Anyone who likes stable, reliable computers has got to love Apple products. And they hardly ever [6)]**crash**. Plus, there are fewer viruses that attack Macs.
等等，我還沒說完。只有設計師喜歡麥金塔電腦是個迷思。喜歡電腦穩定可靠的人都會喜愛蘋果產品。蘋果電腦幾乎不會當機，而且麥金塔電腦較少受到病毒攻擊。

M/男 I guess you have a point. That's why I need a new computer. My PC kept getting [7)]**infected** with viruses.
我想妳說得有道理。所以我才需要新的電腦，我的電腦一直中毒。

F/女 See? Switching to a Mac ought to be a [8)]**no-brainer**! All you need to do is get used to using **OS X**.
看吧？換成麥金塔電腦應該是毫無疑問的！你只要習慣用 OS X 作業系統就行了。

M/男 I just hope most of the [9)]**software** I use is Mac [10)]**compatible**.
我只希望麥金塔電腦能跟我用的大部分軟體相容就好了。

Vocabulary

1) **(a) drag** [dræg] (n.)（口）令人厭倦、煩惱的事
2) **user-friendly** [ˌjuzəˋfrɛndli] (a.) 方便用戶的，便於使用的
3) **graphics** [ˋɡræfɪks] (n.) 繪圖，影像，圖像）
4) **bias** [ˋbaɪəs] (n.) 偏見，傾向
5) **myth** [mɪθ] (n.) 迷思，神話
6) **crash** [kræʃ] (v.)（電腦或系統）當機
7) **infect** [ɪnˋfɛkt] (v.)（電腦）中毒
8) **no-brainer** [ˌnoˋbrenə] (n.)（口）非常簡單的問題、答案、決定等

9) **software** [ˋsɔftˌwɛr] (n.)（電腦）軟體
10) **compatible** [kəmˋpætəbəl] (a.) 相容的，協調的

進階字彙

11) **Mac** [mæk] (n.) Mac 電腦，蘋果電腦，全名為 **Macintosh** [ˋmækɪnˌtɑʃ]
12) **SSD** (n.) 固態硬碟，全名為 **solid-state drive** 或 **solid-state disk**，是一種主要以快閃記憶體 (flash memory) 作為永久性記憶體的電腦儲存裝置

Problems with ¹⁾Pirated Software
盜版軟體的問題

文／ Kenneth Paul

 Hey, Tony, I got this prompt to ²⁾**download** ³⁾**updates** for this software, but when I click on it I get an error message and it shuts down.

嘿，東尼，有個視窗跳出來要我下載軟體更新，但我點擊後出現錯誤訊息，然後軟體就關閉了。

 I've been having the same problem. We're probably using a pirated version.

我也遇到同樣問題，我們大概用到盜版了。

 Was it installed by the ⁴⁾**IT** department?

這是資訊部安裝的吧？

 As far as I know the computers came **LG pre-installed** with the software when we bought them last year.

據我所知，我們去年買電腦時，這軟體就已經安裝在裡面了。

 So the retailer sold us computers installed with illegal software?

所以廠商賣給我們的電腦裡面安裝了盜版軟體？

 Looks that way. Maybe we should just ignore the update message and keep using the old version.

看起來是。也許我們該忽視更新訊息，繼續用舊版。

 But that may make our computers more ⁵⁾**vulnerable** to viruses, and the software may be disabled eventually.

但這樣可能會讓我們的電腦更容易中毒，軟體最後也會被禁用。

 You're right. Let's go talk to Michael in IT and see what he says.

妳說得對，我們去跟資訊部的麥可談談，看他怎麼說。

Language Guide

pre-installed software
預裝的軟體

又稱為配套軟體 (bundled software)，為向廠商購買時，已經事先安裝與授權 (licensed) 在電腦或智慧手機上的軟體。通常作業系統是預先安裝好的，但由於作業系統為基本需求，這個詞通常會用來表示其他非必須性的軟體。

Vocabulary

1) **pirated** [ˈpaɪrətɪd] (a.) 盜版的

2) **download** [ˈdaʊnˌlod] (v.) （電腦）下載

3) **update** [ˈʌpˌdet] (n. / v.) 更新

4) **IT** [ˌaɪˈti] (v.) 全名為 **information technology** 資訊技術，**IT department** 指「資訊部」，也可簡稱為 **IT**

5) **vulnerable** [ˈvʌlnərəbəl] (a.) 易受傷害的

How to [1)]Drive Facebook Traffic

如何增加臉書流量

文／Brian Foden

 M/男 Hey Tammy. How are things in marketing?

嘿，泰咪，行銷的情況如何？

 F/女 It's [2)]**tough** these days. My [3)]**supervisor** is constantly 🔤 **on my case** about reaching more people through Facebook. We're not getting as many page views as we used to on that platform.

最近比較辛苦。我的主管一直在嘮叨，要我設法增加臉書的流量，我們臉書的瀏覽次數沒有以前這麼多了。

 M/男 I think it's partly because Facebook has tweaked its algorithms. They're trying to make content more [4)]**relevant** for users.

我想部分是因為臉書調整了演算法，他們想讓用戶看到更適合的內容。

 F/女 Sure, but it's affecting our [5)]**reach**. What do you guys do in the [6)]**editorial** department?

是沒錯，但這影響到我們的瀏覽人數，你們編輯部是怎麼做的？

 M/男 The secret is to come up with posts that drive traffic. For example, give them useful tips, especially industry-related ones. That's the best way to get more [7)]**followers**—and good [8)]**leads**.

秘訣是發表能吸引流量的貼文，例如提供他們有用的情報，尤其是跟業界有關的。這是吸引更多追蹤者的最好辦法，也能吸引更多潛在顧客。

 F/女 We keep [9)]**recycling** our content year after year.

我們每年都重複使用內容。

 M/男 That's part of the problem. Facebook users want fresh information. There's so much [10)]**competition** out there. People are becoming [11)]**pickier** and pickier about what they choose to read. You need to [12)]**tailor** your content to your target audience.

這就是問題所在。臉書用戶想看新的資訊。競爭對手很多，大家對於所選擇閱讀的內容就越來越挑剔。你要為目標族群量身打造內容。

 F/女 Speaking of useful tips, that's actually really helpful. Thanks!

說到有用的情報，這真的很有用，謝謝！

 M/男 Don't thank me—thank the person who wrote the blog post I got them from!

不用謝我，這是我從部落格文章看來的，要謝謝那位部落客！

Language Guide

be on sb.'s case 嘮叨，埋怨

不停的批評某人或因某事而嘮叨、碎念。

A: **How come you decided to move out of your parents' house?**
你為何決定要搬出你爸媽家？

B: **They're always on my case about settling down and getting married.**
他們總是對我碎碎念，叫我安定下來，趕快結婚。

Vocabulary

1) **drive** [draɪv] (v.) 驅動，促進

2) **tough** [tʌf] (a.) 困難的，辛苦的

3) **supervisor** [ˋsupɚˏvaɪzɚ] (n.) 主管，上司

4) **relevant** [ˋrɛləvənt] (a.) 相關的，切題的

5) **reach** [ritʃ] (n.) 觸及人數

6) **editorial** [ˏɛdəˋtorɪəl] (a.) 編輯的

7) **follower** [ˋfɑləwɚ] (n.) 粉絲，追隨者

8) **lead** [lid] (n.) 潛在客戶，銷售機會

9) **recycle** [riˋsaɪkəl] (v.) 再次利用

10) **competition** [ˏkɑmpəˋtɪʃən] (n.) 競爭，競賽

11) **picky** [ˋpɪki] (a.) 挑剔的

12) **tailor (to)** [ˋtelɚ] (phr.) 量身訂做，使適應特定需要

Marketing with YouTube

用 YouTube 行銷

M/男 Did you hear that the manager wants us to 2)**put together** a YouTube marketing plan?
你知道經理要我們做 YouTube 行銷計畫嗎？

F/女 Yeah. I'**m on it** already. Tom in 3)**Graphics** has a friend who's a YouTube influencer, and he gave us some helpful 4)**pointers**.
嗯，我已經在進行了。平面設計部的湯姆有個朋友是 YouTube 意見領袖，他給了我們一些有用的撇步。

M/男 Wow, that's great! Like what?
哇，太棒了！比如呢？

F/女 For our product videos, he said to choose short, clear titles with good 5)**keywords** so viewers can find them.
以我們的產品影片來說，他說要選擇簡短清楚的標題和好的關鍵詞，這樣觀眾才方便搜尋。

M/男 Great idea. Search engine 6)**optimization** is really important. What else?
好主意。搜尋引擎最佳化很重要。還有呢？

F/女 We also need to keep each video short—under five minutes, and include 7)**links** to our website and social media accounts on our YouTube channel homepage…
我們也要讓每部影片保持在五分鐘內，在 YouTube 頻道首頁加入我們網站的連結和社群媒體帳號……

M/男 OK. What about content?
好，那內容呢？

F/女 I was thinking we could get Tom's friend to do some unboxing videos for us. He has over a million subscribers.
我在想可以請湯姆的朋友幫我們做一些開箱影片，他有超過一百萬名訂閱戶。

Language Guide

be on it 正要去辦

be on it 是個蠻口語的說法，表「正要做」、「正在處理」的意味。

A: We should book our air tickets while they're still cheap.
我們應該趁著機票便宜的時候趕緊下訂。

B: Yeah, I know. I'm on it.
嗯，我知道，我已經在看了。

Vocabulary

1) **marketing** [ˋmɑrkɪtɪŋ] (n.) 行銷，促銷

2) **put together** (phr.) 籌劃，安排，設計

3) **graphics** [ˋɡræfɪks] (n.) 平面設計，為 graphic design 的簡稱

4) **pointer** [ˋpɔɪntɚ] (n.) 指點，撇步，秘訣

5) **keyword** [ˋki͵wɝd] (n.) 關鍵字

6) **optimization** [͵ɑptəməˋzeʃən] (n.) 最佳化，最優化

7) **link** [lɪŋk] (n.) 網站連結

Learning to Use the Cloud

學習使用雲端

文／ Brian Foden

 F/女 Hey, Simon. Do you know where we keep the blank CDs?
嘿，賽門，你知道空白光碟收在哪裡嗎？

 M/男 You mean like for [1]**burning** songs on?
你要燒錄歌嗎？

 F/女 No. I have to send a file to a client, and it's too big to send by e-mail.
不是，我要寄個檔案給客戶，檔案太大，無法用電郵傳送。

 M/男 So you want to put it on a [2]**CD-R** and then send it by courier?
所以你要寫入空白光碟裡，讓快遞送去？

 F/女 Yep, that's the plan.
對，我是這麼想的。

 M/男 But that's so expensive—and [3]**inefficient**. Why not just use a **LG** **file hosting service**? Do you have a Gmail account?
但成本太貴了，速度又慢。為何不用檔案上下載服務？你有 Gmail 帳號嗎？

F/女 Sure, but it has a 25 **LG** **megabyte** limit, and the file is nearly a **LG** **gigabyte**.
有，但有 25MB 的限制，檔案有將近 1GB。

 M/男 But you can upload files to Google Drive right from your Gmail account. They give you 15 gigabytes of **LG** **cloud** storage.
但你可以從 Gmail 帳號上傳檔案到 Google 雲端硬碟，雲端容量有 15GB。

 F/女 How much do you have to pay for that?
這要花多少錢？

M/男 It's completely free. But if you need more capacity, you can get it for a small fee.
這完全免費，但你若需要更多容量，可以付少許費用獲得。

 F/女 Wow, great. But how does my client receive the file?
哇，太棒了，但我的客戶要怎麼收到檔案？

M/男 You just send them a link, and they can use it to download the file onto their computer.
你只要把連結傳給他們就好，他們可以透過連結把檔案下載到他們的電腦。

Language Guide

cloud computing 雲端運算

「雲端運算」其實就是「雲端」這個概念，「雲端」指的是網路上資料存放的空間，而這個空間就位於提供檔案寄存服務（**file hosting service**）的伺服器裡面，「雲端」的作用為讓人在任何地方皆可存取資料或是共享檔案等。像是微軟的 **OneDrive**、**Google** 雲端硬碟以及 **Dropbox**…等都是知名的雲端儲存平台。

數位資訊的計量單位

多以 **megabyte**（百萬位元組，縮寫為 **MB**）和 **gigabyte**（十億位元組，縮寫為 **GB**）來表示，1 GB=1024 MB，1TB = 1024GB，市面上的隨身碟大約是 8~16G，由此可見 Gmail 信箱的容量幾乎相當於一個隨身碟的儲存空間。

Vocabulary

1) **burn** [bɜn] (v.)（光碟）燒錄

2) **CD-R** [ˌsidiˋɑr] (n.) 可錄式光碟，全名為 **compact disc-recordable**，為可單次錄寫的唯讀記憶光碟。CD-R/CD-RW 和 DVD-R/DVD-RW 的唯一差異在於容量，CD-R/CD-RW 大約 700MB，而 DVD-R/DVD-RW 有 4.7GB，另外 CD-RW 和 DVD-RW 皆為可重複讀寫光碟，RW 指 rewritable（可重寫），CD-R 和 DVD-R 只能單次錄寫。

3) **inefficient** [ˌɪnɪˋfɪʃənt] (a.) 無效率的，效能差的

Getting Organized with Google Sheets

Google 試算表讓工作井然有序

文／Brian Foden

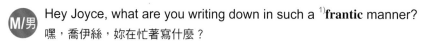

M/男 Hey Joyce, what are you writing down in such a [1]**frantic** manner?

嘿，喬伊絲，妳在忙著寫什麼？

F/女 I'm putting my order for afternoon snacks on this list before it's too late.

我在列出下午要訂的點心，免得來不及。

M/男 That's so **LG** old school! Why don't you guys upgrade to a better system – **LG** Google Sheets, for example. That's what we use in the IT department.

這太老派了！你們怎麼不升級用更好的方法，例如 Google 試算表。我們資訊部都用這個。

F/女 Never heard of it. What is it?

從沒聽過，那是什麼？

M/男 It's a [2]**spreadsheet** app. It's like [3]**Excel**, but you can access it online.

是一種試算表應用程式，就像 Excel，但可以在線上作業。

F/女 Is it tricky to use?

會很難用嗎？

M/男 Nah. It's a [4]**breeze**. You just set up the [5]**cells** to suit what you need.

不會，很容易上手，只要設定好符合妳所需的儲存格就行。

F/女 So people just type in what they want to order on the spreadsheet?

所以大家只要把他們想訂的東西打在試算表上就好？

M/男 Exactly. No more trying to [6]**figure out** everybody's [7]**sloppy** [8]**handwriting**!

沒錯，這樣就不用去辨認大家潦草的字跡了！

Vocabulary

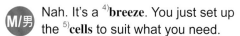

1) **frantic** [ˈfræntɪk] (a.) 緊張忙亂的

2) **spreadsheet** [ˈsprɛdˌʃit] (n.) 試算表

3) **Excel** [ɪkˈsɛl] (n.) 微軟電子表格軟體

4) **breeze** [briz] (n.) （口）輕而易舉的事

5) **cell** [sɛl] (n.) （電子試算表的）儲存格

6) **figure out** (phr.) 找出（答案），理解

7) **sloppy** [ˈslɑpi] (a.) （字跡）潦草的，草率的，邋遢的

8) **handwriting** [ˈhændˌraɪtɪŋ] (n.) 字跡，書寫

Top 科技焦點品牌
Tech Brands

你使用的電腦或手機是 Apple 嗎？每天會在 Facebook 上滑幾個小時？會看 Netflix 打發時間？要叫車的時候，會使用 Uber App 嗎？來看這 10 大佔據你食衣住行的科技品牌。

Amazon
Selling to the World

亞馬遜：賣到全世界

文章 pp.82-86

Born in Albuquerque, New Mexico and raised in Houston and Miami, Jeff Bezos showed promise from an early age. Although his teenage parents [1]**divorced** when he was just a baby, his stepfather, Mike Bezos—a poor [2]**immigrant** from Cuba who became an engineer at Exxon—provided him not only with his last name, but also a role model for success. Bezos got straight A's at Miami Palmetto High School, where he developed an interest in science and computers. After graduating at the top of his class, Bezos studied electrical [3]**engineering** and [4]**computer** science at Princeton.

傑佛瑞貝佐斯出生於新墨西哥州阿布奎基，在休士頓和邁阿密長大，從小就展現前途無量的潛力。雖然他的父母在青少年時剛生下他後就離婚，但他的繼父麥可貝佐斯不但讓他繼承姓氏，也是他日後功成名就的榜樣。麥可貝佐斯是貧窮的古巴移民，後來在埃克森美孚（編註：為世界上總市值最大的上市石油公司）擔任工程師。貝佐斯在邁阿密就讀帕梅托高中時成績優異，並培養出對科學和電腦的興趣。以全班第一名畢業的貝佐斯到普林斯頓大學攻讀電機工程和資訊工程。

A [5]promising career
職場前途無量

Graduating from Princeton with a 4.2 GPA, Bezos was offered jobs at top companies like Intel and Bell Labs, but he decided to join a financial startup called Fitel. After helping them build a trading network, he worked at a bank and then

New York investment management firm D.E. Shaw & Co., where he made senior vice-president at the age of 30. But Bezos wanted to have his own business, and impressed by the rapid growth of [6]**dot-com** companies, he decided to start his own. So in 1994, he quit his job, moved to Seattle and began writing a business plan.

貝佐斯以成績平均績點 4.2 分的成績從普林斯頓大學畢業，獲得英特爾和貝爾實驗室等頂尖公司延攬，但他決定加入新創金融公司費特。貝佐斯協助費特建立電子交易平台後，在一家銀行工作，然後到紐約的德劭投資管理公司，以 30 歲年齡擔任資深副總。但貝佐斯想自己創業，他注意到網路公司的快速成長，因此決定自行創辦網路公司。於是他在 1994 年辭職並搬到西雅圖，開始撰寫創業計畫。

Jeff Bezos 傑佛瑞貝佐斯

超越比爾蓋茲成為世界首富的傑佛瑞貝佐斯，近日鬧出婚變，和結婚 25 年的妻子簽字離婚，不過，財產就算分了一半出去，貝佐斯的身價排名依然沒有落出五名之外，不難看出貝佐斯的實力堅強。

Anton_Ivanov / Shutterstock.com

Vocabulary

單字 pp.82-86

1) **divorce** [dɪˋvors] (v./n.) 離婚

2) **immigrant** [ˋɪmɪɡrənt] (n.) 移民，僑民

3) **engineering** [͵ɛndʒəˋnɪrɪŋ] (n.) 工程，
   electrical engineering [ɪˋlɛktrɪkəl ͵ɛndʒəˋnɪrɪŋ] 即「電機工程」

4) **computer science** [kəmˋpjutəˋsaɪəns] (n.) 電腦科學，資訊工程

5) **promise** [ˋpramɪs] (n.) 前途，指望，
   形容詞為 **promising** [ˋpramɪsɪŋ] (a.)
   有前途的，大有可為的

6) **dot-com** [ˋdɑtˋkɑm] (n./a.) 網路公司（的）

amazon

🅛🅖 Striking out on his own
自行開創新事業

Bezos knew he wanted to market products over the Internet, so he created a list with 20 items, including CDs, computer software and [1)]**hardware**, videos and books. He [2)]**eventually** chose books because there are more 🅛🅖 **in print** than any bookstore could ever [3)]**carry**, making them an ideal product to sell on the Internet. Bezos chose the name Cadabra for his company, but after a lawyer [4)]**misheard** it as "[10)]<u>**cadaver**</u>," he changed it to Amazon. Why Amazon? He wanted his bookstore to be the biggest in the world, just like the Amazon is the biggest river.

貝佐斯知道自己想要透過網路行銷產品，所以列出一份包含 20 項商品的清單，包括音樂光碟、電腦軟體和硬體、影片和書籍。他最終選擇書籍，因為市面上所出版的書籍數量是任何實體書店都裝不下的，是網路銷售的理想產品。貝佐斯一開始為公司命名為卡達巴，但有個律師誤聽成「屍體」後，便改名為亞馬遜。為何取名為亞馬遜？他希望這間書店能成為世上最大的書店，就像亞馬遜河是世上最大的河流。

Amazon's rapid growth
亞馬遜的快速成長

[5)]**Fortunately** for Bezos, his dream soon came true. Although he told [6)]**investors** there was a 70% chance they would lose their money, within two months of beginning service in July, 1995, Amazon was selling books in all 50 states and 45 countries around the world. Amazon added CDs and videos to its product list in 1998, and then toys, software, video games and consumer [7)]**electronics** in 1999. But books were still the company's biggest seller, and when 🅛🅖 **e-books** started becoming popular, Bezos decided to [8)]**manufacture** an 🅛🅖 **e-reader** customers could use to buy books directly from

Amazon by wireless download. The Amazon 🅛🅖 **Kindle's E ink** design made reading easy on the eyes, and although it wasn't the first e-reader when it [9)]**hit** the market in 2007, it quickly became the most popular.

貝佐斯很幸運，他的夢想很快實現了。雖然他告訴投資者有七成的虧損機率，但亞馬遜從 1995 年 7 月開始推出服務後，兩個月內在全美 50 州和世界 45 個國家賣出書籍。亞馬遜於 1998 年在產品清單中加入音樂光碟和影片，接著在 1999 年加入玩具、軟體、電玩和消費性電子產品。但書籍仍是公司最暢銷的商品，電子書開始流行時，貝佐斯決定製造電子書閱讀器，讓顧客可以直接從亞馬遜購買和無線下載電子書。亞馬遜的 Kindle 電子墨水設計閱讀起來不費眼力，雖然在 2007 年上市時並非首款電子書閱讀器，但很快成為最受歡迎產品。

And the Kindle was just the first of many Amazon products. The Kindle was followed in 2011 by the 🅛🅖 **Kindle Fire**, a tablet computer designed to compete against Apple's iPad. That same year, Bezos also started the Amazon

Video service, which allowed members to ⓛⓖ **stream** movies and TV shows—some of which are even produced by Amazon—to any device connected to the Internet. Next came the ⓛⓖ **Amazon Echo**, a smart speaker, in 2014. What makes a speaker smart? All you have do to is give voice commands to ⓛⓖ **Alexa**—the Echo's digital assistant—and you can play music or ⓛⓖ **audiobooks**, listen to weather or traffic reports, and even control other smart devices.

Kindle 只是眾多亞馬遜產品中的第一款，之後在 2011 年推出 Kindle Fire，這是為了跟蘋果的 iPad 競爭而設計的平版電腦。同年貝佐斯也推出亞馬遜影音服務，讓會員用任何裝置上網即時串流電影和影集，有些內容甚至是由亞馬遜製作。接下來是 2014 年推出的亞馬遜智慧音箱 Amazon Echo。怎麼讓音箱變得有智慧？你只要用聲音下指令給 Echo 的數位助理 Alexa，然後就能播放音樂或有聲書，聽氣象預報或路況報導，甚至能控制其他智慧裝置。

Vocabulary

1) **hardware** [ˈhɑrdˌwɛr] (n.)（電腦）硬體
2) **eventually** [ɪˈvɛntʃuəli] (adv.) 最後，終究，形容詞為 **eventual** [ɪˈvɛntʃuəl]
3) **carry** [ˈkæri] (v.)（商店）備有，販售
4) **mishear** [mɪsˈhɪr] (v.) 誤聽，聽錯
5) **fortunately** [ˈfɔrtʃənɪtli] (adv.) 幸運地，僥倖地
6) **investor** [ɪnˈvɛstə] (n.) 投資者，出資者
7) **electronics** [ɪlɛkˈtrɑnɪks] (n.) 電器用品，電子科技
8) **manufacture** [ˌmænjəˈfæktʃə] (v.) 製造，名詞為 **manufacturer** [ˌmænjəˈfæktʃərə] 製造商
9) **hit** [hɪt] (v.)（產品）上架

進階字彙

10) **cadaver** [kəˈdævə] (n.) 屍體，死屍

The world's largest Internet company
世界上最大的網路公司

Finally, Amazon has also made use of technology in how it [1]**distributes** its products. Bezos had long received complaints that he treats his employees like robots, so why not just use robots instead? Much of the work at Amazon [2]**warehouses** is now done by robots, and the company is planning to start delivering products by [3]**drone**. By 2015, Amazon had more employees than any other company in the United States—in spite of all the robots— and had become the largest Internet company in the world. This has also made Bezos the world's richest man, and he hasn't just ⓛⓖ **let his money sit in the bank.** He not only bought the Washington Post, but also founded his own space company, ⓛⓖ **Blue Origin,** which plans

to offer space flights to the public starting in 2019.

最後亞馬遜也在產品分銷上運用了技術。貝佐斯長期以來被批評對待員工如同機器人，所以為何不直接用機器人？亞馬遜倉庫的許多工作現在都是由機器人完成，公司也正計畫由無人機運送產品。儘管用了那麼多機器人，到了 2015 年，亞馬遜的員工人數是全美公司中最多的，也成了世上最大的網路公司。這也讓貝佐斯成了世上最富有的人，而且他也不只是將錢存在銀行。他不僅買下《華盛頓郵報》，也自行創辦航太公司藍色起源，計畫自 2019 年起為大眾提供太空飛航的服務。

Mini Quiz 閱讀測驗

( ) 1. **Which of the following is true about Jeff Bezos?**
   (A) He graduated from Harvard University.
   (B) His first job after college was at Intel.
   (C) Books were the first thing he sold on the Internet.
   (D) He studied finance and electrical engineering.

( ) 2. **Which of the following are NOT manufactured by Amazon?**

   (A) e-reader
   (B) smart phone
   (C) smart speaker
   (D) tablet computer

( ) 3. **What do people mean when they say Bezos treats his employees like robots?**
   (A) He doen't treat them like humans should be treated.
   (B) He assigns appropriate tasks to his employees.
   (C) He thinks his employees are smart.
   (D) The employees work in a high-tech environment.

Vocabulary

1) **distribute** [dɪˋstrɪbjut] (v.) 經銷，配銷，配送

2) **warehouse** [ˋwɛr͵haʊs] (n.) 倉庫

進階字彙

3) **drone** [droʊn] (n.) 無人機，空拍機

strike out on one's own 獨立開創新事業

形容著手新任務或開啟新冒險，尤其「獨立完成」的意味濃厚，常用在創業方面。

A: Why did Bill quit his job?
為何比爾離職？

B: He decided he wanted to strike out on his own.
他決定要獨立開創新事業。

in print 已出版

print 除了有「列印、印刷」的之意，也能當作名詞「印刷品」。in print 用來表示書本等出版品可以在市面上買到，反義詞 out of print，就是指絕版品。

A: I'm looking for a book, but I'm not sure if it's still in print.
我在找一本書，但我不確定它是否還買得到。

B: If it's out of print, the library may still have a copy.
如果已經絕版，圖書館裡可能還是找得到。

e-book / e-reader 電子書 / 電子書閱讀器

電子書就是將書籍內容數位化，以電子檔的形式儲存在電子閱讀裝置中，不需要把大小厚重的書本都帶在身上，就能輕輕鬆鬆閱讀。專門設計來看電子書的電子產品就是電子閱讀器，設計與一般螢幕不同，長時間使用眼睛也不會痠，除了亞馬遜的 Amazon Kindle 系列，美國知名書店品牌邦諾 (Barnes & Noble) 出品的 Nook 閱讀器也很知名。

Kindle 電子閱讀器

Kindle E ink Kindle 電子墨水

一般背光顯示的螢幕會發亮，看久了眼睛容易疲勞，但閱讀使用電子墨水的電子紙螢幕時，感覺與傳統紙張相似，在大太陽下一樣看得清楚，可視角也達一百八十度，且只有改變顯示內容時會消耗電力，所以使用時間比一般平板電腦多了好幾倍，但缺點是目前只有黑白螢幕較普及，反應速度也稍微慢了一點。

Kindle Fire

為了要和蘋果競爭，2011 年推出的 Kindle Fire 平板電腦，大小為 7 吋，採用彩色觸控螢幕，是 Amazon Kindle 電子書閱讀器系列中唯一未使用 E ink 電子墨水的閱讀器。

Amazon Echo 聲控揚聲器

Echo 是一款擁有數位語音助理 Alexa 的智慧音箱，外觀跟一般藍牙喇叭沒有什麼不同，但只要接收到語音指令，就會開始行動，舉凡撥放音樂、聽新聞還是要外送披薩，只要你開口，它都能做到！幾乎全能的 Echo 支援多項裝置，幫忙開關燈還是烤箱定時都不是問題，同時它也有不同的系列產品，不斷推陳出新，讓你的生活更智能。對了，現在最新系列還可以和螢幕連結，試想一下，當你做菜下廚時，還可以請 Alexa 幫你播放食譜教學，是不是真的超級方便的呢！

audiobook 有聲書

以聲音為媒介來呈現書的內容，用朗讀、對話、廣播劇或報導等方式讓聽眾「閱讀」，格式有 CD 或是數位檔（如 mp3），對於盲人或是想邊開車邊聽書的人非常有用，常見於語言學習、童話故事，近年來也有商業資訊及名人演講的相關作品。除了可以下載或轉載至個人的手機，透過配音員 (voice-over actor) 朗讀與後製也使內容更活潑多元。

let one's money sit in the bank 錢存在銀行裡

這個片語是在暗喻沒有把錢用在更好的用途或投資上，反而放在銀行，這裡的 sit 有「閒置未用」意味

Blue Origin 藍色起源

執迷於太空的貝佐斯，為了圓夢，在2000年創辦了這家太空航空公司，並以出售亞馬遜股票來注資。致力於發展能重複使用且可靠的火箭飛行器，期許將航行太空的成本降得更低。藍色起源目前獲得美國空軍授予為國家安全任務開發火箭系統的合作公司之一，並且制定期望在2023年進行載人登月的新計畫，要將月球建立為永久性的居住地。

閱讀測驗解答 1 (C) 2 (B) 3 (A)

Facebook
—A Social Network Goes Global

臉書：使用者遍布世界的社群網站

Mark Zuckerberg was born in 1984 to Karen and Edward Zuckerberg, a [9]**psychiatrist** and a dentist. Growing up in Dobbs Ferry, a small town just north of Manhattan, he developed a strong interest in computers as a kid. Zuckerberg got his first PC when he was 10, and his dad taught him to [1]**program** in ⑯ BASIC when he was 12. He immediately used the language to create ZuckNet, a program that allowed all the computers in

their house—and his dad's [2]**dental** office—to communicate with each other. And while other kids played video games, Zuckerberg *designed* them. His dad even hired a computer tutor for him, and while attending high school at the [10]**exclusive** Phillips Exeter [3]**Academy**, Zuckerberg designed a music player so good that several top tech firms offered him jobs.

馬克祖克柏生於 1984 年，父母凱倫和愛德華祖克柏分別是心理醫師和牙醫。祖克柏在曼哈頓以北的小鎮多布斯費里長大，從小就對電腦培養出濃厚的興趣。祖克柏十歲時有了第一台個人電腦，十二歲時他爸爸教他用 BASIC 語言寫程式。他立刻用這語言編寫出 ZuckNet，這程式能讓他家中所有電腦和爸爸牙醫診所的電腦互相通訊。當其他小孩在打電玩時，祖克柏已經在設計電玩了。他爸爸甚至幫他聘電腦家教，而且他在高級的菲利普斯埃克塞特學院就讀高中時，已經設計出優秀的音樂播放器，以至有幾家頂尖科技公司延攬他。

A 🔟 hacker at Harvard
哈佛駭客

But Zuckerberg already ⁴⁾**had his sights set on** the 🔟 **Ivy League**, and was accepted to Harvard in 2002. In spite of his busy schedule studying ⁵⁾**psychology** and computer science, he still found time for ¹¹⁾__extracurricular__ programming. First he wrote CourseMatch, a program that helped students pick classes, and then Facemash, which let people vote on the ⁶⁾**attractiveness** of female students. The site was so popular that it ⁷⁾**crashed** the Harvard network, and the school shut it down days later because Zuckerberg had hacked into dormitory computers and used student photos without permission. Although Facemash failed in the end, it gave him the ⁸⁾**fame** on campus that

led to his next project, which would be successful 🔟 **beyond his wildest dreams**.

但祖克柏已經將目標鎖定常春藤盟校，並於 2002 年獲得哈佛錄取。儘管在攻讀心理系和資訊工程系時課業繁忙，他仍在課外抽出時間寫程式。他先寫了 CourseMatch 程式幫學生選課，接著是 Facemash，能讓同學投票選出外表優的女同學。這網站由於太過受歡迎，導致哈佛校內的電腦網路當機，校方在幾天後關閉 Facemash，因為祖克柏駭入宿舍電腦未經許可使用學生照片。雖然 Facemash 最後失敗了，但讓他在校內聲名大噪，促成他下一步計畫，其成就也超乎他的想像。

Mark Zuckerberg 馬克祖克柏

難怪人家都說成功的男人背後都有個偉大的女人。臉書教主祖克柏輟學後創業的時期，他的太太一直在背後默默支持他。有段傳聞是他們的愛情邂逅始於排隊等廁所，閒來無事就跟旁邊的人聊聊天吧，沒想到一聊就聊出感情來了。積極參與慈善，即使身價億萬的夫妻檔，生活低調、不愛用奢侈品，珍惜平凡的幸福。

Vocabulary

1) **program** [`progræm] (v.) 為（電腦）編寫程式

2) **dental** [`dɛntəl] (a.) 牙齒的，牙科的

3) **academy** [ə`kædəmi] (n.) 學院，藝術院

4) **have one's sights set on** (phr.) 下定決心，鎖定目標

5) **psychology** [saɪ`kɑlədʒi] (n.) 心理學，心理特質

6) **attractiveness** [ə`træktɪvnəs] (n.) 吸引力，迷惑力

7) **crash** [kræʃ] (v.)（電腦或系統）癱瘓，當機

8) **fame** [fem] (n.) 名聲，聲望

進階字彙

9) **psychiatrist** [saɪ`kaɪətrɪst] (n.) 精神病醫師，精神病學

10) **exclusive** [ɪk`sklusɪv] (a.)（團體，學校等）限制嚴格的，排他性的

11) **extracurricular** [͵ɛkstrəkə`rɪkjələ] (a.) 課外的，課餘的

The Facebook is born
臉書的誕生

After hearing about Facemash, fellow Harvard students and ⓘ **twins Cameron and Tyler Winklevoss** asked Zuckerberg to [1]**take on** programming duties for HarvardConnection, a social networking site that would help students at Harvard and other colleges connect with each other. Zuckerberg agreed to help, but then decided to use their idea to develop his own site— ⓘ **behind their backs**. It was only when he launched The Facebook on February 4, 2004 that the Winklevoss twins realized what had happened. They complained to the school paper, *The Havard Crimson*, which carried out an [2]**investigation**. The twins later filed a [3]**lawsuit**, and eventually won a [4]**settlement** worth $300 million!

在哈佛的雙胞胎同學卡麥隆和泰勒溫克勒佛斯聽說 Facemash 一事後，請祖克柏為 HarvardConnection 寫程式，那是能讓哈佛學生和其他大學互相聯繫的社交網站。祖克柏同意幫忙，但之後決定用他們的創意自行開發網站，而且是背著他們。他在 2004 年 2 月 4 日推出 The Facebook 時，溫克勒佛斯雙胞胎兄弟才發現此事。他們向校刊《緋紅報》投訴，於是報社展開調查。這對雙胞胎後來提出訴訟，最後贏得三億美元和解金！

From Harvard to the world
從哈佛拓展到世界

Within a month of launch, more than half of Harvard's students had joined The Facebook, so Zuckerberg hired several of his classmates and quickly expanded the service to other Ivy League schools and then all colleges in the U.S. and Canada. Next, on the advice of ⓘ **Sean Parker**— creator of the file-sharing service Napster—he moved the company to Palo Alto in Silicon Valley and changed the name from The Facebook to just Facebook. As the company's first president, Parker got PayPal [5]**founder** Peter Thiel to make a $500,000 investment, allowing Facebook to grow even faster. Over the next two years, membership expanded to include high school students, then employees of large companies and finally to anyone over 13 with an e-mail address. By the end of 2007, Facebook had 50 million active users.

The Facebook 推出後一個月內，超過一半哈佛學生加入，因此祖克柏聘請幾位同班同學，並隨後將服務擴大到其他常春藤盟校，然後是全美和加拿大所有大學。接下來在檔案分享服務 Napster 的創辦人西恩帕克的建議下，他將公司遷到矽谷的巴洛阿圖，並將公司名稱改為只有 Facebook。身為公司第一位總裁的帕克說服 PayPal 創辦人彼得泰爾投資五十萬 1 美元，讓 Facebook 能夠成長更快速。接下來兩年，會員資格擴大到高中學生，然後是大公司員工，最後是 13 歲以上且有電郵的人。到了 2007 年底，Facebook 已有五千萬活躍用戶。

How was Facebook able to grow so rapidly? The site kept adding features that not only attracted new users, but also encouraged them

to bring in their friends. Starting out with a basic profile, Facebook soon allowed users to add as many photos as they wanted, and then "tag" their friends. In 2006, the site added the News Feed, which informs users of changes in their friends' profiles and status, and in 2009 came the like button, which lets them instantly give approval and share liked content with friends. Launched in 2008, Facebook's chat feature could be used to make video calls by 2011. That same year, Facebook also introduced the ⑯ **Timeline**, which arranged all content by date, allowing users to ⁶⁾**scroll** through it conveniently.

Facebook 是怎麼能如此迅速成長？該網站不斷增加功能，不但吸引了新用戶，也鼓勵他們把朋友也帶進來。Facebook 一開始只有基本資料，然後很快讓用戶盡可能增加照片，接著能「標記」朋友。2006 年，Facebook 加入動態消息功能，有朋友更新資料和狀態就會通知用戶，2009 年推出按讚功能，讓用戶能立刻讚同並跟朋友分享喜歡的內容。2008 年 Facebook 推出的聊天功能，到了 2011 年已可以打視訊電話。同年，Facebook 也推出動態時報，按日期排列所有內容，讓用戶方便瀏覽。

Vocabulary

1) **take on** 接受、承擔（挑戰、責任、任務等）
2) **investigation** [ɪnˌvɛstəˋgeʃən] (n.) 調查，研究
3) **lawsuit** [ˋlɔˏsut] (n.) 法律訴訟案
4) **settlement** [ˋsɛtəlmənt] (n.) 和解，和解金
5) **founder** [ˋfaʊndə] (n.) 創立者，創辦人
6) **scroll** [skrol] (phr.) 滾動，瀏覽

臉書動態消息 (news Feed)

Facebook goes public
臉書上市

With all the basic features [1]**in place**, Zuckerberg decided to ⓛⓖ **take his company public**. On May 17, 2014, Facebook was valued at $104 billion—the highest amount ever for a newly ⓛⓖ **listed company**. Later that year, the site reached a billion active users. Now that he had lots of money to play with, Zuckerberg began buying other companies, including photo-sharing service Instagram, mobile messaging company WhatsApp and VR headset maker Oculus. Recently, while continuing to add new features— like Facebook Live—he's also started to think about giving back to society. In 2015, Zuckerberg started a [2]**charity** with his wife, Dr. Pricilla Chan, which will use 99% of his wealth to improve health and education around the world.

祖克柏和妻子普莉希拉陳

　　所有基本功能都已經具備了，祖克柏決定讓公司上市。2014 年 5 月 17 日，Facebook 的價值達 1040 億美元，是新上市公司的最高紀錄。那年年底，網站達到十億活躍用戶。現在祖克柏手頭有很多錢可運用，他開始收購其他公司，包括照片分享服務 Instagram、手機通訊公司 WhatsApp 和虛擬實境頭戴式裝置製造商傲庫路思。近年來仍持續增加直播等新功能的同時，他也開始思考回饋社會。2015 年，祖克柏開始與妻子普莉希拉陳醫生一起創辦慈善機構，未來將把自己 99％的財富用來提升世界各地的衛生和教育。

Mini Quiz 閱讀測驗

( ) 1. **Which is closest in meaning to the word "exclusive" in the first paragraph?**
   (A) restricted
   (B) famous
   (C) ordinary
   (D) academic

( ) 2. **Why was the site Facemash shut down?**
   (A) It didn't meet students' needs.

(B) Zuckerberg used student photos without permission.
(C) Some female students complained about the site.
(D) It was difficult to use.

( ) 3. **Who came up with idea that inspired Facebook?**
   (A) Mark Zuckerberg
   (B) Sean Parker
   (C) Cameron and Tyler Winklevoss
   (D) Zuckerberg's tutor

Vocabulary

1) **in place** (phr.) 在正確的位置，準備就緒
2) **charity** [ˈtʃærəti] (n.) 慈善，慈善事業

2012 年 5 月 18 日，Facebook 通過首次公開募股正式在納斯達克上市，美國紐約市湯森路透大樓外歡迎 Facebook 加入納斯達克的看板。

Language Guide

BASIC 培基程式語言

BASIC 是 Beginner's All-purpose Symbolic Instruction Code（初學者全功能指令代碼）的縮寫。一九六四年由 John George Kemeny 和 Thomas Eugene Kurtz 兩人所開發。在此之前，幾乎所有電腦運算功能都必須由電腦科學家及數學家撰寫專用程式，而 BASIC 程式語言的目的，就是要讓非主修科也能夠學習使用，被認為是學習程式設計的入門語言。

hacker 駭客

hacker [ˈhækə]，正面與負面意義兼具的中性詞彙，原意是指程式技術過人的電腦高手，不過也能用來表示藉由破解軟體、解碼入侵電腦，違反資訊安全的涵義，如同網路犯罪份子 (cybercriminal)，這兩種用法都很常見，作動詞時後方要加上 into，成為 hack into。

Ivy League 常春藤盟校

是指由位於美國東北部八所大學組成的名校聯盟，這八所學校都是美國最頂尖、最難進入的私立大學，也是全世界獲得最多捐款的學校，擁有優秀的學生與師資。

八所常春藤盟校依英文首字母排序如下：

● Brown University 布朗大學
● Columbia University 哥倫比亞大學
● Cornell University 康乃爾大學
● Dartmouth College 達特茅斯學院
● Harvard University 哈佛大學
● University of Pennsylvania 賓州大學
● Princeton University 普林斯頓大學
● Yale University 耶魯大學

beyond one's wildest dreams
超乎某人的想像、作夢都沒想到

這裡的 wildest 可不是解釋成「最狂野」喔，wildest dreams 是指想像不受限、期待無上限的事物，經常會說 beyond one's wildest dreams。 另一個類似的說法是 never in one's wildest dreams「想都沒想過，連想都不敢想」。

A: **If you could have one wish, what would it be?**
如果你可以許一個願望，你會許什麼？
B: **I'd want to be rich** beyond my wildest dreams.
我會想要有錢得不得了。

Cameron and Tyler Winklevoss
溫克沃斯雙胞胎兄弟

同樣也念哈佛大學的溫克沃斯雙胞胎兄弟，主修經濟學，為什麼要特別提到他們主修的學系呢？因為這對雙胞胎兄弟可是靠著打官司的和解金成為億萬富翁呢！與祖克柏的訴訟結束後，兄弟倆用這筆錢成立溫克沃斯資本公司 (Winklevoss Capital)，看好虛擬貨幣 (virtual currency) 的未來趨勢，投資比特幣 (Bitcoin)，甚至創立了比特幣交易平台 Gemini，來維護虛擬貨幣的安全性問題。

behind one's back 在別人背後

在人家背後，不敢大大方方，這個片語顧名思義，就是指「偷偷地，不讓人知道」的意思。

A: **How do you know your boyfriend is seeing someone** behind your back?
妳怎麼知道妳男友偷偷和別人約會？
B: **I found a lipstick mark on the collar of his shirt.**
我在他襯衫的領口上發現口紅印。

Sean Parker 西恩帕克

出生於 1979 年的帕克，從小就喜歡寫程式，19 歲創立音樂線上分享服務—— Napster，後來還成立 Plaxo 聯繫管理服務。帕克 25 歲時成為臉書創辦顧問，同時也是臉書的首任總裁，兩年後雖然因為涉及藏毒而卸任，但後續臉書許多的功能開發，帕克都還有參與，是臉書功不可沒的大臣之一。現在的他致力於癌症免疫治療法，希望藉由人體免疫系統來治療癌症。

take company public（公司）上市

這裡的 public 用來表示某公司股票正式上市，也可以說成 go public，成為一般民眾都能投資的公司，我們看財經新聞常聽見的 IPO，是 initial public offering 的縮寫，意思是「首次公開募股」。另一個用詞 list 也有相同意味，listed company 就是指「上市公司」。

Apple
the Company that Made Tech Fashionable
蘋果公司：讓科技變時尚的公司

Humble beginnings
白手起家

On April Fool's Day in 1976, Apple Computer was founded by two college ⁵⁾**dropouts**—Steve Jobs and ⓛ **Stephen Wozniak**—in the garage of Jobs' childhood home in Palo Alto, a small city in Silicon Valley. But Jobs and Wozniak were no ordinary dropouts. Although they went to the same high school, Jobs didn't meet the older Wozniak until a ¹⁾**mutual** friend introduced them. They quickly ²⁾**bonded** over their interest in electronics, and were soon working on their first project: a " ⓛ **blue box**"—an illegal electronic

文章 pp.94-98

device that allows the user to make free long-distance calls. With Woz in charge of design and Jobs handling marketing, their blue box was a big success, but they decided to quit before the police caught up with them.

1976 年 4 月 1 日愚人節這天，史蒂夫賈伯斯和史蒂芬沃茲尼克這兩位大學輟學生，在賈伯斯位於矽谷小城巴洛阿圖的兒時老家車庫創辦了蘋果電腦。但賈伯斯和沃茲尼克不是一般的輟學生，雖然他們上同一所高中，但賈伯斯和較年長的沃茲尼克是後來透過共同朋友介紹認識的。他們很快因為對電子科技都有興趣而結為好友，緊接著便合作研發第一個產品：「藍盒子」——能讓使用者打免費長途電話的非法電子裝置。由沃茲尼克負責設計，賈伯斯負責行銷，藍盒子非常暢銷，但他們決定在被警察抓到前放棄。

After a brief period of study at Reed College, Jobs went on a long [3]**spiritual** trip to India. When he returned, Wozniak was at work on a new project: a personal computer. [4]**Convinced** of its commercial potential, the two started Apple to sell the computer, which they named the Apple I. Although it was basically just a [6]**motherboard**—you had to add your own keyboard and monitor to use it—the Apple I sold so well that they went to work right away on the next model. The Apple II, which came out in June 1977, featured a plastic case, attached keyboard and color graphics. It sold so well that

Apple was able to hire a whole staff of computer designers, but it was the Macintosh that would [7]**revolutionize** the industry.

在里德學院短暫就讀後，賈伯斯到印度進行長期的靈修之旅。他回美國時，沃茲尼克正在研發新產品：個人電腦。由於相信這產品有商業潛力，他們倆創辦了蘋果電腦公司以販售這台電腦，並取名為蘋果一代。雖然這電腦基本上只是主機板，要自己加鍵盤和螢幕，但蘋果一代銷售量很好，於是他們立刻研發下一個機型。1977 年 6 月蘋果二代推出，有塑膠外殼，附有鍵盤和彩色圖形介面。由於電腦很暢銷，因此他們能聘請一群電腦設計員，但徹底改革電腦業的是麥金塔。

Tim Cook 提姆庫克

作為賈柏斯的接班人，提姆庫克難免會不斷被拿來和他比較，認識他們的人都曉得，他們的個性南轅北轍。追求實際、冷靜沉著的庫克，若認真責問起來，整間會議室的空氣都會凝結，威力比破口大罵還驚人！

單字 pp.94-98

Vocabulary

1) **mutual** [ˈmjutʃuəl] (a.) 互相的，共同的

2) **bond** [bɑnd] (v./n.) 建立關係；（人之間的）關係，聯繫

3) **spiritual** [ˈspɪrɪtʃuəl] (a.) 精神上的，心靈的

4) **convince** [kənˈvɪns] (v.) 說服

進階字彙

5) **dropout** [ˈdrɑpˌaʊt] (n.) 中輟生

6) **motherboard** [ˈmʌðɚˌbɔrd] (n.)（電腦）主機板

7) **revolutionize** [ˌrɛvəˈluʃəˌnaɪz] (v.) 徹底變革

A new kind of computer
新型電腦

Launched in 1984, the Macintosh featured a 🅛🅖 **GUI** and a mouse—features that Jobs "borrowed" from 🅛🅖 **Xerox** after a visit to their [1]**research** [2]**lab**. Although it became a model for all the PCs that followed, it didn't become a mass market product because of its $2,495 price tag. And then, following a power struggle with [9]**CEO** 🅛🅖 **John Sculley**—who Jobs had brought over from Pepsi by asking, "Do you want to sell sugar water for the rest of your life or come with me and change the world?"—he left Apple to start another company, 🅛🅖 **NeXT**. Over the next decade, Jobs developed [10]**workstations** for [3]**higher education** at NeXT, and also helped found 🅛🅖 **Pixar**, which would become one of the world's most famous [11]**animation** studios.

1984 年推出的麥金塔有圖形使用者介面和滑鼠，這些功能是賈伯斯參觀過全錄的研究中心後「借來」的。雖然麥金塔成為接下來所有個人電腦的模型，但此時尚未成為大眾市場產品，因為價格高達 2495 美元。之後賈伯斯與執行長約翰史考利經過一番權力鬥爭後離開蘋果，創辦另一家公司 NeXT。而史考利原本是賈伯斯從百事可樂挖來，當時賈伯斯問他：「你要下半輩子繼續賣糖水，還是跟我一起改造這世界？」離開蘋果後十年間，賈伯斯在

NeXT 為高等教育研發工作站，也協助創辦皮克斯，皮克斯後來成為世上最有名的動畫製片廠之一。

Jobs returns 賈伯斯回歸

Meanwhile, Apple wasn't doing so well. Under a [4]**series** of CEOs, the company tried making other products—like digital cameras, CD players and speakers—and began losing money. It was time to bring Jobs back, and Apple CEO Gil Amelio did this by buying NeXT in 1997 and making him an advisor. He was soon CEO again, and working with designer 🅛🅖 **Jonathan Ive**, he began to put together a whole new product line. With the 🅛🅖 **iMac**, a beautiful computer with a built-in screen introduced in 1998, Apple immediately began making money again. This was followed in 2001 by another big hit, the 🅛🅖 **iPod**—a [5]**portable** digital [6]**audio** player that could hold thousands of songs. The iPod was so popular that it sold 100 million units over the next six years, and forever changed the way people listen to and share music.

同時蘋果則表現不佳。該公司在好幾位執行長帶領下嘗試製造其他產品，比如數位相機、CD 播放器和喇叭，卻開始虧損。是時候該請賈伯斯回來了，蘋果執行

由左至右分別為 MacBook、iMac、iPad 和 iPhone

© testing/shutterstock.com

2016 年 9 月，當 iPhone 7 在中國北京西單店上市，民眾排隊搶購的盛況

長吉爾艾米里歐在 1997 年收購 NeXT，請賈伯斯擔任顧問。賈伯斯很快又當上執行長，與設計師強納生艾夫合作，開始研發新的產品線。1998 年推出出色的電腦 iMac 有內建螢幕，蘋果立刻又開始賺錢。接下來在 2001 年推出的 iPod 又成功大賣，那是能容納成千上萬首歌的攜帶式數位音樂播放器。iPod 非常受歡迎，在接下來六年賣出一億個，就此永遠改變了大家聽音樂和分享音樂的方式。

From computers to mobile devices
從電腦到行動裝置

Although Apple continued making [12]**well-liked** computers like the iMac, and laptops like the ⓛⓖ **MacBook**, the great success of the iPod convinced Jobs to [7]**shift** the company's focus to mobile devices. His design team was working on a touchscreen tablet at the time, but when Jobs saw the scrolling function, he immediately thought, "We can build a phone with this!" In his 2007 speech announcing the ⓛⓖ **iPhone**, Jobs said, "Today, Apple is going to [8]**reinvent** the phone, and here it is." The iPhone wasn't the first phone to replace the [13]**keypad** with a touchscreen—that would be the ⓛⓖ **LG Prada**—but it was the first one to catch the public's interest. People formed long lines at Apple stores to buy an iPhone, and new models kept coming out each year, each adding new features—like ⓛⓖ **3G** support, ⓛⓖ **Siri** and ⓛⓖ **Touch ID**.

雖然蘋果仍繼續生產廣受歡迎的電腦，比如 iMac，和 MacBook 等筆記型電腦，但 iPod 的暢銷讓賈伯斯將公司的重心轉往行動裝置。他的設計團隊當時正在研究觸控式平板電腦，但賈伯斯看到滑動功能，立刻想到：「我們可以打造有這種功能的手機！」賈伯斯在 2007 年的 iPhone 發佈會上演講時說：「現在蘋果要重新發明電話，就是這款。」iPhone 並不是第一個用觸控螢幕取代傳統鍵盤的手機，而是 LG Prada，但 iPhone 是第一個引起大眾興趣的觸控螢幕手機。顧客在蘋果商店前大排長龍買 iPhone，而且 iPhone 每年都推出增加新功能的新機型，比如支援 3G、人工智慧助理 Siri 和指紋識別感應等。

While Jobs died of cancer in 2011, he at least lived to see the [1]**phenomenal** success of the iPhone—over 1 *billion* have been sold—as well as the iPad, which is basically a larger iPhone minus the phone. New CEO Tim Cook may not be a creative [2]**genius** like Jobs, but he's done a good job managing Apple [3]**operations**, making sure that new and better iPhone and iPad models come out every year. He must be doing something right—Apple is now the most valuable company in the world!

賈伯斯雖然在 2011 年死於癌症，但至少能活著看到 iPhone 驚人的暢銷現象——賣出超過十億個——以及 iPad 的誕生，那基本上就是比較大型的 iPhone，只是沒有通話功能。新任的執行長提姆庫克可能不像賈伯斯一樣是創意天才，但他將蘋果公司營運得很好，確保每年都能推出更好的 iPhone 和 iPad 新機型。他肯定是做對了，因為蘋果現在是世上最有價值的公司！

Language Guide

Stephen Wozniak 史蒂夫沃茲尼克

蘋果電腦的發明者其實是天才發明家沃茲尼克，他個性內斂不擅長社交，在正式研發蘋果電腦前，就已經設計出一台名為「奶油蘇打」(Cream Soda) 的電腦，當時動輒耗用上百顆晶片 (chip) 的一般電腦，這台奶油蘇打只要 20 顆就組裝完畢，算是當時很轟動的事蹟。「發明」是他這輩子都會一直做的事，設計出一、二代蘋果電腦後，沃茲尼克離開蘋果，1987 年，他製作了一台只有 20 個按鍵的萬用遙控器 (universal remote control)，這支遙控器可以控制電視機、錄影機和音響。

blue box 藍盒子

賈伯斯和沃茲尼克合作研發的第一個產品，藉由模仿訊號控制接線總機 (switchboard) 來撥打免費電話，不過隨著通訊數位化，現今藍盒子已普遍無法使用。

GUI 圖形化使用者介面

全名為 graphical user interface，是指電腦的操作介面採用圖形顯示，能藉由滑鼠移動及操作，而不是透過輸入指令，相較於早期的命令列使用者介面 (command line interface，簡稱 CLI) 較容易使用，DOS 系統就是 CLI 的一種，而 window 作業系統則是屬於 GUI。

Xerox 全錄印表機

讀做 [`zɪrɑks]，是影印裝置公司——全錄的品牌名稱，Xerox 跟 Google 一樣變成動詞，為「影印 (photocopy)」的口語用法。說到全錄，它可以說是發展個人電腦 (personal computer) 的背後功臣，為什麼這麼說呢，全錄開發個人電腦早於蘋果跟微軟，它最早建立圖形化的 GUI 介面，也最早開始接觸人工智慧研究，可惜的是，當時公司的重心全都集中在他們的主業印表機上，沒有好好經營個人電腦的領域，還開放最高機密的研究室給蘋果和微軟的工程師看，讓他們學到了技術，也因而錯失比肩科技龍頭公司的地位。

John Sculley 約翰史考利

約翰史考利雖然是賈伯斯挖角來的,但經營理念卻和他相去甚遠,在他執掌蘋果期間,公司的銷售額從 8 億美元上升至 80 億美元。不過他也因為背離了賈伯斯所定的銷售結構,特別是他決定與 IBM 競爭相同的客戶群體,從而受到爭議,最後離開了蘋果。後來的史考利,參與投資數間公司都有不錯的成績,其中還有跟他的兄弟一起合夥的公司。2014 年,當時已經 74 歲的史考利再度投身新事業——Obi Worldphone,跨足至智慧型手機的產業。

NeXT

賈伯斯在 1985 年成立的一間工作站製作的軟體公司,主要是服務高等教育研發。不敵虧損的 NeXT,決定捨棄硬體的銷售策略,轉型販售 NeXTSTEP 作業系統,這個系統後來被蘋果看上,現今蘋果的作業系統都有其影子,以 NeXTSTEP 做為設計的藍圖。

Pixar 皮克斯

賈伯斯 1986 年收購盧卡斯影業 (Lucasfilm) 的電腦動畫部,成立皮克斯動畫工作室,後來又為迪士尼買下。截至目前為止,皮克斯共發行 20 部動畫長片,第一部就是大家耳熟能詳的《玩具總動員》(Toy Story),天外奇蹟 (Up)、怪獸電力公司 (Monster Inc.)、腦筋急轉彎 (Inside Out) 等,都是家喻戶曉的著名作品,甚至多次奪下奧斯卡最佳動畫片獎。

位於美國加州愛莫利維爾市 (Emeryville) 的皮克斯動畫工作室

Jonathan Ive 強納森艾夫

鑽研工業設計的艾夫,是蘋果公司的首席設計師,同時被認為是成就蘋果的重要人物之一。他的設計風格為極簡、典雅且易上手,曾參與設計多項具代表性的產品,例如 iPod、iPhone 及 Apple Watch 等,還有 iOS7 介面的規劃設計。

Apple 代表商品

現在年輕人幾乎人手一支 iPhone,不過在智慧型手機時代來臨之前,當時的年輕人手上可是人手一支 iPod。iPod 是數位音樂播放器,將音樂檔案數位化,不用 CD 就能隨時隨地聽音樂,在當時可是很夯的,隨著手機平板的出現,iPod 才逐漸被取代。除了 **iPhone**、iPad,也不忘要提到蘋果電腦的演進,從麥金塔到現在的 Mac 系列,如筆記型的 **MacBook**、一體化的 **iMac**。Macintosh 的出現,使得 GUI 界面和滑鼠成為電腦的基本配備,直覺性操作的麥金塔被認為是改革電腦業的重要發明。

LG Prada

LG 電子 (LG Corporation) 與時尚品牌 Prada 共同發表的觸控螢幕手機,第一代在 2007 年開始販售,是世界首創觸控螢幕手機,可聽音樂可拍照,集多功能於一身,帶領手機走向新的里程碑。

Siri

在蘋果正式收購 Siri 之前,原本是一款主攻旅遊規劃的助理應用程式,蘋果買下重新開發後,成為內建在蘋果 iOS 系統中的人工智慧助理。

Touch ID

內建在蘋果手機、平板中的指紋辨識 (fingerprint recognition) 系統,省去按密碼的步驟,簡化螢幕解鎖 (unlock) 程序。後來 touch ID 也能當作身分驗證的一種安全機制,例如在 iTune Store、APP Store 購買下載 app 時或是登入銀行理財 app 等。現在更發展出 face ID「臉部辨識功能」,在 2017 年公開的 iPhone X 首次登場,未來技術若發展得更成熟,說不定會全面取代 touch ID 呢!

Google the King of Search

谷歌：搜尋之王

Like another famous tech company, Google was also founded in a garage. But unlike most large tech companies, Google started as a research project. The company's two founders, Larry Page and Sergey Brin, met at Stanford University in 1995 and soon became good friends. They were both Ph.D. candidates in computer science, and Page invited Brin to join him on a project studying the links between web pages. Realizing that the number and quality of links to web pages was a good [1]**measure** of their importance, they created an algorithm called **ℓ PageRank** to rank pages based on this information. And they soon realized something even more important—

PageRank could be used to provide better results than existing search engines.

Google 就像另一間知名科技公司，也是在車庫創辦的。但跟大部分大型科技公司不同的是，Google 一開始是一項研究計畫。Google 的兩位創辦人，賴利佩吉和謝爾蓋布林是 1995 年在史丹福大學認識，隨後變成好朋友。他們都是資訊工程學的博士候選人，佩吉邀請布林加入他的網頁連結研究計畫。他們瞭解到網頁連結的數量和質量是評估網頁重要性的衡量方式後，便設計出名為「佩奇排名」的演算法，並根據這項資訊為網頁排名。他們很快發現一件更重要的事，比起現有的搜尋引擎，佩奇排名可以用來提供更好的搜尋結果。

From dorm to garage 從宿舍到車庫

So Page and Brin changed the focus of their project to developing a search engine, which they called BackRub. Working from Page's dorm room, they put their search engine online in 1996, and by 1997 it was so popular that it took up most of the ⓖ **bandwidth** on Stanford's network. After changing the name from BackRub to Google—which came from *googol*, a mathematical term for the number ten followed by 100 zeros—Page and Brin decided to turn their project into a business. With a $100,000 investment from Andy Bechtolsheim of Sun Microsystems, in August 1998 they set up their first office in the Menlo Park garage of their friend ⓖ **Susan Wojcicki**,

who would later become CEO of YouTube. That same year, they posted the first Google 2)**Doodle**, a figure to let users know that the whole staff was away at the 3)**Burning Man festival.**

於是佩奇和布林更改研究計畫的重心，研發出一個搜尋引擎，並命名為「搓背」。他們在佩奇的宿舍房間研發的搜尋引擎於 1996 年上線，到 1997 年時已經非常受歡迎，佔了史丹福電腦網路的大部分頻寬。在將「搓背」改名為 Google 後——源自數學術語「古戈爾」，意指 10 的 100 次方——佩奇和布林決定將這項計畫發展成事業。在昇陽電腦的安迪貝托爾斯海姆投資十萬元下，他們於 1998 年 8 月在朋友蘇珊沃西基位於蒙洛公園市的車庫成立第一間辦公室，她後來成為 YouTube 的執行長。那年他們發表第一個 Google 塗鴉，是一個讓使用者知道所有員工都去參加燃燒人節的人形圖案。

Larry Page and Sergey Brin
賴利佩吉和謝爾蓋布林

你們知道嗎，初識的佩吉和布林，其實互看不順眼！不過正確說法應該他們有許多共通點，尤其都對於事物有很強烈的意見，所以很難一拍即合。生性害羞的二人認為自己不一定是個優秀的管理者，為了公司好他們退居幕後，專注於產品與技術。

© anjamalaicse/flickr.com

左為賴利佩吉，右為謝爾蓋布林

Vocabulary

1) **measure** [ˈmɛʒɚ] (n./v.) 測量方法；測量

進階字彙

2) **doodle** [ˈdudəl] (n./v.)（無聊、心不在焉地）塗鴉

3) **Burning Man Festival** (n.) 燃燒人節慶
又稱「火人祭」，是美國內達華洲黑石沙漠（Black Rock Desert）舉辦的慶典，祭典的宗旨是盡情展現自我，其中因營火晚會燃燒一具木製難行雕像而得名。

Google

An advertising goldmine
廣告金礦

Page and Brin were against using annoying 🔴 **pop-up ads**, but they had to figure out a way to monetize the growing number of eyeballs—so many people were using the site that "google" became a verb. In 2000, Google came up with the perfect solution: 🔴 **AdWords**, an advertising platform that displays simple text ads linked to the search terms typed by users. This turned out to be a [6]**goldmine**, and Google began spending its money on a variety of new services. First came Google Images in 2001, and next Google News in 2002. Then came Gmail in 2004, which quickly became the most popular e-mail service by offering an [1]**unheard of** 1 GB of storage (now 15 GB).

佩奇和布林反對使用惱人的彈出式廣告，但隨著使用人數越來越多，他們要設法將人潮變成錢潮，而且因為有太多人使用 Google，使「google」一詞演變成動詞。2000 年，Google 想到一個完美辦法：AdWords，這是一種廣告平台，所顯示的簡單文字廣告與使用者輸入的搜索詞相連。結果證實這是個金礦，Google 也開始將錢花在各種新服務上。首先是在 2001 年推出 Google 圖片搜尋，接著是 2002 年的 Google 新聞。然後是 2004 年的電子郵件 Gmail，藉由提供前所未聞的 1GB 容量信箱（現在已增至 15GB），迅速成為最受歡迎的電郵服務。

Google also added new services by [2]**acquiring** other companies, like Keyhole, which developed the technology for Google Earth, a 3D map of the globe created from [3]**satellite** images, and Where 2 Technologies, which created the program that became Google Maps. But perhaps their most successful [2]**acquisition** was that of video-sharing site YouTube in 2006. Although many questioned the purchase at the time, YouTube is now the second most popular website in the world, with 400 hours of content uploaded each minute, and one *billion* hours of content being watched every day. Also introduced in 2006 were Google Calendar and Google Docs—a set of web-based office software similar to Microsoft Office. It may not provide the full [7]**functionality** of Office, but it's completely free!

Google 也藉由收購其他公司增加新服務，例如研發 Google 地球技術的 Keyhole，運用衛星圖像設計 3D 全球地圖，以及 Where 2 Technologies，其創造的程式後來成為 Google 地圖。但最成功的可能是在 2006 年收購影音分享網站 YouTube。雖然當時引起許多人質疑，但現在 YouTube 是世上第二大受歡迎的網站，每分鐘有 400 小時內容上傳，每天有十億小時的點閱。同樣在 2006 年推出的是 Google 日曆和 Google 文件，Google 文件是一套類似微軟 Office 的線上辦公室軟體。這套軟體或許無法提供完整的 Office 功能，但它是完全免費的！

Entering the mobile market
進軍行動市場

There were [4]**rumors** that Google would introduce a smartphone in 2007, but instead it released Android, an open mobile platform meant to compete against those put out by companies like Microsoft and Apple. And compete it did—

within a few short years Android became the most used mobile platform in the world, which has [5]**ensured** that the mobile versions of Google's apps are used on as many smartphones and tablets as possible. But not every attempt by Google to enter a new market has been this successful. With an eye on Facebook, Google launched social networking site **LG Orkut** in 2004 and social network **LG Google+** in 2011. While Orkut was popular for a time in India and Brazil, it was shut down in 2014 due to low user numbers, and Google+ is due to meet the same fate in 2019.

曾有傳聞說 Google 會在 2007 年推出智慧手機，結果卻發表了 Android 作業系統，那是為了與微軟和蘋果等公司推出的平台競爭而研發的開放式行動裝置平台。在這場競爭中，Android 短短幾年內成了全世界使用量最大的行動平台，使得多數智慧手機和平板都使用 Google 的行動版應用程式。但 Google 並非每次都能成功進軍新市場，在注意到 Facebook 的發展後，Google 在 2004 年推出社群網站 Orkut，並在 2011 年推出。雖然 Orkut 曾在印度和巴西流行一陣子，但因為使用者數量較少而在 2014 年結束，而 Google+ 也在 2019 年將遭遇同樣命運。

AdWords

2013 年 6 月於紐西蘭基督城施放的熱氣球

Eyes on the future
放眼未來

In addition to developing products for the current market, Google also has its eyes set on the future. Through its research and development [1]**arm**, Google X (now called just X), the company is working on projects like Weymo ([3]**driverless** cars), Loon (balloons that bring Internet [2]**access** to remote areas), and Wing (flying delivery vehicles). And looking even further into the future are Google-funded Verily, which is using technology to develop new medical solutions, and Calico, a company that is working to slow down, or even stop, human aging.

除了為目前的市場研發產品外，Google 也放眼未來。Google 正透過研發部門 Google X（現只稱為 X）進行幾項計畫，例如 Weymo （自動駕駛汽車）、 Loon （用熱氣球將網路帶到偏遠地區）、Wing（送貨無人機）。為了展望更遙遠的未來，Google 贊助生命科學研究機構 Verily，利用科技研發新的醫療方法，以及生物科技公司 Calico，是研究延緩甚至阻止人類老化的公司。

Mini Quiz 閱讀測驗

( ) 1. **Which of the following is true about Google?**
   (A) The founders met at Sun Microsystems.
   (B) It was first named PageRank.
   (C) Its name came from the word "googol."
   (D) It became a business in 1996.

( ) 2. **Which of the following is NOT a company that Google bought?**

   (A) Keyhole
   (B) Where 2 Technologies
   (C) YouTube
   (D) Orkut

( ) 3. **Which of the following is NOT a successful Google product?**
   (A) Google+
   (B) Google Calendar
   (C) Google Docs
   (D) Android

PageRank 佩吉排名

是 Google 對其搜尋引擎分析排名的一種演算法，以創始人之一的佩吉來命名，這項技術成為評估 SEO 成效的方式之一。SEO 是 search engine optimization 的簡稱，意思是「搜尋引擎最佳化」，將排名規則進行優化，將資料內容作比對，以最快且最完整的方式呈現。

bandwidth 頻寬

傳輸訊號最大的吞吐量 (throughput)，也就是指能有效接受訊號的最大寬度。我們打個簡單的比方：把頻寬比喻為道路，路如果寬敞就不會塞車，行車速度就越快，因此頻寬越寬，資料傳輸速度也就越快。

Susan Wojcicki　蘇珊沃西基

© Krista Kennell/shutterstock.com

要談起蘇珊和 Google 的淵源，一切都要從她的車庫開始，為了紓解經濟壓力的蘇珊，將她的車庫租給佩吉和布林。一次 Google 伺服器大當機，讓當時在英特爾 (Intel) 有穩定工作的蘇珊體悟到對 Google 引擎的依賴性，毅然決然地加入團隊。作為 Google 的第 16 號員工，同時也是市場推廣經理，主導廣告業務，蘇珊的部門成為撐起 Google 營收的大支柱，領導買下 Youtube，現在是 Youtube 的執行長。

Google Doodle

doodle 有「塗鴉」的意思，Google 的首頁標誌會為了紀念名人、節日等而臨時調整的特別設計。1998 年為了慶祝燃燒人節所誕生的第一個塗鴉。起初的塗鴉大部分是以靜態圖片為主，後來開始加上動畫或超連結，還可以互動。第一個互動式塗鴉是 2010 年為了紀念小精靈 30 週年而出現，能直接在首頁標誌上玩小遊戲，頗受好評。不過塗鴉偶爾也為 Google 引來一些評論，例如 2014 年發布紀念日本圍棋手的塗鴉，卻未考慮到適逢諾曼地登陸 70 週年而飽受抨擊，最後只好將原先的塗鴉撤下，並為諾曼地登陸重新設計。

第一個 Google 塗鴉，為了讓使用者知道所有員工都去參加燃燒人節的人形圖案

pop-up ad 彈出式廣告

廣告和網頁連結，當用戶在進入網頁時，會自動開啟瀏覽視窗，吸引使用者的目光，以達到行銷的廣告手法。不過彈出式廣告被認為是最惱人的廣告手段，有時還會造成當機 (crash)，目前的瀏覽器 (browser) 幾乎都有支援封鎖 (block) 彈出式廣告，因此這樣類型的廣告方式也逐漸減少。

AdWords 關鍵字廣告

當我們在 Google 搜尋引擎上輸入「關鍵字」(keyword) 時，關鍵字廣告會出現在搜尋結果頁面中的最上面，提高商家資訊和商品訊息的曝光率，是一種計算點擊次數的網路廣告，稱作 pay per click（每點擊付費）。這樣類型的廣告手法，主要是因應資訊爆炸的時代，當使用者透露感興趣的商品或是主題，進而篩選提供相關內容，把廣告發送給適合的使用者，以達到最佳的廣告效益。2018 年，Google AdWords 更名為 Google Ads。

Orkut 我酷

是 Google 在 2004 年推出的社交網路服務，大部分的用戶來自於印度及巴西，使用者可以依照興趣創建虛擬社團 (virtual community)，在裡頭留信息，與好友互動，可說是 Google+ 的前身。

Google+

Google Plus 的簡稱，可說是整合 Google 所有社交服務的核心，如 Circles（社交圈）、Hangouts（多人視訊）、Sparks（話題靈感）等多項功能，讓社交應用的服務不再侷限於單一功能。原本肩負能與當時聲勢當紅臉書匹敵的使命，卻沒想到模糊的定位，無法拉攏原先臉書上活躍的用戶，也沒有讓新使用者註冊的動力，尚未帶起轟動便退流行。自 2011 上線，不到十年的時間，Google 宣布將在 2019 年的 4 月關閉所有相關服務。

閱讀測驗解答 1 (C) 2 (D) 3 (A)

DJI
—the First Chinese Global Brand

大疆創新：中國第一個全球品牌

A dream of flight
飛航夢想

Born in 1980 to an engineer and a teacher, Frank Wang grew up in the historic Chinese city of Hangzhou. His [7]**fascination** with aircraft began in [1]**elementary** school when he read a comic book that featured a red [2]**helicopter**. He dreamed of having his own flying robot that could follow him around taking pictures, and when he did well on an exam in high school, his parents [3]**rewarded** him with an 🔤 **RC helicopter**. Unfortunately, he immediately crashed it and had to wait months for new parts to arrive from Hong Kong. But this didn't [8]**dampen** his [4]**enthusiasm** for flying machines.

父母分別為工程師和教師的汪滔生於 1980 年,在中國古都杭州長大。他在小學時看了一本關於紅色直升機的漫畫後就迷上了飛行器。他夢想能有自己的飛行機器人,可以跟著他到處拍照,他在高中考試成績好時,父母獎勵他一架遙控直升機,可惜立刻被他撞壞,等了好幾個月,新零件才從香港寄來。但他對飛行器的熱情並沒有就此消退。

An engineer with potential
潛力無窮的工程師

Wang 🔤 **had his heart set on** attending a top college in the U.S., but with his average grades he ended up at the Hong Kong University of Science & Technology, where he studied electronic engineering. In his senior year, he got closer to his dream, choosing to build a helicopter 🔤 **flight-control system** for his final project. Although the [5]**hovering** function failed before Wang's presentation, his [6]**professor** recognized his potential and arranged for him to continue the project in graduate school. After successfully completing the 🔤 **UAV** flight controller for his [9]**thesis**, he knew it was time to set up a company.

汪滔一心想就讀美國的頂尖大學,但因成績平庸,最後只能進入香港科技大學,主修電機系。他在大四的期終報告選擇打造直升機飛行控制系統,距離夢想成真更近了。雖然在汪滔發表報告前,盤旋功能故障,但他的教授看出他的潛能,安排他進研究所後繼續這項計畫。在完成無人飛行載具飛行控制器的論文後,他知道是該創業的時候了。

Frank Wang 汪滔

不走一般 CEO 的標準路線,低調的穿衣風格,鴨舌帽是他的必要配件,鮮少露面媒體的汪滔,連劃時代的產品發表會都不一定會有他的身影,不過追求完美產品的執著,被公認是超級工作狂。他在 2013 年推出的「精靈」系列無人機,與蘋果 iPhone 6s、iPad Air 2 還有運動攝影神器 GoPro 等一同入選為「十大科技產品」,是頗具代表性的表現。

Vocabulary

1) **elementary** [͵ɛlə`mɛntəri] (a.) 基本的,初級的。 **elementary school** 即「小學」

2) **helicopter** [`hɛlɪ͵kɑptə] (n.) 直升機

3) **reward** [rɪ`wɔrd] (v./n.)(提供)獎賞,報償

4) **enthusiasm** [ɪn`θuziͺæzəm] (n.) 熱忱,熱衷的事物

5) **hover** [`hʌvə] (v.) 盤旋,停懸

6) **professor** [prə`fɛsə] (n.) 教授

進階字彙

7) **fascination** [͵fæsə`neʃən] (n.) 陶醉,迷戀

8) **dampen** [`dæm͵pən] (v.) 對…潑冷水

9) **thesis** [`θisɪs] (n.) 論文,畢業論文

So in 2006, Wang went across the border to Shenzhen, China's main manufacturing center, and used what was left of his scholarship money to start Dajiang [5]**Innovations** Technology Co., better known as DJI. During its early years, the company just made flight controllers, which were mostly sold to [6]**hobbyists** building DIY **drones**. And as drones with multiple **rotors** became popular, DJI started making more advanced controllers with **autopilot** functions, and also **gimbals** that allowed cameras [1]**attached to** drones to take smooth videos.

於是在 2006 年，汪滔離開了香港到深圳，那是中國的製造重鎮，他用剩下的獎學金創辦大疆創新科技有限公司，更為人所熟知的名稱為 DJI。公司早期只製造飛行控制器，主要賣給自製無人機的業餘愛好者。隨著多軸無人機越來越盛行，DJI 開始製造更先進且有自動駕駛功能的控制器，並附有平衡環架，讓機上的攝影機拍攝更流暢的影片。

Drones for the masses
無人機大眾化

But by 2011, Wang realized that there was more money to be made in drones than flight controllers, so he set to work putting all the pieces together. Two years later, in January 2013, DJI launched **the** [7]**Phantom**, the first ready-to-fly drone with a GPS system, making it stable and easy to fly. Even though it had no camera—most users added a **GoPro**—and a flight time of under 10 minutes, it was a huge hit. And it kept improving with each new version. The current version, the Phantom 4, features a 3-[8]**axis** gimbal system with a built-in camera that can film **4K** video, a five km range and up to 27 minutes of flight time. It can also stream video directly to a screen on the controller so you can see exactly what you're filming.

但到了 2011 年，汪滔發現製造無人機比飛行控制器更賺錢，於是他著手整合。兩年後，在 2013 年 1 月，DJI 推出「精靈」，是第一架配備 GPS 的免組裝無人機，讓飛行更穩定容易。雖然這款無人機沒有攝影機，大部分使用者會加裝 GoPro 攝影機，而且飛行時間不到十分鐘，但仍然大賣。而且每次推出的新版本都不斷在改進。目前的精靈四代配備三軸穩定器，內建攝影機，可拍攝 4K 影片，航程五公里，飛行時間長達 27 分鐘，也可以直接把影片串流傳輸到控制器的螢幕上，這樣就能看到正在拍攝的畫面。

Encouraged by the great success of the Phantom, Wang decided to create a smaller and cheaper model to capture an even larger market share. Released in September 2016, the **Mavic Pro** could be folded to the size of a water bottle, but still had powerful features like a 3-axis gimbal system and 4K video. And the [2]**Spark**,

安裝了 GoPro HERO 4 的無人機

DJI's smallest model yet, features an [9]**infrared** camera for obstacle avoidance and can be controlled using hand gestures. In addition, the company also makes advanced models like 🔴 **the** [3]**Inspire**, aimed at professional filmmakers and photographers, and 🔴 **the Matrice**, designed for applications like firefighting and search and [4]**rescue**.

Mavic Pro

　　因精靈大獲成功而受到鼓舞的汪滔決定打造更小、更便宜的機型，以攻佔更大的市場佔有率。2016 年 9 月推出的 Mavic Pro 無人機可折疊成水瓶般大小，但仍具備強大的三軸穩定器和 4K 影片功能。還有 DJI 最小的機型「曉」，具備紅外線攝影機，可避開障礙物，還可用手勢控制。此外，公司也推出高階機型，例如針對專業電影製作人和攝影師的「悟」，還有為了消防和搜救等用途而設計的「經緯」款。

Vocabulary

1) **attach (to)** [əˋtætʃ] (v.)（使）依附，繫上
2) **spark** [spɑrk] (n.) 火花，火星
3) **inspire** [ɪnˋspaɪr] (v.) 賦予⋯靈感，激勵
4) **rescue** [ˋrɛskju] (n./v.) 營救，援救

進階字彙
5) **innovation** [ˌɪnəˋveʃən] (n.) 新想法，創新
6) **hobbyist** [ˋhɑbɪɪst] (n.) 沉迷於某嗜好者
7) **phantom** [ˋfæntəm] (n.) 幻影，幽靈
8) **axis** [ˋæksɪs] (n.) 軸
9) **infrared** [ˌɪnfrəˋrɛd] (a.) 紅外線的

摺疊與展開後的 Mavic Pro

位於捷克布拉格，官方的大疆販賣店。

China's youngest billionaire
中國最年輕的億萬富翁

DJI's strategy of putting out newer and better drones every year has definitely [1)]**paid off**. The company is now the world's top seller of drones, with a 70% global market share. But this success hasn't come without its share of problems. In 2015, a Phantom drone containing [4)]**radiation** was flown onto the roof of Japanese PM Shinzo Abe's office, and another crash-landed on the White House lawn, causing a big panic. Having people use your products to [2)]**commit** crimes may seem like a [3)]**nightmare** for a CEO, but Wang just calmly responded by changing to [5)]**firmware** so his drones wouldn't be able to fly in ⓛⓖ **restricted areas**. No wonder he's now China's youngest [6)]**billionaire**, and the first to create a successful global brand.

加拿大卡加利 (Calgary) 國際機場旁的圍牆上寫著「無人機禁入區」(No Drone Zone)

DJI 每年推出更新、更好的無人機，這項策略確實獲得回報。該公司目前的無人機是全球最暢銷，全球市佔率達七成。但往成功的道路並非一帆風順。2015 年，一架帶有輻射的精靈無人機飛到日本首相安倍晉三的辦公室屋頂，也有一架墜落在白宮的草坪上，造成大恐慌。對執行長來說，有人用你的產品犯罪似乎是個夢魘，但汪滔藉由修改韌體冷靜應對這個問題，這樣他的無人機就無法飛入禁區。也難怪他現在是中國最年輕的億萬富翁，也是中國成功打造全球品牌的第一人。

Mini Quiz 閱讀測驗

( ) 1. **Where was DJI founded?**
(A) Shenzhen
(B) Hangzhou
(C) Hong Kong
(D) Shanghai

( ) 2. **Which of the following models can be folded?**
(A) The Phantom
(B) the Mavic Pro
(C) the Spark
(D) the Matrice

( ) 3. **Which of the following statements is false?**
(A) DJI is China's first successful global brand.
(B) Wang got interested in helicopters when he was in elementary school.
(C) DJI sells more flight controllers than drones.
(D) The Inspire is aimed at professional filmmakers and photographers.

Vocabulary

1) **pay off** [pe ɔf] (phr.) 得到好結果，取得成功

2) **commit** [kəˋmɪt] (v.) 犯（罪、過失等）

3) **nightmare** [ˋnaɪt͵mɛr] (n.) 夢魘，惡夢

進階字彙

4) **radiation** [͵rediˋeʃən] (n.) 輻射，放射

5) **firmware** [ˋfɝm͵wɛr] (n.) 韌體（將程式指令寫進晶片體中，協助硬體載入執行，作為軟體和硬體之間的橋樑。）

6) **billionaire** [ˋbɪljə͵nɛr] (n.) 億萬富翁

RC helicopter 遙控直升機

是 radio-controlled helicopter 的簡稱，和遙控飛機 (RC airplane) 都是屬遙控模型的一種。飛行原理與真實直升機相同，只是遙控直升機是以無線電波控制，因此操作起來相當不易。

have one's heart set on 渴望

set 在這裡當形容詞，意思是「下決心的」，have one's heart set on sb./sth. 就用來形容一心想要達成的事情，或是傾心於某物。你也可以說 have one's mind set on sb./sth.，或是把 set 改為動詞用法，說成 set one's mind on sb./sth.。

A: Did you hear? Michael didn't get accepted to Stanford.
你有聽說嗎？麥可沒有被史丹佛錄取。

B: That's too bad. He really had his heart set on going there.
真可惜。他一心一意想上那所學校。

flight-control system 飛行控制系統

也就是操縱飛航的系統。早期是機械式控制系統，飛行員藉由操作控制桿，運用繩索、滑輪或是鍊條來掌控飛行。發展至今，已能使用電腦控制的系統來飛行。飛行控制器 (flight controller)，被認為是飛行器的大腦，是控制飛行狀態的核心，讀取傳感器 (sensor) 的數據，做出各樣的飛行動作，達到穩定機體的作用。

UAV 無人機

UAV 是 unmanned aerial vehicle 的縮寫，照字面翻是「沒有人的空中交通工具」，也就是「無人駕駛飛機」，drone 也有一樣的意思，通常利用遙控設備或是自控的程式設備操縱飛行。

無人機的飛行原理

講到無人機就不能不跟大家聊聊 autopilot（自動駕駛裝置，automatic pilot 的縮寫），千萬不要被 automatic 給誤導，autopilot 並非「全」自動化的駕駛裝置，而是「輔助」駕駛控制，不需要一直由「人」做干預的系統。無人機和自動駕駛的結合，就是能使無人機自行判斷環境及飛行路徑的安全，自行飛往目的地，通常會和遙控裝置搭配使用，以應即時的監控。

無人機的用途相當廣泛，從早期的軍事方面到現在生活科技的應用，它能幫助我們完成拍照、探勘或是搜查等功能。無人機主要是依靠馬達 (motor) 和旋翼 (rotor) 產生動力，是無人機推進系統的主要成員，目前常見的大多是多軸 (multi rotor) 飛行器，就是有 2 個旋翼以上的飛行器，不同的旋翼產生互相抵銷的作用力，以便達到平衡的效果。為了擁有更流暢穩定的空拍畫面，有些機型會加裝平衡環架 (gimbal) 來固定攝影機。

飛機（無人機）專有的三軸 (axis)，跟大家所知的立體空間的三軸空間 (XYZ) 相同，像是機翼的左右旋轉、機頭上下抬頭或是左右偏擺，有效實行操縱姿態才能平穩飛行。

DJI 超熱門無人機款

「未來無所不能」的大疆將無人機推向大眾，Phantom（精靈）就是首推的消費級產品，不光是精靈系列，還推出其他系列給不同需求的玩家，例如：Mavic（御）系列是主打輕巧可折疊，但專業功能皆具備的口袋型無人機；Spark（曉）是比水瓶還小的掌上無人機。當然不只這樣，大疆為了給不同程度的玩家都能擁有完美、適合的產品，推出 Inspire（悟）系列，能拍出更專業的影視效果，而 Matrice（經緯）則是為消防搜救的行業專用款。

Matrice 2000 在極端的環境下搜尋和救援

GoPro

GoPro 一款專為運動視角出品的攝影器材，泛舟、跳傘、衝浪、滑板還是越野，無論上山下海都能拍出令人驚豔的戶外運動影片。以 Be a Hero 為宗旨，捕捉極限運動玩家的冒險時刻，被譽為極限運動攝影神器。

restricted area 禁區

未經許可不得隨意進入的特殊區域，禁區有分很多種類，這裡指的是禁止任何航空器進入的空中區域，像是無人機、熱氣球還是飛機等等，英文也可以叫做 no-fly zone。

Alibaba
—Opening Doors for Businesses and Consumers
阿里巴巴：開啟企業和消費者之間的大門

淘寶網（天貓）於 2018 年 11 月 11 日光棍節，開賣 2 分鐘銷售額即超過 100 億人民幣。

A talent for English
英文天分

Like DJI's Frank Wang, Ma Yun was also born in Hangzhou, but 16 years earlier, at the height of ⓁⒼ ¹⁾**communism**. He began studying English as a kid by talking to foreign visitors and taking them on free tours of the city. Because his name was hard to pronounce, one of these tourists gave him the English name "Jack." Despite his success in learning English, Ma was a poor student, and it took him three tries to pass the college entrance exam. After graduating from Hangzhou Teachers College with a degree in English in 1988, he was rejected for many jobs—including one at KFC—before becoming an English ²⁾**lecturer** at a local technical ³⁾**institute**.

馬雲和 DJI 的汪滔一樣，也在杭州出生，不過是早了 16 年，正是共產主義的高峰時期。他小時候靠著和外國遊客說話並免費帶他們遊覽城市學英語。因為他的名字不好發音，有個遊客替他取英文名為「傑克」。雖然馬雲學英語有成，但他的成績不佳，考了三次高考才考上大學。1988 年從杭州師範學院外語系畢業後，他被許多工作回絕了，包括肯德基，然後在當地一所工業學院當英語講師。

Ma meets the Internet
馬雲遇上網路

Ma was good at his job, and popular with students, but pay for teachers was extremely low at that time. So Ma quit his job and in 1994 started his first business, the Haibo [4)]**Translation** Agency. On a business trip to Seattle the following year, he had his first contact with the Internet. When he did a search for beer, he got no results for Chinese beer, and realized that this represented a big business opportunity. When he returned to China he started his second [5)]**venture**, **🄻🄶 China Pages**, to create websites for Chinese companies to promote their products overseas. But within a year, government-run Hangzhou Telecom had taken control of China Pages, and Ma went to work for an Internet advertising agency in Beijing run by the [6)]**Ministry** of Commerce.

馬雲書教得很好，很受學生歡迎，但當時教師的薪水極低，於是馬雲在 1994 年辭職後第一次創業，創辦海博翻譯社。隔年他到西雅圖出差，第一次接觸到網路。他在搜尋啤酒的資料時，沒搜尋到中國啤酒，於是意識到這代表一個大商機。他回到中國時，第二次創業，創辦了「中國黃頁」，為中國的公司架設網站，將他們的產品推廣到海外。但不到一年，國營的杭州電信接管了中國黃頁，然後馬雲到北京一家由對外經貿部經營的網路廣告公司上班。

Jack Ma 馬雲

真性情瀟灑的馬雲，其實是個金庸武俠小說迷，年少時常為朋友伸張正義，不因身材瘦小而膽怯，懂得化缺點為優勢，這樣的性格對於他日後創業也有很大的助益，2018 年時馬雲被評選為中國最佳的 CEO。但就在此刻他丟出一枚震撼彈，決定卸下這個職位，投身於教育及公益上，不過他表示自己永遠都屬於阿里巴巴。

單字 pp.112-116

Vocabulary

1) **communism** [ˈkɑmjʊˌnɪzəm] (n.) 共產主義

2) **lecturer** [ˈlɛktʃərə] (n.) 講師

3) **institute** [ˈɪnstɪˌtut] (n.) 學院，機構

4) **translation** [trænsˈleʃən] (n.) 翻譯

5) **venture** [ˈvɛntʃə] (n.) 新創事業，投資事業

6) **ministry** [ˈmɪnəstri] (n.)（政府的）部

Luckily, 🔵 **the third time was the charm**. Tired of working for the government, Ma quit his job and in February 1999, with a group of 17 friends and former students, founded Alibaba in his Hangzhou apartment. Why Alibaba? Because everybody knows the story of 🔵 **Ali Baba**, the man who magically opens doors. And that's what Ma wanted to do as well—open doors between businesses by creating a 🔵 **B2B** platform to connect Chinese sellers with local and overseas buyers. Impressed by Ma's [1]**drive**, investors lined up to give him money. Goldman Sachs invested $5 million, followed by a $20 million investment from Mahayashi Son, [2]**chairman** of Japan's SoftBank and one of the world's richest men.

　　幸好第三次創業成功了。厭倦為政府工作的馬雲在 1999 年 2 月辭職，跟 17 名朋友和以前的學生一起在杭州的自家公寓創辦阿里巴巴。為什麼取名阿里巴巴？因為大家都知道阿里巴巴的故事，他能施魔法開門。這也是馬雲想做到的，建立讓中國賣家能夠接觸本地和海外買家的企業對企業平臺，打開企業之間的大門。投資家欣賞馬雲的魄力，紛紛提供他資金。高盛銀行投資 500 萬美元，接著日本軟銀集團總裁孫正義投資 2000 萬美元，他是世上最富有的人之一。

A new C2C platform
消費者之間交易新型態

Alibaba charged a membership fee to businesses that advertised on the 🔵 **e-commerce** platform, a strategy that made the company [3]**profitable** by 2002. In 2003, with another investment from SoftBank, Ma created 🔵 **C2C** platform Taobao to compete against 🔵 **eBay**, which was expanding into the Chinese market. Unlike eBay, which was mainly an [4]**auction** site at the time, Taobao allowed individual sellers and small businesses to sell products, and didn't charge transaction fees either. In 2004, Ma made shopping even more convenient by launching

his own online payment platform, Alipay, and a messaging service called 🔵 **Aliwangwang** that allowed buyers and sellers to communicate in real time. This strategy was a huge success—Taobao was the largest e-commerce site in China within two years, and eBay left the Chinese market soon after.

　　阿里巴巴向在電子商務平臺打廣告的企業收取會員費，這項策略讓公司在 2002 年開始獲利。2003 年時，軟銀集團再次注入資金，讓馬雲能夠創辦消費者對消費者平臺淘寶網，與在中國擴張市場的 eBay 競爭。跟拍賣網站 eBay 不一樣的是，淘寶網讓個人賣家和小型企業賣產品，也不收取交易費用。2004 年，馬雲推出自己的線上支付平臺支付寶，讓購物更便利，還有即時通訊服務阿里旺旺，讓買家和賣家能即時溝通。這項策略是一大成功，淘寶網在兩年內成為中國最大的電子商務網站，eBay 隨後也退出中國市場。

Ma's expansion plans were so successful that he continued to add new services and increase

Alibaba's share of the e-commerce market. In 2008, Taobao introduced a new 🔠 **B2C** platform called Taobao Mall (later Tmall), allowing online retailers to sell products to consumers in mainland China, Hong Kong, Macau and Taiwan. And in 2010, Taobao launched eTao, a shopping search engine that consumers can use to compare prices from different sellers, and 🔠 **Juhuasuan**, a group shopping website that [5]**specializes in** 🔠 **flash sales**. Ma next began opening retail stores—where people could pick up online [6]**purchases** and even buy products directly—in 2011, and started the Cainiao delivery company in 2013. Alibaba now had control of every stage of the sales process, completing what Ma called the "🔠 **iron triangle**" of e-commerce, finance and logistics.

由於馬雲的拓展計畫非常成功，因此繼續增添新服務，並增加阿里巴巴在電子商務市場上的市佔率。2008年，淘寶網推出新的企業對消費者平臺，淘寶商城，後來稱為天貓，讓線上零售商向中國大陸、香港、澳門和台灣的消費者販賣產品。2010年，淘寶推出一淘網，那是讓消費者用來比較不同賣家價格的購物搜尋引擎，以及聚划算，那是專門提供限時優惠的團購網站。馬雲接下來在2011年開始開設零售店，讓顧客領取線上購物的貨品，甚至能直接購買商品，並在2013年推出物流公司菜鳥網絡。阿里巴巴現在掌控了銷售過程的每個階段，完成了馬雲所說的「鐵三角」，即電子商務、金融和物流。

Vocabulary

1) **drive** [draɪv] (n.) 魄力，幹勁
2) **chairman** [ˋtʃɛrmən] (n.) 主席，主任，董事長
3) **profitable** [ˋprɑfɪtəbəl] (a.) 有利可圖的，賺錢的
4) **auction** [ˋɔkʃən] (n./v.) 拍賣
5) **specialize (in)** [ˋspɛʃəˌlaɪz] (v.) 專門從事，專攻
6) **purchase** [ˋpɚtʃəs] (n./v.) 購買之物；購買

The world's largest retailer
世界最大的零售商

How successful has this strategy been? When Ma took Alibaba public in 2014, the company raised $25 billion, the highest amount in history. And the company is now worth $352 billion, making it one of the top 10 most valuable in the world. Alibaba is not only the world's largest e-commerce company—it's the largest retailer of *any* type. Since 2015, the company's online sales and profits have been higher than that of all U.S. retailers—including Amazon, Walmart and eBay—combined. Ma has obviously achieved everything he wanted to with the little company he started in his apartment two decades ago. In September 2018, he announced that he would [1]**retire** from Alibaba in the coming year and [2]**devote** his efforts to charity.

這項策略有多成功？馬雲在 2014 年將阿里巴巴上市時，公司募得 250 億美元，是史上最高金額。該公司現值 3520 億美元，名列世界十大最有價值的公司。阿里巴巴不只是世上最大的電子商務公司，也是最大的零售商。自 2015 年，該公司的線上銷售量和營收都比美國所有零售商加起來還要高，包括亞馬遜、沃爾瑪和 eBay。從 20 年前在公寓創辦小公司到現在，馬雲顯然實現了他所想要的一切。2018 年 9 月，他宣布來年要從阿里巴巴退休，並投身慈善事業。

Mini Quiz 閱讀測驗

(   ) 1. **Which of the following is NOT true about Ma?**
(A) He was born in Hangzhou.
(B) He used to be a tour guide.
(C) He once worked at KFC.
(D) He taught English at a local institute.

(   ) 2. **What does B2C stand for?**
(A) Business to business
(B) Business to consumer
(C) Consumer to consumer
(D) Business to computer

(   ) 3. **Which is NOT true about Alibaba?**
(A) Its online sales and profits are higher than that of all U.S. retailers combined.
(B) It is the largest retailer in the world.
(C) It is world's largest e-commerce company.
(D) It went public in 2015.

Vocabulary

1) **retire** [rɪ`taɪr] (v.) 退休
2) **devote** [dɪ`vot] (v.) 將⋯奉獻給，致力於

Language Guide

communism 共產主義

共產主義追求整體的「一致性」，要求每個人都一樣，賺的錢一樣，連想法也一樣。經濟共享是對資本主義 (capitalism) 的反衝，消弭自由經濟，強調財富共享共有；思想方面，不容許異端言行，當有人出現不合政府期待的言論或思想，共產政府會罰以體力勞動，藉此懲治管理這些人。目前除了中國奉行共產主義，還有寮國、越南及古巴。

China Pages 中國黃頁

還記得網路尚未出現的時期，家中總會有一本厚厚的像字典般的黃色電話目錄，裡頭滿是各個公司及商業團體的電話，稱作 Yellow pages（黃頁）。

the third time is the charm 第三次會成功的

charm 這裡解釋為「魔力，咒語」，第三次就會有魔力到底是在説什麼？！the third time is the charm 用來鼓勵不輕易放棄，經過前兩次的努力，第三次一定能成功，會開花結果。

A: **I can't believe you're getting married again after two divorces!**
我不敢相信你離了兩次婚，現在還要再結婚！

B: **You know what they say—the third time is the charm.**
你知道人們總是説：「第三次會成功的。」

Ali Baba 阿里巴巴

出自《阿里巴巴與四十大盜》(*Ali Baba and the Forty Thieves*)，收錄於《一千零一夜》或稱《天方夜譚》的其中一篇阿拉伯民間故事。故事主要是在講述男主角阿里巴巴無意間發現四十名強盜的藏寶洞穴，並得知開啟咒語：「芝麻開門！」(Open, Sesame!)，而他哥哥因為太過貪心又忘記咒語最後被強盜們殺死的故事。

e-commerce 電子商務

電子商務有多種經營模式，「to」的發音跟「two」一樣，因此被簡寫為「2」。

- C2C「consumer to consumer」：消費者之間的交易活動，例如拍賣網出售二手品
- B2B「business to business」：企業間上下游關係的買賣交易
- B2C「business to consumer」：企業架設官方網站，提供商品或服務給消費者選購
- C2B「consumer to business」：不同於上面的「誰銷售商品給誰」，C2B 並不是指消費者銷售給廠商，

商業模式的核心掌握在消費者上，由消費者主導企業提供的服務，例如團購，透過匯聚需求，進而得到更優惠的價格

- B2B2C「business to business to consumer」：電子商務企業整合的網路商業模式，作為供應商和消費者的橋樑，提供更統一完整的服務。第一個 B 是指「供應商」；第二個 B 是「電子商務企業」；C 則是「消費者」，其中像是 momo 摩天商城或是 PC Home 商店街等，就是很標準的 B2B2C 的例子。

eBay

是 1995 年設立的全球線上拍賣網站，前身為 AuctionWeb，每天有數以百萬的商品被刊登及售出，你想的到的，通通都能在這裡找到，只要不是違禁商品，什麼都能賣。2002 年買下 PayPal，成為 eBay 主要付款的途徑之一。

Aliwangwang 阿里旺旺

是淘寶網上買賣家用來聯繫的通訊軟體，可線上洽談購買及訂單的相關事宜，對話內容也都會被記錄保存，對於買賣雙方都多一層保障。這個聊天工具都是以淘寶網為主，又暱稱為「淘寶旺旺」。

Juhuasuan 聚划算

阿里巴巴旗下的團購 (group buying) 網，是全球最大的團購網站。看中規模經濟 (economics of scale) 帶來的效益，買量衝高，才能壓低價格。2016 年，阿里巴巴將聚划算整併進天貓網，希望能為消費者帶來更完善的網路消費服務。

flash sale 限時優惠

flash 原意為「閃光」，也能用來形容迅雷不及掩耳，像閃光一樣掠過。這個字的用法非常廣泛，能延伸出很多不同的詞彙，例如 flash mob。flash mob「快閃族」就是一群人透過網路，在指定時間和地點集合，做完特定動作後再急速消失。又譬如本文提到的 flash sale「限時優惠」，就像「限時下殺」般的短時間促銷優惠，不去搶購就沒了。

iron triangle 鐵三角

用來形容強而有力的三方面，結合而成堅強陣容。以打造電商強國的馬雲來説，鐵三角是指：電子商務、金融服務及物流。多元性的消費需求，網路購物平台的全面性，不論想買什麼「淘寶網」通通找得到；提供第三方支付「支付寶」，保障交易的金流服務，不管是買家還是賣家都安心；再來，收發貨的效率也要顧及，投資快遞業者「菜鳥網絡」，整合訂單及掌握運送狀態，降低貨運延遲率及損壞的風險，提升服務品質。

Netflix
—Entertaining the World

網飛：提供世界觀賞娛樂的新方式

A [8]privileged [9]upbringing
享有特權的教育環境

Wilmot Reed Hastings, Jr. was born in Boston, Massachusetts in 1960. His father, Wilmot Reed Hastings, Sr., was a [1]**prominent** lawyer who served in the Nixon [2]**administration**. After attending [3]**elite** private schools around Boston, the young Reed entered Bowdoin, a small **16 liberal arts** college in Maine, where he majored in math. He was a hardworking and talented student, twice receiving math department awards for his [4]**academic** achievements.

威摩里德海斯汀二世一九六〇年出生於麻州波士頓。他的父親威摩里德海斯汀一世是任職於尼克森政府的知名律師。念完波士頓附近的菁英私立學校，年輕的里德進入緬因州小規模的鮑登文理學院就讀，主修數學。他是一位既用功又有天分的學生，兩度因學業成績優秀獲頒數學系書卷獎。

A desire to serve others
為民服務的欲望

Upon graduation, Reed joined the [5]**Marines** and [6]**underwent** officer training. But when he discovered that asking questions wasn't encouraged, he decided that the military life wasn't for him. Reed's desire to serve was still strong, however, so he signed up for the **16 Peace Corps**. From 1983 to 1985, he taught high school math in [7]**rural** Swaziland, where he had no electricity, cooked his meals over a wood fire, and slept on a [9]**cot** in a [10]**thatched** hut.

里德一畢業後便進入美國海軍陸戰隊服役，接受軍官訓練。然而他卻發現軍方不鼓勵發問，於是他便確定軍事生活不適合他。不過里德為民服務的欲望還是很強烈，因此他報名加入美國和平工作團。從一九八三至一九八五年，他在史瓦濟蘭農村教高中數學，那裡沒有電，只能用木柴生火煮飯，還得睡在茅頂屋的帆布床上。

Wilmot Reed Hastings, Jr.
威摩里德海斯汀二世

不一樣的富二代，出身名門的海斯汀沒有按照原本人生勝利組的劇本演出，不當老師反倒跨足成為影視大亨！新創的線上 DVD 租賃服務打擊了傳統錄影帶的老大哥百視達 (Blockbuster)，為了擺脫版權限制，影視製作他自己來，《富比士》雜誌 (Forbes) 曾評價「海斯汀改變了全世界觀賞娛樂節目的方式」。

@re:publica/flickr.com

Vocabulary

1) **prominent** [ˋprɑmənənt] (a.) 著名的，重要的
2) **administration** [ədˌmɪnəˋstreʃən] (n.)（某位總統的）政府、任期
3) **elite** [ɪˋlit] (a./n.) 菁英的，頂尖的；菁英
4) **academic** [ˌækəˋdɛmɪk] (a.) 學術的
5) **Marines** [məˋrinz] (n.)（美國）海軍陸戰隊，全名為 **U.S. Marine Corps**
6) **undergo** [ˌʌndəˋgo] (v.) 接受（訓練、治療等），經歷
7) **rural** [ˋrʊrəl] (a.) 鄉下的，農村的

進階字彙

8) **privileged** [ˋprɪvəlɪdʒd] (a.) 享有特權的，上流社會的
9) **upbringing** [ˋʌpˌbrɪŋɪŋ] (n.) 養育，教養，培養
10) **cot** [kɑt] (n.) 帆布床，行軍床
11) **thatched** [θætʃt] (a.)（屋頂）茅草蓋的

119

NETFLIX

A rising tech star
科技新星

Back in the U.S., Reed continued his education at Stanford, earning a master's degree in computer science in 1988. It wasn't long before he became one of  Silicon Valley's rising tech stars. At the age of 37, he sold his startup, Pure Software, for $700 million. As the story goes, Reed was searching for his next big idea when he received a $40 late fee for an [1]overdue movie—a VHS cassette of *Apollo 13*. This everyday [2]occurrence led to Reed's eureka moment, inspiring the idea that would forever change the way people enjoy watching movies at home.

回到美國後，里德進入史丹佛大學深造，於一九八八年拿到電腦科學碩士學位。不久後，他成為矽谷的科技新星。三十七歲時，他以七億美元轉售他創建的「純粹軟體」公司。後來，里德在尋找下一個不得了的構想時，他因為租電影逾期未歸還（《阿波羅十三》的 VHS 影帶）而被追討四十美元的逾時費。這種稀鬆平常的事讓里德靈機一動，啟發了一個構想，就此改變了人們在家觀賞電影的方式。

A better business model
更好的商業模式

How could the video [3]rental store charge a late fee that was three times what the cassette cost in the first place? It just didn't seem fair. Later, on his way to the gym, Reed realized that they had a much better business model. Gym members pay a [7]**flat** fee each month and can [4]**work out** as much—or as little—as they like. So why not apply a similar model to movie rentals? What's more, VHS cassettes were being replaced by DVDs in the late 90s, which would make it [5]feasible to mail movies to customers, saving them a trip to the video store. Just like that, the idea for Netflix was born.

錄影帶店怎麼可以收取影帶原價三倍的逾時費？這一點也不公平。後來，在前往健身房的途中，里德想到他們有更好的經營模式。健身房會員可以每個月付均一費用，然後想健身多少次就去多少次。那麼影片出租為什麼不能用類似的模式呢？此外，至九〇年代晚期，VHS 影帶已逐漸被 DVD 所取代，這讓把影片郵寄給顧客這件事變得可行，顧客可以不必親自到錄影帶店。Netflix 的概念於焉誕生。

A simple idea
簡單的概念

With an investment of $2.5 million, Reed and his partners launched Netflix in 1998. The idea was simple: members could rent as many DVDs as they wanted for a flat monthly rate, and there were no late fees. At first, Netflix had only 30 employees and 925 titles for rent. But the company grew rapidly, going public in 2002 and reaching $272 million in [6]**revenues** in 2003. By 2005, Netflix was mailing a million DVDs per day, and in 2007 the company delivered its billionth disc.

Netflix 位於加州的總公司

里德投資兩百五十萬美金,與合夥人在一九九八年創立 Netflix。概念很簡單:會員只要每月繳定額的費用,想租多少影片就可租多少影片,且不必支付逾時費。當時 Netflix 只有三十名員工和九百二十五部片子。但公司成長迅速,在二○○二年公開上市後,二○○三年的營收達到兩億七千兩百萬美元。到了二○○五年,Netflix 每天要寄送一百萬片 DVD,二○○七年,該公司寄出第十億片光碟。

Vocabulary

1) **overdue** [ˌovɚˋdu] (a.) 逾期的,過期的
2) **occurrence** [əˋkɝəns] (n.) 事情,事件,發生
3) **rental** [ˋrɛntəl] (n./a.) 租賃(的)
4) **work out** (phr.) 健身,鍛鍊身體
5) **feasible** [ˋfizəbəl] (a.) 可行的,行得通的
6) **revenue** [ˋrɛvənu] (n.) 營收,收入

進階字彙
7) **flat** [flæt] (a.)(費用、價格等)均一的,一律的

Netflix 寄送的信封,包含《卡特教頭》的 DVD

In 2008, Netflix began changing home movie and TV viewing as we know it, introducing a new Internet video streaming service allowing subscribers to watch movies and TV shows [1]**on demand**. And in 2011 Netflix, like HBO, began producing its own content, branded as ⑯ **Netflix Originals**—including series, specials, films and [2]**documentaries**. This has made Netflix so popular that during [3]**prime time** hours, the service [4]**accounts for** a third of all North American Internet traffic. And Nexflix isn't just popular in North America. It's now available in over 190 countries around the world, including Taiwan. That's ⑰ **not too shabby** for an idea that was inspired by a video rental late fee.

Netflix 開始自製影片，就像 HBO 一樣，以 Netflix 原創作為品牌名，製作影集、特別節目、電影和紀錄片。這使 Netflix 在黃金時段極受歡迎，該時段的 Netflix 使用流量占了北美網路總流量的三分之一。而且 Netflix 不是只在北美受歡迎，現在在世界 190 多國皆可收看，包括台灣。就一個由影帶出租逾時費啟發的構想而言，這數字還不賴。

二○○八年起，正如我們知道的，Netflix 改變了家家戶戶觀賞電影與電視的習慣，推出新的網路影片串流服務，讓會員依照需求看電影及電視影集。二○一一年，

Mini Quiz 閱讀測驗

( ) 1. **What inspired Reed's eureka moment?**

(A) *Apollo 13*
(B) A VHS cassette
(C) A fine
(D) A movie

( ) 2. **When can Netflix subscribers enjoy movies?**

(A) When they are scheduled
(B) Whenever they want
(C) When the DVDs are mailed
(D) Only during prime time

( ) 3. **Which of the following about Netflix is true?**

(A) It mailed VHS cassettes to its customers.
(B) It was launched in 1998.
(C) Customers have to pay late fees.
(D) It is Reed's first company.

Vocabulary

1) **on demand** [an dɪˋmænd] (phr.) 隨選的

2) **documentary** [ˌdɑkjəˋmɛtəri] (n.) 紀錄片

3) **prime time** (phr.)（電視、廣播）黃金時段

4) **account for** (phr.) 佔據

Language Guide

liberal arts 通識教育

這個詞彙最早可追溯到古希臘時期柏拉圖 (Plato) 提出的「七藝」(seven liberal arts)，即文法 (grammar)、修辭 (rhetoric)、辯證 (dialectic)、算術 (arithmetic)、

愛荷華大學 (University of IA) 通識教育側廳的外觀

幾何 (geometry)、天文 (astronomy) 及音樂 (music) 這七種學科，當時被認為是應具備的基礎知識。現今我們所說的通識課程則是指大專院校所提供的基礎教育，像是語言、哲學、文學、或科學等一般知識，藉以提升整體的智性發展，並訓練判斷和思考能力。本文中提到的 liberal arts college 是以人文科目為主的文理學院，通常是私立的小型學院，不以研究為目的，採小班授課為主，大部分只有大學部。

Peace Corps 和平工作團

一九六〇年由正在競選總統的甘迺迪 (John F. Kennedy) 發起的志工團，主要宗旨在於促進世界的和平及友誼。和平工作團的志工 (volunteer) 至今活躍在一百三十九個國家，從事的內容包括將受訓的志願人士送到發展中國家 (developing country) 提供教育、醫療、農業等、促進各國人對美國人民的瞭解，同時也促進美國對別國人士的瞭解。參加和平工作團的志工必須融入當地生活，和當地人做同樣的工作，吃一樣的食物，說相同的語言，努力為世界和平作出貢獻。

Silicon Valley 矽谷

翻遍全美國地圖，就是找不著矽谷，究竟矽谷在哪裡？原來矽谷並不是一座城市，坐落在北加州舊金山灣區的南部一帶，由聖荷西 (San Jose)、桑尼維爾 (Sunnyvale)、門洛

帕克 (Menlo Park)、聖塔克拉拉 (Santa Clara) 等多座城市組成。早期當地大多為製造電腦、電路板的半導體 (semiconductor) 產業，屬於高濃度矽的工業製造，因此得名「矽」。目前是高科技資訊業的重鎮，許多知名的科技公司像是蘋果、谷歌、英特爾還有 IBM 等的總部都設立於此，是科技行業人都嚮往的聖地。

VHS 家用錄影帶

全稱為 Video Home System，是 JVC 公司所推出的一種家用錄影帶規格，在一九八〇年代到一九九〇年間蔚為流行，當時幾乎獨

佔居家觀看影片的市場，和另一種錄影帶規格 Betamax 相互競爭，不過最後由 VHS 勝出，支配了當時的錄影帶市場，直到 DVD 出現後才式微。

Eureka 我發現了

希臘數學家阿基米德在泡澡時，浴缸會溢出多餘的水，讓他靈機一動，解開他棘手的問題，找到可以精準計算不規則物體的體積，讓他高興的從浴缸跳出來，喊著：「Eureka! Eureka!」——也就是古希臘語的「我發現了！」。

Netflix Originals 網飛原創

Netflix 推出一波波獨家製作，追劇趕不及上架速度的原創影集、電影及節目，只有 Netflix 的訂閱戶才看得到，無法透過電視或其他頻道觀看。其中

人氣最高的自製影集就是《紙牌屋》(House of Cards)，二〇一三年第一季首推出就替 Netflix 增加了三百萬的新訂戶。不只有影集，《埃及廣場》(The Square) 甚至是 Netflix 原創製作中首度獲奧斯卡提名的電影作品。近年來 Netflix 作品不斷，《怪奇物語》(Strange Things)、《王冠》(The Crown) 以及電影《蒙上你的眼》(Bird Box) 等，都是不容錯過的佳作！

not too shabby 還不賴

形容詞 shabby [ˈʃæbi] 意思是「破舊的、寒酸的」，因次直譯 not too shabby 就是「不會很爛」，言下之意當然就是「還不賴」囉！

A: Our team won the game seven to four.
我們的隊伍以七比四的比數贏了比賽。

B: That's not too shabby, considering our best player was out with an injury.
我們的最佳選手因傷無法上場還能有如此的表現，這樣的成績算不錯了。

Airbnb
—Feel at Home While Traveling

Airbnb 民宿網站：讓旅客賓至如歸

Brian Chesky was born in 1981 and grew up in a small town in New York State. At age eight, he became interested in [1]**landscape** [2]**architecture** after seeing plans [3]**drafted** by his friend's father. Just for fun, he began drawing his own plans for gardens, houses and even cities. Chesky also developed an interest in product design. Every year, he asked to receive 🅻🅶 **a poorly-designed toy** for Christmas. Rather than play with the toy, he would focus on improving its design.

布萊恩切斯基生於 1981 年，在紐約州一座小鎮長大。八歲時看到朋友的父親畫的平面圖草稿後，對景觀設計產生興趣。他開始為了好玩而繪製自己的花園、房子，甚至城市的平面圖。切斯基也對產品設計產生興趣。他每年會要求收到設計不佳的玩具當耶誕禮物，他的重點不是玩玩具，而是改良設計。

An early career in industrial design
早期的工業設計職涯

After high school, Chesky attended the Rhode Island School of Design, where he studied industrial design, learning to create products 🅻🅶 **from scratch.** 🅻🅶 **On** earning his [4]**bachelor**'s degree in 2004, he moved to Los Angeles and pursued a career as an industrial designer. A few years later, he went to San Francisco to live with his friend and former classmate, Joe Gebbia. Living in one of the most [6]**affluent** cities in the U.S., Chesky and Gebbia struggled to pay their rent. They soon came up with a money-making [5]**scheme** that would change their lives forever.

高中畢業後，切斯基就讀羅德島設計學院，修讀工業設計，學習從無到有創作產品。他在 2004 年取得學士學位後，搬到洛杉磯當工業設計師。幾年後，他到舊金山，跟朋友和老同學喬傑比亞同住。住在全美最富裕的城市之一的切斯基和傑比亞要為付房租而煩惱。他們很快想到一個賺錢的方法，繼而永遠改變了他們的人生。

Brian Chesky 布萊恩切斯基

切斯基曾經靠著刷爆信用卡，只為了要讓 Airbnb 生存下來，他曾比喻自己是一隻打不死的小強，任何艱難環境都經歷過了，切斯基用他的故事告訴大家，誰說只有工程師才能創業？！Airbnb 目前榮登為獨角獸企業的成員之一（編註：獨角獸企業（unicorn）、是指市值達美元十億以上，尚未上市的科技新創公司）。

Vocabulary

1) **landscape** [ˋlænd͵skep] (n.) 風景，景色
2) **architecture** [ˋɑrkɪ͵tɛktʃə] (n.) 建築，建築學
3) **draft** [dræft] (v./n.) 起草，設計；草稿，草圖
4) **bachelor** [ˋbætʃələ] (n.) 學士，單身漢
5) **scheme** [skim] (n.) 計畫，計謀

進階字彙
6) **affluent** [ˋæfluənt] (a.) 富裕的

125

Money in mattresses
靠床墊賺錢

In 2007, the Industrial Designers Society of America held a [1)]**conference** in San Francisco, and every hotel room in the city was **LG** **booked solid**. Chesky and Gebbia realized they could make money by sharing their apartment with conference [2)]**attendees**. So they bought three air [3)]**mattresses** and created a website to advertise their service. When this scheme was successful, Chesky and Gebbia decided to turn the idea into a business. The two friends, along with their roommate, Harvard graduate Nathan Blecharczyk, created an Internet platform to help other people find paying guests to stay in their homes. Airbnb was born!

2007 年，美國工業設計師協會在舊金山舉辦會議，城市裡的旅館房間都訂滿了。切斯基和傑比亞發現到他們可以把公寓分租給參加會議的人，藉此賺錢。於是他們買了三張充氣床墊，架設網站宣傳他們的服務。這個辦法成功後，切斯基和傑比亞決定把這想法發展成事業。這對朋友跟他們的室友，哈佛畢業生納森布萊克奇一起架設一個網路平臺，幫助其他人尋找房客，將自家分租出去，Airbnb 民宿網站就此誕生！

Saved by breakfast cereal
靠早餐穀片解救

Airbnb was not, however, an immediate success. By early 2008, Chesky and his team were [4)]**desperate** to [14)]**pay down** the debt they had [15)]**racked up** founding the company. To raise money, they created and sold special edition breakfast cereal boxes—Obama O's and Cap'n McCains—featuring pictures of the two American [5)]**presidential** candidates, Barack Obama and John McCain. They earned about $30,000 selling the cereal, but more importantly, their [6)]**determination** and [7)]**creativity** impressed

investors. Airbnb soon received funding to expand and improve its website, attracting new users as well as new investors. The company grew steadily for the next few years, and in 2014 launched a more user-friendly website and mobile app.

但 Airbnb 沒有立刻成功。到了 2008 年初，切斯基和他的團隊急需錢來償還創辦公司時所累積的債務。為了湊錢，他們設計並販賣特製版的早餐穀片盒——歐巴馬圈圈和馬侃船長——主打兩位美國總統候選人的照片，巴拉克歐巴馬和約翰馬侃。他們靠著賣穀片賺了三萬美元，但更重要的是，他們的決心和創意吸引了投資者的注意。Airbnb 隨後獲得資金，得以擴展和改善網站，繼而吸引了新用戶和新投資者。接下來幾年公司穩定成長，並在 2014 年推出更好用的網站和行動 app。

Homes away from home
四海為家

The founders of Airbnb made it their goal to help curious travelers connect with local people willing to share their homes. Property owners, called "hosts" on the Airbnb site, earn money by renting extra bedrooms or empty apartments to travelers. In return, travelers who stay in these properties **LG** **get a taste of** local living. Among the millions of properties on Airbnb,

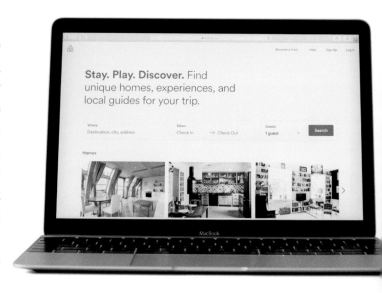

there are houses, apartments, castles, boats and even private islands. For hosts, the [8]**incentive** to use Airbnb is not just extra income, but also the chance to meet new people. The company earns a [9]**commission** every time a property is rented.

民宿網站創辦人的目標是協助好奇的遊客與有意分租自家的當地人聯繫。在 Airbnb 網站上稱為「房東」的屋主靠著分租多餘的房間或空置的公寓給遊客來賺錢,入住民宿的遊客則可藉此體驗當地生活。Airbnb 網站上有數百萬筆房地產,有房子、公寓、城堡、船,甚至私人島嶼。對房東來說,使用 Airbnb 網站不只是為了賺外快,也有機會認識新朋友。公司則從出租的民宿抽取佣金。

A global [10]community
全球社群

Since its founding, Airbnb has expanded around the globe, and now offers properties in nearly 200 countries. By 2012, 10 million nights' [11]**accommodation** had been booked on Airbnb. Although it is based in the United States, 75% of the company's business currently comes from other countries. One of Airbnb's fastest-growing market [12]**segments** is Africa, where Airbnb now has more than 130,000 [16]**listings**. This is [13]**remarkable** growth for a company that nearly went out of business just a decade ago.

Airbnb 網站自創辦以來已擴大到全球,在近兩百個國家提供民宿。到了 2012 年,民宿網站已累積一千萬晚的住宿預訂。雖然公司設在美國,但有 75% 的業務是來自其他國家。其中發展最快的市場是非洲,那裡的民宿登記現已超過 13 萬筆。對十年前幾乎要倒閉的公司來說,這樣的成長相當驚人。

印有歐巴馬歐圈圈和馬侃船長的早餐穀片盒

More than a place to stay
不只是住宿

From the beginning, Airbnb has hoped to connect travelers and local people. Recently, it created a new way to do this by offering "experiences," which are tours, classes and other events led by local guides. 🔵 **Through Airbnb experiences, travelers can** [1]**surf in California, tour a coffee farm in Kenya, learn to make traditional Italian** [2]**pasta in Rome, and take part in many other interesting local activities.** Recognizing that its global reach gives it the potential to effect positive change in the world, the company also offers "social [3]**impact** experiences," helping travelers find [4]**volunteer** activities wherever they go.

Airbnb 網站一開始是希望能協助遊客和當地房東聯繫，近來也以新的方式提供「體驗」，就是由當地導遊帶領的遊覽、課程等活動。透過 Airbnb 體驗，遊客可以在加州衝浪、在肯亞遊覽咖啡農場、在羅馬學習製作傳統義大利麵，參與許多其他有趣的當地活動。在瞭解到 Airbnb 遍布全球可為世界帶來正面改變後，該公司也提供「社會影響體驗」，協助遊客無論到何處都能尋找義工活動。

More than 600,000 hosts currently offer properties on Airbnb. The company itself has over 3,000 employees. It reported almost US$3 billion in 🔵 **revenue** in 2017 and has been using its 🔵 **war chest** to acquire smaller companies in the travel industry. For example, in 2012 it bought a website that collects information on city neighborhoods. Airbnb then used this information to create "Neighborhoods," which are detailed neighborhood travel guides offered on its site. Airbnb has also hinted that the company may one day start its own airline. It seems that for Airbnb, the sky's the limit!

現在 Airbnb 網站有超過 60 萬名房東提供民宿，該公司本身有超過三千名員工，2017 年公司的營收近 30 億美元，並利用其雄厚財力持續收購旅遊業的較小公司。例如 2012 年收購了一個收集城市鄰里資訊的網站。Airbnb 於是利用這些資訊在網站上建立「社區」，提供詳細的社區旅遊指南。Airbnb 也暗示公司可能有一天會創辦航空公司。看來 Airbnb 的發展是無可限量的！

Mini Quiz 閱讀測驗

( ) 1. **What did Chesky and his team do to pay down their debt?**
(A) They helped Obama to run for president.
(B) They sold special cereal.
(C) They worked as industrial designers.
(D) They launched a mobile app.

( ) 2. **Which of the following are NOT mentioned as Airbnb listings?**

(A) Houses
(B) Castles
(C) Airplanes
(D) Boats

( ) 3. **Which is NOT true about Airbnb?**
(A) They have over 100,000 listings in Africa.
(B) Most of the company's business currently comes from the U.S.
(C) It offers properties in nearly 200 countries.
(D) It offers social impact experiences.

Vocabulary

1) **surf** [sɝf] (v.) 衝浪

2) **pasta** [ˋpɑstə] (n.) 義大利麵食

3) **impact** [ˋɪmpækt] (n./v.) 影響，衝擊

4) **volunteer** [ˌvɑlənˋtɪr] (n./v.) 義工；自願服務，擔任義工

複合形容詞

「複合形容詞」就是由兩個字，中間加上連字號而成的形容詞。用法和一般形容詞相同，作用卻等同於用「一句話來形容」，能讓文章句子更到位。複合形容詞的組合有很多種，可以是「名詞＋動詞」、「形容詞＋動詞」或是「副詞＋動詞」…等等。

要加強形容詞，我們只能找副詞來幫幫忙，不過形容詞中該選主動進行的 Ving 還是被動的 p.p. 型態，都須視形容詞後方的名詞來決定，就拿本文的句子來舉例，a poorly-designed toy（設計不良的玩具），玩具是被人設計，所以這裡的 design 改為 p.p. 的形式。

from scratch 從頭做起

scratch 當名詞有「起跑線」的意思，from scratch 就表示「從頭開始」，用來描述一樣東西從最基本的食材、原料做起。經常搭配的動詞有 bake/do / make / start sth. from scratch。

A: This cake is delicious! What's your secret?
這個蛋糕好好吃！你的祕訣是什麼？

B: I baked it from scratch.
我用食材從頭烤起。

On+Ving/N 放句首

這個用法和 As soon as 一樣，表「一…就…」的意思。句型為「As soon as 主詞 + 動詞, 主詞 + 動詞」，為修飾主要子句所用。

例 **On receiving his Chinese New Year bonus, Michael quit his job.**
麥克一收到他的年終獎金，就離職了。

booked solid 客滿

book 做動詞用時，意思為「預訂，預約」，而這裡的 solid 解釋為「沒有空隙」，為形容詞的用法，booked solid 常用來描述餐廳、旅館店、電影院或車位被訂滿的狀態，意思就是 completely full。

get a taste of 體驗

我們都曉得 taste 解釋為「品嚐」，不過 get a taste of 就不一樣了，變成「體驗」的意思。

A: Why is it dangerous to visit Hawaii?
去夏威夷玩為什麼很危險？

B: Once you get a taste of island life, you'll never want to leave!
一旦體驗過海島生活，可能就不會想離開了！

Airbnb 品牌故事

切斯基期許 Airbnb 能打造一個四海有家的世界，為了體現人與人之間的歸屬感，設計了一個名為 bélo 的標誌，也就是切斯基的理念「belong anywhere」，這個標誌是由四個圖像文字所組成，分別為：雙手高舉說嗨的人 (people)、標示地點符號 (places)、愛 (love) 以及 Airbnb 的 A。

平行結構

寫作的平行結構，英文專業術語為 parallelism，也就是句子中相對位置的字詞是以同樣的文法、語法來呈現。文中用來描述可藉由 Airbnb 來體驗的活動種類，皆是以 **travelers can surf** in California；**travelers can tour** a coffee farm in Kenya…… 這樣的句子來形容，語法的結構都相同，只不過為了不讓文章顯得冗長，將後方的 travelers can 都省略。

revenue

revenue 指的是公司的總收益，有「營業額」的意思，也可以用 turnover 來表示。這類型的商業會計用語，雖然稍微艱澀，但在一般文章裡也很常出現，現在我們來看看還有那些常見的財務術語吧！break even 意思為「收支平衡」，就是公司沒賺錢也沒虧損 (loss)；profit 是指「利潤」，net profit 就將所有成本和開支 (expense) 都全部扣除的「淨利」。

war chest 戰爭基金

本意是為了漫長的征戰所做的財力儲備，現在常用在公司企業方面，因應無法預期的營運問題或是投資機會，所預留募集的資金，也能用來表示為特定活動準備的活動基金。

科技焦點品牌

Tesla, Inc.
Leader in Electric Cars
特斯拉：電動車的領導者

Early dreams of escape
早期夢想為逃離

Elon Musk was born in 1971 in Pretoria, South Africa to Errol Musk, an engineer, and Maye, a Canadian model. Growing up, he loved reading—mostly science fiction—and computer programming, two activities that made him the target of [1]**bullies**. In one [2]**incident**, Musk had to be [3]**hospitalized** after a group of boys attacked him at school. It is perhaps no wonder he dreamed of escaping to a different place. Because Musk's mother is Canadian, he was able to move to Canada to attend university. He later [4]**transferred to** the University of Pennsylvania, where he completed two bachelor's degrees, one in [5]**economics** and another in [6]**physics**. For Musk, the U.S. turned out to be a place where the success he [9]**envisioned** was indeed possible.

伊隆馬斯克 1971 年生於南非普利托利亞，父親埃羅爾馬斯克是工程師，母親梅爾是加拿大模特兒。成長過程中他喜歡閱讀——大部分是科幻小說——和寫電腦程式，這兩樣消遣活動都讓他成為霸凌的目標。在一次事故中，馬斯克在學校被一群男孩打傷後住院。也難怪他夢想逃到另一個地方。由於馬斯克的母親是加拿大人，他得以前往加拿大就讀大學。他後來轉學到賓州大學，完成雙學士學位，分別是經濟學和物理學。對馬斯克而言，美國確實能實現他所嚮往的功成名就。

　　1995 年，馬斯克和弟弟創辦網路軟體公司 Zip2，為報社提供線上城市指南。Zip2 於 1999 年被康柏電腦收購時，馬斯克因賣出自己的股份而賺得 2200 萬美元。馬斯克用這筆收益創辦了網路支付公司 X.com，並於 2001 年改名為 PayPal。隔年將 PayPal 賣給 eBay 後，馬斯克創辦了 SpaceX 公司，致力於改進火箭技術，希望能讓一般人負擔得起太空旅行，最終能將拓荒者送上火星。由於馬斯克認為在火星上旅行要靠電動車，而且他對環保科技也有濃厚的興趣，因此他接下來將目標瞄準電動汽車製造商特斯拉，也是完全合理的。

A young entrepreneur
年輕企業家

　　In 1995, Musk and his brother started Zip2, a web software company that provided online city guides to newspapers. When Zip2 was acquired by Compaq in 1999, Musk earned $22 million for his share of the company. Musk used his profits to start Internet payment company X.com, which became 🔟 **PayPal** in 2001. After selling PayPal to eBay the following year, Musk founded 🔟 **SpaceX**, a company devoted to improving rocket technology in the hopes of making space travel [7]**affordable** for average people and eventually sending [8]**settlers** to Mars. Because Musk believes that travel on Mars will depend on electric vehicles, and has a strong interest in environmentally-friendly technology, it makes perfect sense that he would next set his sights on electric car manufacturer Tesla.

Elon Musk 伊隆馬斯克

引領科技先鋒，從電動車到太空計畫，據說電影《鋼鐵人》(*Iron Man*) 中東尼史塔克的形象是根據馬斯克的形象所創造出來的。有趣的是，他本人也有客串電影的演出喔，甚至在 SpaceX 的總部取景。這個真實版「鋼鐵人」，在員工眼中也宛如鋼鐵人，好像不用睡覺似的，工作常超時，累了就直接在公司打地鋪。

Vocabulary

1) **bully** [ˈbʊlɪ] (n.) 惡霸

2) **incident** [ˈɪnsədənt] (n.) 事件，事變，衝突

3) **hospitalize** [ˈhɑspɪtə͵laɪz] (v.) 讓人住院接受治療

4) **transfer (to)** [ˈtrænsfɚ] (v.) 轉學，調動，調任

5) **economics** [͵ɛkəˈnɑmɪks] (n.) 經濟學

6) **physics** [ˈfɪzɪks] (n.) 物理學，**physicist** [ˈfɪzəsɪst] (n.) 物理學家

7) **affordable** [əˈfɔrdəbəl] (a.) 負擔得起的

8) **settler** [ˈsɛtələ] (n.) 拓荒者，移民，殖民者

進階字彙

9) **envision** [ɪnˈvɪʒən] (v.) 想像，展望

Early investment in Tesla
早期對特斯拉的投資

Though Elon Musk is now the 🄶 **public face** of Tesla, he didn't join the company until around nine months after its [1]**establishment**. Originally known as Tesla Motors, Inc., the company was founded by engineers 🄶 **Martin Eberhard and Marc Tarpenning** in July 2003. The two men had previously [10]**collaborated** on an early version of an e-book reader called Rocket eBook. Sales were [2]**modest**, but the pair's work on improving battery technology for the e-book reader was [3]**crucial** to their move into electric cars. After starting Tesla, Eberhard and Tarpenning began drawing up plans for an electric sportscar. In 2004, when they began seeking venture capital, Musk invested millions of dollars, winning him the position of chairman of the board. This gave him a controlling interest that allowed him to influence the direction of the company, and even gave him the right to be considered a co-founder.

雖然伊隆馬斯克現在是特斯拉的公共形象代表人，但他是在該公司創辦約九個月後才加入。該公司最初名為特斯拉汽車公司，由工程師馬丁艾伯哈德和馬克塔彭寧於 2003 年 7 月創辦。兩人曾合作研發名為火箭電子書閱讀器的早期版本。雖然銷售情況普通，但兩人改進電子書閱讀器電池技術的成果，對他們日後進軍電動汽車至關重要。創辦特斯拉後，艾伯哈德和塔彭寧開始製定電動跑車的計畫。2004 年，他們開始尋求創業資金，馬斯克投資了數百萬美元，贏得董事長的職位，也讓他擁有控制股權，可左右公司的發展方向，甚至讓他有權成為共同創辦人。

Release of the Roadster
發表 Roadster 跑車

With financing in place, the company began designing the Tesla [11]**Roadster** [12]**in earnest**. Released in 2008, the Roadster was a sportscar with a [13]**hefty** price tag. This model was aimed at 🄶 **early adopters** eager to end their [4]**reliance** on gasoline vehicles. The [14]**premium** price paid by those wanting to own the first model helped fund the creation of [5]**subsequent** mainstream Tesla models. True to the company's name, the Roadster used a motor directly based on one designed by physicist 🄶 **Nikola Tesla** in 1882. It was the first highway legal production automobile to use [15]**lithium-ion battery** cells, and also the first to travel over 200 miles on a single charge. But more importantly, it was fast. Not many electric vehicles could [6]**accelerate** from 0 to 60 mph in 3.7 seconds!

隨著資金到位，公司開始慎重設計特斯拉全電動敞篷跑車 Roadster。於 2008 年推出的 Roadster 價格非常昂貴。這款車型是針對渴望停止依賴汽油車的嘗鮮者。想擁有第一款車型的顧客所支付的昂貴價格，成為該公司打造後續特斯拉主流車型的資金來源。正如公司的名稱，Roadster 使用的引擎，是根據物理學家尼古拉特斯拉 1882 年發明的馬達所設計。這是第一輛使用鋰離子電池的合法上路量產汽車，也是第一輛續航里程超過 200 英里的電動車。但更重要的是，車子的速度很快，能在 3.7 秒內從時速 0 加速到 60 英里的電動車並不多！

物理學家尼古拉特斯拉

A move to the mainstream
邁向主流

The success of the Roadster led to investment by prominent tech [16]**entrepreneurs** like Google founders Larry Page and Sergei Brin. Yet despite receiving over US$100 million in funding by 2007, the company was not profitable. After Musk became CEO in 2008, he [7]**laid off** a quarter of Tesla's workers to avoid going bankrupt. When Tesla began releasing its cars to the mass market in 2012, its [17]**bottom line** finally began to improve. The mid-size **Model S** was a major hit with both consumers and automobile experts. Tesla's first [18]**SUV**, the **Model X**, released in 2015, was similarly well received. And the introduction of the **Model 3** [8]**luxury sedan** in 2016 resulted in more orders than expected, forcing Tesla to speed up [9]**production** to meet demand. By 2018, the Model 3 was the top-selling [19]**plug-in** electric car in the U.S.

Roadster 的成功吸引了知名科技企業家的投資，例如 Google 創辦人賴利佩吉和謝爾蓋布林。儘管到了 2007 年，公司收到超過一億美元資金，卻沒有獲利。馬斯克在 2008 年當上執行長後，裁減特斯拉四分之一員工以避免破產。特斯拉於 2012 年開始向大眾市場推出汽車，淨收益終於開始好轉。中型的 Model S 轎車深受消費者和汽車專家的喜愛。特斯拉於 2015 年推出第一款休旅車 Model X，同樣受歡迎。2016 年推出的 Model 3 豪華轎車收到的訂單比預期還多，迫使特斯拉加速生產以滿足需求。到了 2018 年，Model 3 已是美國最暢銷的插電式電動車。

暢銷的 Model 3 車款

電動車從電池插座充電的示意圖

Innovation and ambition
創新與野心

Over the past several years, Tesla has been developing technology to make cars completely ⓖ **self-driving**. Musk has predicted that within a few years, Tesla owners will be napping in their cars when they travel instead of driving them. All drivers will need to do is [1]**input** their [2]**destination**, and Tesla's ⓖ **Autopilot** software, with the help of eight cameras [3]**mounted** to the car, will drive them there automatically. Tesla has been [4]**criticized** in the past for making promises it can't keep, such as [5]**neglecting** to deliver new vehicles on time and failing to increase the number of charging stations in certain areas. But considering what Musk has achieved so far in his [6]**career**, it may not be wise to bet against him. He may even put people on Mars one of these days!

自動駕駛的車上路，綠色線條為機器人所偵測到的影像。

特斯拉過去幾年一直在研發完全自動駕駛汽車的技術，馬斯克預估幾年內，特斯拉車主將可在行進中的車子裡小睡，不用自己開車。駕駛人只要輸入目的地，特斯拉的自動駕駛軟體就會在八個車上攝影機的幫助下，自動載車主到達目的地。特斯拉過去因為未盡到承諾而受到批評，例如未準時交付新車、未在特定區域增加充電站。但鑒於馬斯克目前職涯中所達到的成就，不看好他或許並不明智。他還是有可能在未來將人類送上火星！

Mini Quiz 閱讀測驗

( ) 1. **Who is NOT one of Tesla's founders?**
(A) Elon Musk
(B) Nikola Tesla
(C) Martin Eberhard
(D) Marc Tarpenning

( ) 2. **Which company was NOT founded by Elon Musk?**
(A) eBay
(B) Zip2
(C) PayPal
(D) SpaceX

( ) 3. **Which is true about Tesla?**
(A) The mid-size Model S was its first model.
(B) It doesn't have a sportscar line.
(C) Its cars require gasoline.
(D) It is developing self-driving cars.

Vocabulary

1) **input** [ˋɪnˌpʊt] (v.) （將資訊）輸入
2) **destination** [ˌdɛstəˋneʃən] (n.) 目的地，去處
3) **mount** [maʊnt] (v.) 固定在⋯上，鑲嵌
4) **criticize** [ˋkrɪtɪˌsaɪz] (v.) 批評，指責
5) **neglect** [nɪˋglɛkt] (v.) 忽視，忽略
6) **career** [kəˋrɪr] (n.) 職業，生涯

PayPal

馬斯克與合夥人在 1998 年創立的網路第三方支付平台，與電子商務網合作的安全付費機制，最後在 2002 年賣給 eBay。

SpaceX

追求太空探索運動新趨勢，馬斯克在 2002 年成立的太空公司稱作 SpaceX，致力於發展低成本的太空運輸，旗下的龍飛船

SpaceX 龍號正在繞地球軌道行進

(Space X Dragon) 與獵鷹 9 號運載火箭 (Falcon 9) 皆為目前唯一能重複使用之太空載具，未來將以此為設計基礎，開發載人的龍飛船。

public face 公眾形象代表人

千萬不要解釋成「大眾臉」啊，這裡的 face 解釋為「形象」，public face 代表來面對大眾，就是「公眾形象代表人」。

Martin Eberhard and Marc Tarpenning 艾伯哈德和塔彭寧

兩人當時在評估各種電池能源後，發現鋰離子電池 (lithium-ion battery) 最適合做為電動車的動力來源，能改善鉛酸蓄電池 (lead-acid battery) 蓄電力不足的問題，成就了現今 Tesla 的輝煌成就。他們向外尋求資金，馬斯克入主 Tesla，但沒多久他們倆都離開了 Tesla，有人說是馬斯克與他們的成本控管理念不合，也有人說是因為光芒被馬斯克奪去，他們不被受尊重而選擇退出，眾說紛紜，實際原因不得而知。

特斯拉的兩位創辦人艾伯哈德（左）和塔彭寧（右）

early adopter 創新擴散理論

由美國埃佛雷特羅傑斯 (Everett Rogers) 提出的創新擴散理論，探討新概念或新科技的普及化過程，並將使用者分為五種人，分別為 innovator（創新者）、early adopter（早期採用者）、early majority（早期大眾）、late majority（晚期大眾）及 laggard（落伍者）。越早期接納新科技的人比例越少，但卻是散播新技術的重要推手，大家可以想想，自己屬於五種族群中的哪一種？

Nikola Tesla 尼可拉特斯拉

發明出交流電 (alternating current) 和感應馬達 (induction motor) 的天才科學家，個性孤僻又古怪，常被冠上瘋狂科學家的稱號，今日許多電影漫畫中出現的科學家形象，常以他的樣貌為藍圖。他發明的電力系統，至今仍照亮全世界，除此之外，發電機 (generator)、遙控器 (remote control)、醫療器材 X 光都是他的發明之作。

特斯拉如何充電

特斯拉的充電站大約分為三種：長途旅程超充站、抵達目的地充電站還有停車即可充電。超充站就是快速充電的概念，雖然目前台灣有 12 個超充站，在低電量的狀態下充個 10 分鐘就夠跑到下一個超充站了！抵達目的地充電提供壁掛式充電座，大部分是有合作的飯店、百貨商場都有設置。在你常停車的公司或家用車位，設置充電座，讓車子充電如同手機充電一樣簡便，使用 220V 電源，跟一般大型家電沒有什麼不同。

特斯拉具代表性的車款介紹

· Model X

Tesla 首款安全性以及功能性兼備的運動休旅車，乘坐空間寬敞，且能彈性配置座位，要 6 人座還是 7 人座都可以，尤其它的招牌鷹翼車門別具特色，相較於滑動式車門，便利性更為提升。

· Model S & Model 3

除了休旅車款，經典轎車款當然也不能少，英文中的 sedan 就是在指這種後方有行李空間，可以載 4~5 人的的雙門或四門車。Tesla 的旗艦豪華轎車款——Model S 採雙馬達全輪驅動的掀背轎車 (hatchback)，堪稱為市面上續航力最佳的純電動車。作為新一波主推車款 Model 3，很多人誤以為它是 Model S 的新代旗艦車款，但較為輕巧簡潔的 Model 3 其實是 Tesla 推出的入門車款，價格也較為平民。

self-driving / Autopilot 自動駕駛

不需要人類介入的自動化系統，不過目前市面上並沒有「全」自動駕駛配備款，Tesla 的 Autopilot 其實只是駕駛「輔助」系統，必要時還是須及時掌控方向盤。

Uber, the [1]Ridesharing Giant
優步：共乘鉅子

A family of [2]refugees
難民家庭

Uber CEO Dara Khosrowshahi was born in Iran in 1969, and is the youngest of three children. His parents, Lili and Asghar Khosrowshahi, were very [3]**well-off**, having founded a [8]**conglomerate** involved in [9]**pharmaceuticals**, food, packaging, and other areas. In 1978, on the [4]**eve** of the ⓛⓖ **Iranian Revolution**, his family's wealth made them targets of [10]**persecution**. Khosrowshahi's parents decided to leave everything behind, [5]**fleeing** first to France and later to the United States, where they settled in New York. When Khosrowshahi was 13, his father returned to Iran to care for his own father. Due to the family's history, he was [6]**detained** and not allowed to return to the U.S. for six years. By the time he could come back, Khosrowshahi had already finished high school.

Uber 執行長達拉柯霍斯洛夏西於 1969 年在伊朗出生，是家中三名子女中的老么。他的父母莉莉和阿哈柯霍斯洛夏西原本家境富裕，曾創辦一個企業集團，經營藥廠、食品、包裝等領域。1978 年，在伊朗革命前夕，他們因富裕背景成了迫害的目標。柯霍斯洛夏西的父母決定放棄一切，先是逃到法國，後來到美國，然後定居紐約。柯霍斯洛夏西 13 歲時，父親回到伊朗照顧祖父。因家族背景的關係，他被拘留，並有六年被禁止回美國，等他能回美國時，柯霍斯洛夏西已高中畢業。

From engineering student to [7]analyst to CEO
從工程系學生、分析師一路到執行長

After graduating from the elite Hackley School in 1987, Khosrowshahi earned a [11]**BA** in electrical engineering at Brown University. His first job was not as an engineer, however; instead, he spent seven years as an analyst at New York investment bank Allen & Company. One of Khosrowshahi's clients there, media [12]**mogul** ⓛⓖ **Barry Diller**, made him president of USA Networks, and then [13]**CFO** of media company IAC, which purchased travel booking company ⓛⓖ **Expedia** in 2001. Khosrowshahi became CEO of Expedia in 2005, and by 2016 he had doubled Expedia's earnings and become one of the highest-paid CEOs in the U.S. Given this [14]**track record** at Expedia, it's no wonder Uber recruited Khosrowshahi in 2017 to replace co-founder ⓛⓖ **Travis Kalanick** as CEO.

1987 年從貴族學校哈克利中學畢業後，柯霍斯洛夏西從布朗大學取得電機工程學士學位。但他的第一份工作不是工程師，而是在紐約投資銀行艾倫公司擔任七年的分析師。柯霍斯洛夏西的客戶，媒體大亨巴瑞迪勒請他擔任 USA 電視台的總裁，接著擔任媒體公司 IAC 的財務長，該公司在 2001 年收購旅遊預訂公司智遊網。柯霍斯洛夏西於 2005 年擔任智遊網的執行長，到了 2016 年已替智遊網增加兩倍營收，成為美國薪水最高的執行長之一。有鑑於在智遊網的業績，也難怪 Uber 會在 2017 年延攬柯霍斯洛夏西，取代共同創辦人特拉維斯卡拉尼克成為執行長。

單字 pp.136-140

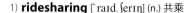
Vocabulary

1) **ridesharing** [ˈraɪdˌʃɛrɪŋ] (n.) 共乘
2) **refugee** [ˈrɛfjuˌdʒi] (n.) 難民
3) **well-off** [ˌwɛlˈɑf] (a.) 富有的，有錢的
4) **eve** [iv] (n.) 前夕，前日
5) **flee** [fli] (v.) 逃跑，逃脫
6) **detain** [dɪˈten] (v.) 拘留，扣留
7) **analyst** [ˈænəlɪst] (n.) 分析師

進階字彙

8) **conglomerate** [kənˈglɑmərɪt] (n.) 企業集團，聯合大企業
9) **pharmaceutical** [ˌfɑrməˈsutɪkəl] (n./a.) 藥物（的），製藥（的）
10) **persecution** [ˌpɜsɪˈkjuʃən] (n.) 迫害，動詞為 **persecute** [ˈpɜsɪˌkjut]
11) **BA** [ˌbiˈe] (n.) 文學士，全名為 **Bachelor of Arts**
12) **mogul** [ˈmoɡəl] (n.) 巨擘，大人物
13) **CFO** [ˌsi ɛfˈo] (n.) 首席財務官，全名為 **chief financial officer**
14) **track record** (phr.) 過去的業績、工作紀錄

Uber

An idea that changed an industry
足以改變產業的想法

Kalanick, who remains a board member at Uber, founded the company in 2009 with computer [11]**programmer** Ⓛ **Garrett Camp** after the two paid an [12]**exorbitant** fee to hire a private driver on New Year's Eve. The co-founders realized that the cost of ride [1]**hailing** could be lowered by using a smartphone app to pair drivers with nearby passengers, and by [2]**splitting** the cost among different parties. Uber officially launched in San Francisco in May 2011, but at that time the app could only be used to hail black luxury cars, with rides costing 1.5 times the average cost of a taxi. But within a year, Uber's luxury car service—now called UberBLACK—had Ⓛ **taken a back seat** to its main ride sharing service, UberX, which allows owners of any type of car to drive for the company as independent [3]**contractors**, earning income for each ride driven.

仍在 Uber 保有董事會席位的卡拉尼克，在 2009 年與電腦程式設計師加瑞特坎普在除夕付了過高費用聘請私人司機後，兩人一起創辦了 Uber。這兩位共同創辦人發現用智慧手機 app 幫汽車駕駛和附近的乘客配對並以此分擔成本，叫車成本便能因此降低。Uber 是 2011 年在舊金山正式推出，但當時的 app 只能用來召黑色豪華轎車，車資比一般計程車高 1.5 倍。但在一年內，Uber 的豪華轎車服務——現稱為尊榮優步——已退居次位，現以共乘服務菁英優步為主，讓各類車主以獨立承包的身分為公司接案，按每趟車程賺取收入。

A successful business model
成功的商業模式

Uber's success can be [13]**attributed to** several factors. First, scheduling a ride through the Uber app makes ride hailing more [4]**predictable**; passengers no longer need to wait on the [5]**curb** in the hopes of [14]**flagging down** a taxi. Second, the app displays the price of the ride before the driver is engaged, so passengers know [15]**upfront** how much they'll have to pay, instead of only learning the price upon reaching their destination. Also, transactions are handled on the Uber app, so no cash [16]**changes hands**. This offers convenience for passengers and security for drivers, who needn't worry about carrying cash that could be stolen. Finally, Uber uses a [6]**dynamic** pricing model, meaning prices for the same trip vary based on Ⓛ **supply and demand**. This creates an incentive for drivers to head to areas experiencing increased demand, ensuring passengers will be able to find rides at peak times.

Uber 的成功要歸功於幾個因素。首先，透過 Uber app 安排車程使叫車服務更容易預測；乘客不再需要到路邊等車，希望能招到一輛計程車。第二，app 會在司機接手前顯示車資，因此乘客會預先知道要付多少錢，不用等到達目的地才知道。而且交易是在 Uber app 上完成，所以不用現金交易。這對乘客來說相當方便，對司機來說也安全，身上不用帶著現金而擔心被偷。最後，Uber 使用動態定價模式，這表示同一趟車程的車資可根據供需而改變。這鼓勵司機前往需求量增加的區域，以確保乘客在尖峰時刻可叫到計程車。

停放在路邊的 Uber 電動滑板車

Worldwide expansion and new [7]offerings
全球擴張和新服務

In the past few years, Uber has both expanded its ride hailing services and developed beyond this [8]**core** business. In taking Uber to over 70 countries worldwide, the company has even [9]**adapted to** local modes of [10]**transportation**. For example, UberAUTO offers auto [17]**rickshaw** rides in India and Pakistan. In the U.S., the Uber app can be used to rent JUMP electric bicycles in nine cities, and Lime electric [18]**scooters** all over the country. In 2014, the company moved into meal delivery with Uber Eats, allowing customers to order food online from participating restaurants have it delivered to their door by car, bike, scooter, or even courier on foot.

過去幾年 Uber 持續擴大叫車服務，發展範圍也超越了這項核心業務。全世界已超過 70 個國家接受 Uber，該公司甚至為適應當地的交通模式而調整，例如在印度和巴基斯坦提供嘟嘟車搭乘服務的 UberAUTO。美國有九座城市可用 Uber app 租 JUMP 電動自行車，在全美都可租到 Lime 電動滑板車。2014 年，Uber 公司轉戰美食外送服務，讓顧客上網從合作的餐廳點餐，然後透過汽車、自行車、滑板車，甚至步行的方式送餐。

Disrupting the taxi industry
顛覆計程車業

Industry analysts say Uber [8]**disrupted** the taxi industry in the same way Airbnb disrupted the hotel industry: by allowing ordinary people to use their private property—their vehicle or home—to earn income. Uber's next move will likely disrupt the auto industry itself. Uber began developing [9]**autonomous**, self-driving vehicles in 2015, and has been testing them on the roads of several American cities. Working with Ford and Volvo, Uber has [1]**equipped** a [2]**fleet** of cars **with** GPS, radar and [10]**lidar** technology and begun testing them in real-world conditions, with human drivers inside to monitor performance and [11]**take the wheel** in case of an emergency. The program suffered a major [3]**setback** when one of these cars killed a [4]**pedestrian** in 2018. The criticism of Uber following this incident added to existing scandals over sexual [5]**harassment** within the company and [6]**aggressive** business practices. It's no doubt that new CEO Dara Khosrowshahi has a number of challenges to [7]**overcome** to ensure Uber continues [12]**capitalizing on** its early successes.

行業分析師表示，Uber 顛覆了計程車業，就像 Airbnb 民宿網站顛覆了旅館業，因為他們都讓一般人利用自己的汽車或住宅等私人物業賺外快。Uber 下一步可能會撼動汽車業。Uber 已於 2015 年開始研發自動駕駛車，並已在美國幾座城市的道路上測試。Uber 與福特和富豪汽車合作，為一批汽車隊配備全球定位系統、雷達和光學雷達技術，開始在真實世界的環境下測試，讓駕駛員坐在車內監控，在發生緊急狀況時接手。這項計畫在 2018 年遭到重挫，有一輛自駕車撞死了一名路人。Uber 公司內部原本就有性騷擾和經營方式強勢的醜聞，這起事故更讓該公司飽受批評。新任執行長柯霍斯洛夏西無疑有許多挑戰要克服，以確保 Uber 能在創業初期成就的基礎上繼續前進。

Vocabulary

1) **equip (with)** [ɪˋkwɪp] (v.)（使）具有工具、裝備、能力等

2) **fleet** [flit] (n.) 車隊，艦隊，機群

3) **setback** [ˋsɛt͵bæk] (n.) 挫折，失敗，阻礙

4) **pedestrian** [pəˋdɛstrɪən] (n.) 行人

5) **harassment** [həˋræsmənt] (n.)（不斷）騷擾，攻擊

6) **aggressive** [əˋgrɛsɪv] (a.) 強勢的，咄咄逼人的

7) **overcome** [͵ovɚˋkʌm] (v.) 克服，戰勝

進階字彙

8) **disrupt** [dɪsˋrʌpt] (v.) 顛覆，破壞

9) **autonomous** [ɔˋtɑnəməs] (a.) 自主的

10) **lidar** [ˋlaɪ͵dɑr] (n.) 光學雷達，光達，全名為 **light detection and ranging**

11) **take the wheel** (phr.) 掌控方向，開車

12) **capitalize (on)** [ˋkæpətəl͵aɪz] (v.) 積累資本，利用

Iranian Revolution 伊朗革命

一九七〇年代，反伊朗君主體制，宗教勢力與政治對立，以什葉派 (Shia) 宗教領袖霍梅尼 (Ayatollah Khomeini) 為首的反政府行動及言論奠定伊朗革命的基礎，推翻自 1953 年由美國支持的當權沙王──巴列維 (Shah Pahlavi)，隨後即誕生政教合一的伊朗伊斯蘭共和國。

Barry Diller 巴瑞迪勒

是 IAC 和 Expedia 的董事長，這名影視大亨巴瑞迪勒同時也是福克斯電視台 (FOX) 和美國廣播公司 (USA Broacasting) 的創始人，風靡超過 30 年的國民卡通《辛普森家族》(The Simpsons) 也是他一手推動，卡通中一角色──伯恩斯老闆據說就以巴瑞迪勒當原型創作。迪勒甚至在 1994 年入選為電視名人堂的成員之一，推崇其對於美國電視的非凡貢獻。

Expedia 智遊網

網站名稱為 exploration 和 speed 組合而成的字，全球最大旅遊平台，推出套裝服務，找飯店、訂機票，機加酒一個網站就能搞定，旗下還有 Trivago、Hotels.com、TripAdvisor… 等多元的旅遊服務平台。

Travis Kalanick 特拉維斯卡拉尼克

曾在路上和計程車司機大打出手，甚至半路跳車，讓卡拉尼克想到計程車就討厭，也因為這樣的經歷，讓卡拉尼克有了創造 Uber 的想法。從上述的過程，我們能看到卡拉尼克性格豪放、瘋狂又有點魯莽，爭議事件層出不窮，雖然他將 Uber 帶領至事業的高峰，但卻也因負面形象而蒙上陰影，被認為是位極為矛盾的企業家。

Garrett Camp 加瑞特坎普

加瑞特坎普是位另類風格的富商，2015 年成為加拿大第三富有的人，他闊氣宣誓加入巴菲特和比爾蓋茲發起的

「贈與誓言」(Giving Pledge)，鼓勵富豪參與慈善，所以他將一半以上的財產都捐出去，雖然沒有直接管理 Uber，坎普一直都是董事會的成員之一，同時計畫推出 ECO 加密貨幣，希望能實現虛擬貨幣即時便利。

take a back seat (to) 退居次要位置

back seat 原本是指「汽車後座」，這裡就用來表示在組織中退居次要的位置，不是作主的人；相反地，be in the driver's seat「坐在司機的位置上」，掌控方向盤的人，當然就是擁有主導權、當家的人囉！

A: What advice did your lawyer give you?
你的律師給你什麼意見？

B: He said to just take a back seat and let him do the talking.
他叫我少發言，讓他主導局面。

supply and demand 供給與需求

供給 (supply) 與需求 (demand) 是經濟學中一門探討市場價格與產量的原理模型，這兩者成反比，意思是當消費者的需求量增加，價格就會往上攀升，出產的供貨量就會減少，也就是「物以稀為貴」的概念。

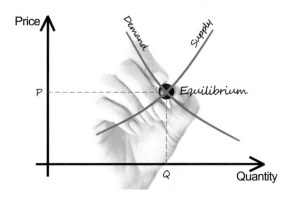

Uber 公司內部醜聞

性平醜聞不斷，Uber 形象傷到不能再傷，高層主管的隱匿，性騷擾事件不斷被「擺平」，最後也都一一露出檯面。歧視女性的觀點風波不斷，早先卡拉尼克提及為女性的專屬服務稱作「Boober」也再度引發撻伐聲浪，英語中 boob 有女性胸部的意思。身陷風暴的前執行長卡拉尼克，危機意識低，甚至流出與 Uber 司機對罵的影片，形象大大受損，為平息風聲，宣布無限期休假。

EZ 叢書館 34

科技世代一定要會的英文
EZ TALK 總編嚴選特刊

科技世代一定要會的英文：EZ TALK 總編嚴選特刊 /
EZ 叢書館編輯部作 . -- 初版 . -- 臺北市：日月文化，
2019.04
　　面；　公分 . -- (EZ 叢書館；34)
ISBN 978-986-248-792-1

1. 英語　2. 科學技術　3. 讀本

805.18　　　　　　　　　　　　108000342

總　　編　　審：Judd Piggott
撰　　　　稿：Sandi Ward、Brian Foden、Kenneth Paul、Leah Zimmermann
專 案 企 劃 執 行：潘亭軒
校　　　　對：潘亭軒
封　面　設　計：謝捲子
版　型　設　計：蕭彥伶
內　頁　排　版：簡單瑛設
錄　音　後　製：純粹錄音後製有限公司
錄　音　員：Jacob Roth、Leah Zimmermann

發　　行　　人：洪祺祥
副　總　經　理：洪偉傑
副　總　編　輯：曹仲堯
法　律　顧　問：建大法律事務所
財　務　顧　問：高威會計師事務所
出　　　　版：日月文化出版股份有限公司
製　　　　作：EZ 叢書館
地　　　　址：臺北市信義路三段151號8樓
電　　　　話：(02)2708-5509
傳　　　　真：(02)2708-6157
客　服　信　箱：service@heliopolis.com.tw
網　　　　址：www.heliopolis.com.tw
郵　撥　帳　號：19716071日月文化出版股份有限公司

總　　經　　銷：聯合發行股份有限公司
電　　　　話：(02)2917-8022
傳　　　　真：(02)2915-7212
印　　　　刷：中原造像股份有限公司
初　版　一　刷：2019 年 4 月
定　　　　價：350 元
I　S　B　N：978-986-248-792-1

《科技世代一定要會的英文》全書音檔下載

日月文化集團
HELIOPOLIS
CULTURE GROUP

客服專線 02-2708-5509
客服傳真 02-2708-6157
客服信箱 service@heliopolis.com.tw

日月文化集團 讀者服務部 收

10658 台北市信義路三段151號8樓

對折黏貼後，即可直接郵寄

日月文化網址：**www.heliopolis.com.tw**

最新消息、活動，請參考 FB 粉絲團

大量訂購，另有折扣優惠，請洽客服中心（詳見本頁上方所示連絡方式）。

| 日月文化 | EZ TALK | EZ Japan | EZ Korea |

大好書屋・寶鼎出版・山岳文化・洪圖出版

日月文化集團
HELIOPOLIS
CULTURE GROUP

感謝您購買 科技世代一定要會的英文：EZ TALK 總編嚴選特刊

為提供完整服務與快速資訊，請詳細填寫以下資料，傳真至02-2708-6157或免貼郵票寄回，我們將不定期提供您最新資訊及最新優惠。

1. 姓名：＿＿＿＿＿＿＿＿＿＿＿＿＿　性別：□男　　□女

2. 生日：＿＿＿＿年＿＿＿＿月＿＿＿＿日　職業：＿＿＿＿＿

3. 電話：（請務必填寫一種聯絡方式）

　（日）＿＿＿＿＿＿＿＿　（夜）＿＿＿＿＿＿＿＿　（手機）＿＿＿＿＿＿＿＿

4. 地址：□□□＿＿＿＿＿＿＿＿＿＿＿＿＿＿

5. 電子信箱：＿＿＿＿＿＿＿＿＿＿＿＿＿＿＿

6. 您從何處購買此書？□＿＿＿＿＿＿縣/市＿＿＿＿＿＿書店/量販超商

　□＿＿＿＿＿＿網路書店　□書展　□郵購　□其他

7. 您何時購買此書？　　年　　月　　日

8. 您購買此書的原因：（可複選）

　□對書的主題有興趣　□作者　□出版社　□工作所需　□生活所需

　□資訊豐富　　□價格合理（若不合理，您覺得合理價格應為＿＿＿＿＿）

　□封面/版面編排　□其他＿＿＿＿＿＿＿＿＿＿＿＿＿

9. 您從何處得知這本書的消息：　□書店　□網路／電子報　□量販超商　□報紙

　□雜誌　□廣播　□電視　□他人推薦　□其他

10. 您對本書的評價：（1.非常滿意 2.滿意 3.普通 4.不滿意 5.非常不滿意）

　書名＿＿＿＿　內容＿＿＿＿　封面設計＿＿＿＿　版面編排＿＿＿＿　文/譯筆＿＿＿＿

11. 您通常以何種方式購書？□書店　□網路　□傳真訂購　□郵政劃撥　□其他

12. 您最喜歡在何處買書？

　□＿＿＿＿＿＿縣/市＿＿＿＿＿＿書店/量販超商　□網路書店

13. 您希望我們未來出版何種主題的書？＿＿＿＿＿＿＿＿＿＿＿

14. 您認為本書還須改進的地方？提供我們的建議？

＿＿＿＿＿＿＿＿＿＿＿＿＿＿＿＿＿＿＿＿＿＿

＿＿＿＿＿＿＿＿＿＿＿＿＿＿＿＿＿＿＿＿＿＿

＿＿＿＿＿＿＿＿＿＿＿＿＿＿＿＿＿＿＿＿＿＿

＿＿＿＿＿＿＿＿＿＿＿＿＿＿＿＿＿＿＿＿＿＿